FAR WEST

THE DIARY OF ELEANOR HIGGINS

LINELL JEPPSEN

WOLFPACK
PUBLISHING
— EST 2013 —

FAR WEST
The Diary of Eleanor Higgins

Wolfpack Publishing
6032 Wheat Penny Avenue
Las Vegas, NV 89122

wolfpackpublishing.com

Paperback ISBN 978-1-62918-622-1
eBook ISBN 978-1-62918-947-5

PART I
PART ONE

FEB 22, 1876

Dear Diary,

My name is Eleanor Higgins, except that most folks call me Nellie, which I hate. Nelly makes me sound like a little kid but in four days I will turn sixteen. That makes me a woman in my book, although Daddy says I'm still just a stupid child.

My father, Pastor Frank Higgins, is a mean man. He beats my mamma, me and all us kids, even though he dresses up in his black suit every Sunday morning and preaches the word of God on high to the people in my hometown.

My family and I live just outside of Sioux City, Iowa. We live in a nice house (the parish) snugged up close to the Missouri River. Daddy's church is pretty nice too, with two stained-glass windows and solid oak pews but there is always a strange smell inside it-like fish or something equally noisome, has gone bad in some hidden corner. Father says it's the stench of discarded sin.

We have a few acres of land which we could farm, I suppose, but Daddy spends all his time writing sermons for our neighbors up and down the river valley.

There are the Adam's family (they are Scottish, I think) and the Winston's (just plain Americans). They have a crazy old woman living in their upstairs attic. She is Mrs. Winston's mamma, I guess, but she wails and moans like a haint whenever anyone comes to call. I don't like to go there unless my mother is with me.

Then there are the O'Neal's with their brood of thirteen children and the McNabs, a starchy old couple who sit the day long on their front porch glaring out at the world with suspicious eyes.

They are our closest neighbors but there are many more on both sides of the river. There is a church on the other side, too. Episcopal, I think. It is not nearly as big or grand as our church, but many of Daddy's parishioners will head to that church, instead of my father's when they haven't got the nickel to pay for a ferry ride. Daddy says those folks will pay in hell for their fickle ways.

My father is a Lutheran minister and he believes that the fire of hell is always waiting... hidden just beyond sight like a snake in tall grass. That serpent is forever coiled up and ready to strike a sinner with its horrid, juicy fangs. He also believes the most everyone, except for himself, is a sinner just beggin' to be bit.

Me, I have a hard time with that notion. Sure, there are bad people out there-real sinners like bank robbers and bandits, or murderers like that Stanley Winthrop who got hanged by the neck in the town square last year for killing his wife and child. Daddy took me and the rest of the family to see it. I had a good time although, to be honest, I

pretty much looked away when that fat man went dropping through the hole in the floor of the hanging
platform.

My sister Patsy turned kind of green and threw up,
although she claimed it was the heat and "the curse" what
made her go cringy like that. No matter, as soon as we
headed back home, my daddy pulled the wagon to the
side of the road, picked up his wooden paddle and beat
my sis hard on the back of her petticoats for all the
passers-by to see!

I wish I could have done something for Patsy that
day... anything to take away her shame and embarrassment. But I didn't dare and neither did my mamma or
siblings. We knew then, like we've always known, to defy
father's harsh manner means my mamma will suffer for
our sins. That is how Daddy keeps us all in line- by
torturing our mamma, Ellen.

Patsy had stared at me that day while my daddy beat
her, her face red with pain and humiliation. I could tell
she was begging me not to interfere, although I wanted to
scream at him to stop! But I kept my mouth shut and a
month later she up and left home. I thought my heart
would break but she went to live with Chloe Hammond,
my mamma's spinster sister in Chicago, Illinois and she
seems real happy now.

Patsy was seventeen at that time, and my best friend
(she was who gave me this diary). Now she writes regular
and gives me lots of news about the bustling city and
fashions and, although I'm not supposed to tell anyone,
her new beau who goes by the name, Marcus Tremont. He
is studying to be a solicitor and Patsy thinks he's going to
ask her to be his wife.

I won't tell anybody except you, dear diary, especially my father who would, most likely, jump on the wagon and drag Patsy home by the ear if he knew she was sweet on some man!

Anyway, although my birthday isn't until Saturday next, my mother picked up the mail in town this morning and saw this parcel addressed to me. Knowing my daddy would think of a diary as some sort of vain and nasty sin, she snuck it up to my room and told me to hide it away so father would never see it.

So, that's what I did. My mamma gave me an old quill and some ink too and now I'm huddled under the covers writing these thoughts down. I know I'm not a very good writer, but my diary doesn't care about that, I'm sure.

It's wonderful to have someone to talk to... I love my little sister Annie but she's only seven and would not understand the feelings going on in my head... besides she's so scared of Daddy she might accidentally spill the beans about my gift.

My little brother David is sweet but he's only five years old. Of all of us kids, he is the one Father picks on most. Davey's bottom is so black and blue from Daddy's paddle he can barely sit down most days. So, no. If I'm going to get things off my chest, it's going to be here, on these pages, with no one to see my words but me.

I know that, some day, I'll be able to take my leave. Either I will get married, or maybe Aunt Chloe will let me come to stay with her once Patsy gets married and moves into her own home. In the meanwhile, someone needs to stay here and keep an eye out for Mamma and my siblings.

I know that my daddy will beat one of them to death if

someone doesn't keep watch and, for now, that someone is me.

I just wish he wasn't so big... and scary.

Getting tired now. I know that tomorrow will be busy because we're going into town for supplies, so I'd better get some sleep.

Good night Diary,

Nel Higgins

P.S. Lying in the dark and thinking about my daddy, I wish he would just die!

P.P.S. I take that back! Good night again, Diary. I am going to blow out the candle now and pray to God for my wicked thoughts.

Dear Diary,

Well, it turned out to be a horrible day, thanks to Daddy. It started out well enough. Mamma seemed happy and my father had been called in to talk to the Lutheran diocese about his church and congregation. He is always pleased to prove how righteous he is to the church elders.

We headed into town in the wagon and Daddy surprised us by saying we could get two bolts of fabric for new dresses instead of just one. I swear, most of the time Mamma, me and Annie look like cookie-cutter copies of each other, always wearing the same, drab but sturdy gingham.

I gazed at my mamma in surprise and saw her once pretty face blush pink with pleasure and excitement. Looking closer, I saw myself reflected in her visage, although my coloring is more intense. Her faded strawberry-blonde hair is streaked with gray and her dark blue eyes peer bashfully through folds of papery wrinkles.

My hair is as auburn as a copper penny and springs from my scalp in a frenzy of corkscrew curls. My eyes haven't had a chance to fade yet and I know they are my best feature because they are as blue and round as robin's eggs. But, like a robin's egg, my skin is speckled all over in ruddy freckles.

My Daddy once took my chin in his hand and shook his head in disgust. "You are the very definition of 'Jezebel', Nelly," he murmured. "Best take care, girl, afore you burn in hell..."

Anyway, like I said, it was a happy start to the day. It took about an hour to ride into town to the mercantile, and Daddy left for his meeting while we shopped for supplies. Filled with excitement, Mamma and I went immediately to the sewing section in back of the store. Mamma had promised Annie and Davey a penny a piece to buy hard candy so those two were standing in front of the shop-owners counter staring at the colorful display of confections.

The materials were dazzling! There were pink silks and emerald green velvets, lace ribbons and pretty, pearl buttons. I almost drooled with delight but even I knew those beautiful fabrics were out of the question for the likes of us. Going further back, we saw plenty of bolts that were more appropriate for a pastor's wife and children.

There was one that was fairly plain but not too ugly- a gray cotton with darker gray checks. There was a lot of that particular material which meant, if we were careful, we could also fashion a new shirt for Davey from the left-overs. Mamma nodded her head and I picked the roll off the shelf and walked it over to the counter for purchase.

When I walked back, I saw my mamma staring at a

piece of striped, pale peach and green taffeta. The look in her eyes was so wistful, so... desirous I almost gasped out loud. "Oh Mamma, could we? Please?" I said, just barely managing not to jump up and down with excitement.

She looked torn and then, after checking the price tag, she nodded with a smile. "Yes, we shall, Nelly. If I work quickly, you'll have a pretty new dress to wear for your birthday!"

I shrieked with joy and snatched the material out of her arms before she could change her mind. We walked to the counter, paid for the children's peppermint sticks and finished the rest of our more mundane shopping- flour, beans, ink, salt and the like.

After everything was added up and paid for, Mamma asked the shop-keeper if he would please wrap the material in paper so it wouldn't get dusty on the trip home (I knew she was trying to hide it from Daddy's prying eyes). He complied and had just finished wrapping it up tight when father walked in the door.

I knew something was wrong the minute I saw his face. His pleased smile was gone and his brow was lowered like a storm cloud. Mamma's happy grin disappeared instantly and she ducked her head in anxiety. Even the youngsters looked guilty and stared at the dusty floor-boards under their feet.

"Let's go!" he snarled and we all jumped to do his bidding. Within minutes, we were heading back home, although he had promised to buy us ices at the town park before we left town.

Halfway home, he turned to my mother. "They want me to go to California, Ellen. They say the Catholics are taking over out west and they want me-us-to represent God- the real, Protestant God in San Francisco."

My mother turned pale and said, "But, Frank! I thought that ministers with families were not subject to that kind of recruitment. We... I am too old to undertake such a trek!"

In answer, Daddy slapped her so hard she almost flew out the other side of the wagon. The children screamed and I couldn't help myself. I hollered, "Daddy, stop it!"

He yanked up hard on the reins, pulled the wagon to the side of the road and lunged over the driver's bench. I, of course, scrambled backwards as fast as I could but in the process, my feet scraped over the paper wrapping the dress-material and tore it wide open so that the peach and green taffeta gleamed like a jewel in the afternoon's sultry sunlight.

My father stopped and stared down at the fabric in shock. His mouth dropped open and he whispered, "What's this? What in the name of God is this?"

Mamma, who was busy wiping blood away from a split lip, said, "It's taffeta, Frank, that's all. It's very proper and it was on sale!"

"So, wife, the devil bought you cheap, eh?" he grated.

Ellen shook her head. "No! Frank, there is nothing wrong with a tiny bit of color in clothing. It is not a sin to wear the colors of spring, is it?"

Father seemed to be speechless for the moment, but his mouth turned upside down and his cheeks turned brick red. He bent over, picked the parcel up and tossed it to the side of the road. Then, he turned back to me and kicked me in the ribs as hard as he could.

I heard my mamma and siblings cry out in shock but I

had gotten the wind knocked out of me and I spent the rest of the trip curled up in a ball, trying not to vomit on our newly purchased supplies.

We made it back home, eventually, but everyone was sent to their rooms to reflect upon their sins. Once I was alone, I took my old gingham dress off and inspected my ribcage which hurt to the touch and was turning my freckled skin blue, red and purple.

Now, I'm lying in bed and trying not to wail. A sharp pain jabs me if I take too deep of a breath, and my heart aches at the loss of the pretty material. Mainly, though, I am wracked with guilt because Daddy is beating on my mamma again.

In all the hubbub, I had almost forgotten about heading to California. In a way, the trip sounded kind of exciting, but right now all I can feel is despair. My father has always made a show out of punishing my mother, but this time it's going on too long.

I can hear his heavy fists fall and mamma's groans, and all the while his mumbled rants as he reads different passages from his battered, old bible. "The Lord says", Thud... Gasp. "The bible tells us," Crash... Groan.

Oh, Diary, I hate him! I hate him, I hate him!

There, the door to their bedroom just slammed shut and I hear his footsteps heading down the stairs. Straining my ears, I can make out my mother's muffled tears, so at least I can sleep now, knowing she's still alive.

I let the tears come and feel my broken rib(s) grinding against each other as I slowly fall asleep.

Goodnight, dear Diary~ Goodnight.

Dear Diary,

Sorry I didn't get back to you sooner, but it's been a bad couple of days. I think that when Daddy beat my mother two nights ago, he broke something inside her. She hasn't been able to get out of bed since then and the three times I was allowed into her bedroom she just stares with empty eyes at the wall, although I call her name over and over.

Daddy has been quiet- almost too quiet- since then. He does nothing but sit in the parlor for hours on end, reading his bible and jotting long lines of figures down on a sheet of paper.

So, it's up to me to take care of the children, fix the meals, do the laundry and try to care for Mamma, which is hard because my left ribs hurt like the dickens every time I move. Oh well, like I said, someone has to do it and it looks like that someone is me.

The good news- it's my birthday! There will be no celebrating around here though, that's for sure. This has been a somber household since our trip into town, although my brother and sister surprised me this morning with a gift.

I could hardly believe my eyes when Davey shuffled up to me in his shy way and pulled a long braided ribbon from his pants pocket.

"This is from Mamma, Anna and me, sister. Happy birthday," he whispered.

Three lengths of ribbon (red, gold and blue) were braided together to form a chain on which hung a little silver cameo brooch. I opened it with a gasp and saw a tiny drawing of my mamma from when she was younger on one side and a new rendering of Annie and Davey on the other side.

Tears filled my eyes. I don't know how long Mamma, Anna and Davey have been planning this scheme but it must have been for quite a while. The kid's portraits are sketched in new ink, which means my mother drew it on the sly.

My father has been kept in the dark, I know. He believes that personal pictures, paintings ... even mirrors are a testimony to the worst kind of vanity and thus, a sin. He would never have granted permission for such a vain gift, which means that Mamma and the kids have kept this present a secret.

Annie and Davey were staring up at me with wide, hollow eyes and I knelt down and folded them in my arms. "Thank you, thank you! Oh, I love it so much- thank you!" I whispered as they wept and trembled on my shoulders.

Then I heard Daddy say, "What's going on in here? Where's my breakfast!"

I managed to place the necklace in my skirt pocket before the kids sprang away from me like scared mice and went to sit at the table. Standing up, I answered, "The children were just wishing me a happy birthday, Daddy. Breakfast is ready if you would like to sit down."

He glared about suspiciously for a moment and then joined the kids for porridge, apples, bread and jam. He did not wish me a happy birthday. As they ate and Daddy read bible passages between bites, I ran a tray upstairs to my mother, who barely responded when I pulled the necklace out of my pocket and hugged her in thanks.

I was watching her face, though, and for a moment she smiled faintly as if my words had sparked a memory of something she held dear. Maybe she will come back to me... to us, someday soon.

Daddy retired to his office after breakfast, saying he did *not* want to be disturbed. That was fine by us. We kept to ourselves the rest of the day and I spent time teaching the kids sums (which they hated), the alphabet letters M-R, and showing them places on our globe... places like the recorded states and what I thought encompassed the California Territories.

I had a horrible scare after dinner. I had put the children down for bed and crept up to my room after checking on Mamma. She was much the same, although she *did* allow me to lead her to the chamber bowl which was a relief, since daddy is getting angry over the soiled sheets and ticking.

I was lying under the covers and had just lit a candle to write in my diary when Daddy walked in the door. Thank God I had not yet pulled it out from under the mattress or he would have seen!

Anyway, he sat on the one chair in my bedchamber and said, "I need you to help collect the tithe tomorrow at the service, Nelly. I want you to convince those sinners that only God's grace will save them from damnation and that they must pay dearly for his time and benign attention." He glared at me. "Do you understand what I'm telling you, girl?"

Normally, the church elders did that kind of work and I really didn't think it was my place to admonish my elders with threats of God's reprisal if they were not generous, but I nodded and replied, "Yes, Daddy. I do and I will."

He smiled in satisfaction. "Good. We are going to need money and a lot of it for our trip to the California Territories." Standing up, he added, "I noticed when I came in here you have a candle burning. Are you reading your bible?"

"Yes, Daddy. I mean, I was just about to before you walked in..." I fumbled for the Holy Book on my nightstand.

He looked about my room as if he wanted to search for some sort of contraband but then he said, "Very well... that's a good girl, but only a passage or two, you hear me? Candle wax is expensive and right now we need to save every penny we've got."

"Yes sir," I answered. He left the room and I breathed a sigh of relief.

That was close!

I have decided to hide you in my special place down by the river. I have the feeling that Daddy knows- somehow- that I'm hiding something from him and if a suspicion grows in his mind, he will stop at nothing to find out what there is to find.

If he found you- and read all my secret thoughts- I know he will kill me dead.

Tired now, so I will see you tomorrow and tell you all about church.

Good night, dear diary~

Feb 26, 1876
Dear Diary,

I can't write now for crying, but you should know... Both Mamma and little Davey are dead.

I'll write later.

March 5, 1876
Dear Diary,

Okay, I'm better now. I mean, my heart is broke in two but at least I can write about it without ruining the pages of this book with my own tears.

Let me think... Looking back I realize that the last time I wrote was on my birthday- the day before Mamma and Davey died. I could tell you about that, and I will, but first I want to talk about what happened at the church service, before I forget entirely.

We got ready for church that morning in our best clothes, except for Mamma, who would not budge from her bed. In fact, she grew increasingly frenzied, like a wild animal caught in a trap, when I asked her to get up and put on her Sunday best.

Daddy tried to help me, but Mamma was bucking around and baring her teeth at him so fiercely, he almost struck her again. Finally, he gave up and said, "Let her be, Nellie. We'll have Davey stay home with her while we're gone. Won't be more than three or four hours, anyway."

I hated to leave her, but I knew better than to argue. We left Davey sitting by the side of mamma's bed and walked the mile and a half to the Church.

Daddy was in fine form that morning... for all that I know he's a brute, Frank Higgins is also a handsome man with brilliant blue eyes and a thick mane of salt and pepper hair. Every once in a while he *does* seem to be filled with glory and his sermon shook the pews that day.

Afterwards, although I hated to do it, I followed his orders and picked up one of the large, wooden tithing platters. I was as polite as can be and respectful but no one- not one soul- put a coin on my platter.

I was confused and worried, too. If I came back up to the alter with an empty plate, I just knew I was in for a beating, but short of shaking coins out of the parishioner's pockets, I was out of luck. And yes, my daddy was watching, and he frowned horribly when I placed the empty plate on the bench beneath the pulpit.

I sat on the back pew as father finished his sermon, wondering how much more abuse my poor bruised ribs could take when Gertrude McNab turned around on her pew and said, "Girl, I need to go to the privy as soon as this infernal sermon is done. Will you help me?"

Peter and Trudy McNab had glared at me when I tried to collect this morning's tithe but I attempted to turn the other cheek in a Christian manner and replied, "Yes Ma'am, I sure will."

A few minutes passed and then came the final AMEN. Mrs. McNab sprang to her feet in a decidedly un-infirm

way and grasped my right arm with cold, crab-like
fingers. "Let's go," she snapped.

I almost stopped in my tracks. It's accepted that the
minister walks down the aisle first and his flock follows
after him, but Trudy almost bowled my daddy over as she
dragged me out the door.

I mumbled an apology as my father snarled in
outrage but I followed in Trudy's wake as she made
her way to the outhouse behind the church. Once
there, she flung open the door, pulled a snowy white
handkerchief from her pocket, placed it over the
smelly hole on the bench and sat down without lifting
her skirt.

"Stand in the doorway, girl, so if your father looks
over here, it will look like you are guarding my privacy.
Hurry up now!"

I did as she asked and peered inside as she fumbled in
her pocket, pulled a heavy, leather bag of coins and dollar
notes out and handed it to me.

"I know you were embarrassed, girl, when we refused
your tithing plate but this is why we done it. This money
is for you, your mamma and the little'uns. Don't let your
father know you have it, alright?"

Dumbfounded, I nodded even as tears of gratitude
pricked my eyes. I looked over my left shoulder and saw
that a number of women had wandered up close. It was a
long wagon ride back home for many of them and the
privy was an absolute necessity but none of the women
seemed in a particular hurry to get inside the out-house.
In fact, I could tell that two or three of them were squatting, slightly, and letting their bladders go on the grass
under the skirts.

Mrs. McNab spoke again. "I hear you and your family are headed out west?"

I nodded. "Yes Ma'am, We're going to the California territories. Daddy says the elders are sending us there to fight the Catholics."

She rolled her eyes. "The elders are not sending you there, girl, your daddy is. I know, for a fact, that Frank Higgins was fired as pastor here, because I was the one what made it happen!"

I stared at the old woman in shock but heard a ripple of feminine whispers behind me. One of the women stepped up close and said, "Better hurry up Trudy, Higgins is a comin' this way..."

Trudy stood up and tossed the hankie down the privy-hole. Glancing at me, she added, "Don't look so surprised, girl. Do you think we don't know what that man does to you kids and your mamma? Frank ain't no God-fearing man- he's a scoundrel, through and through. This parish and the good people in it deserve a man of God- not a thieving brute like yer pa!"

She took a step forward and put her arms around me in a brief hug. "Our advice to you... take the money we gathered up for you and run! Run away from that evil man before he does you all in. Now, step away and let me pass."

I stumbled backwards as Trudy stepped outside, groaning, "Oh... my rhumatiz... it's killing me, I swear! Henrietta, help me, please."

Suddenly, the hale and hearty little woman was as crippled as could be and leaning heavily on her daughter-in-law's left arm. My father *had* come to check on us, but the women were now moving, as one, toward the front of the church and the many horses and wagons in the driveway.

"What was the hold up?" Daddy snapped.

"Oh, Missus McNab was having some... lady trouble." I answered.

It looked as though he wanted more information but, luckily, an innate sense of common decency took over and he let it go. But that didn't stop him from adding, "You and I are going to have words about that tithing plate once we get home!"

I ducked my head and mumbled, "Yes sir," thinking about the heavy purse in my pocket and about how he was dragging us out west... not on a mission from God, but because he had just been run out of town by our own neighbors.

After the congregation left, Annie and I helped Daddy pick up the church- house pews and sweep the floors. Then we walked back home. My whole body tingled all over- every inch of it wondering where his nasty wooden paddle would land, and hoping it wouldn't land on my already bruised ribcage.

My punishment was put on hold, though, once we got back home. After what we found...

I just realized that I'm not ready to talk about that quite yet. I have to figure out how to get Annie's and my own worldly belongings into two, measly carpet-bags for our trip out west.

Good night, dear diary. Good night.

Dear Diary,

I can't write now for crying, but you should know… Both Mamma and little Davey are dead.

I'll write later.

Dear Diary,

Looking back now, I figure we left our burning house about 3:00 in the afternoon, although I'm not really sure. I don't think I had looked at a time-piece for days. Anyway, Daddy drove our poor old horse almost to death that night as we fled across the high prairies.

We traveled well into the dark hours, not stopping to eat or rest until late that night. I wasn't very hungry but my body was sore, my arms were tired from holding Annie, more or less, upright and my heart broken.

To my surprise, Father had been busy over the last week or so and had packed the wagon full of supplies. I hadn't noticed the crates of food and water, tack, salt, jerked meat, tools and sundries crammed in back and for that, at least, I was grateful. I figured, despite who Annie and I were traveling with, we probably wouldn't starve.

Finally, Frank saw a copse of trees at the top of a hill in the moonlit distance. Peering ahead through the darkness and then turning around so he could gaze back from whence we came, he clicked his tongue, touched his whip to the horse's right flank and moved the wagon up a sloping hillside to a grove of willow trees.

Pulling to a stop, he said, "Nelly, jump down and find some wood for a fire."

I was too weary to answer, but after placing my sister on the bench and pulling an old blanket over her so she could stay warm, I walked slowly around the area collecting fallen branches and dry bark for a campfire.

I found a fairly clear space on the ground and placed the damp branches in a pile, hoping Daddy had brought a flint along. He was rummaging around in back of the wagon and after a few minutes he walked up with a plug of paper and a small cup of kerosene.

It seemed like a waste of expensive resources to use kerosene in that way, especially since he kept harping on about our lack of money, but I dared not say anything and simply sat in exhausted silence as Daddy added more wood to the fire. The flames rose so high, I couldn't help but stare past the blaze into the distance, wondering if hostile Indians were also staring into our fire with anger in their hearts.

It was not lost on me that we were traveling alone, in the dark, in a land of many Indian nations. The Sioux, of course, but also the Dakota and remnants of the Iroquois and Algonquin tribes had moved into these parts and more than a few altercations had taken place in and around my hometown over the last few years.

Still, I was incapable of adding worry over my own personal safety to the long list of things that had gone wrong. Much like my little sister, the only thing I wanted to do at that moment was close my eyes, sleep and wake up to a whole new and better reality. Shrugging my fears off, I stared into the flames and felt my eyelids grow heavy.

My father was silent as well, moody and withdrawn. I wondered, briefly, if he felt any remorse over Mamma and Davey's passing but knew, deep down, that he was only worried over what he, himself, was going to do next.

Feeling myself drift off to sleep, I was startled when he said, "Nelly, go to the wagon and fetch a pan, some bread and bacon out of the crate closest to the tailgate. I'm hungry and I'm betting you two are too."

The last thing I wanted to do was cook dinner but the mention of bacon made my stomach twist in hunger. I got up and started rummaging around in the crate. Finding the necessaries, I jumped to the ground and started walking back to the fire.

That's when I noticed my father was gone. Staring around at the shadows that seemed all the darker for the flames I called out, "Daddy? Where are you?"

I hated my father most of the time, and even more so now but I was not ready for him to up and disappear either. "Daddy!"

"Shhh!" I heard him growl from a distance. "There's some sort of critter moving around out here!"

Heart pounding, I moved toward the wagon. I knew there were all kinds of wildlife in these parts... bears, wolves, big cats; any one of which could *and would* eat the bunch of us for dinner given half a chance.

Climbing into the wagon, I found Annie sitting up and staring out into the darkness with wide eyes. "It's okay, Annie," I murmured. "Daddy's got his rifle."

"I hope he gets et by a bear," she rasped.

I couldn't help myself... I laughed out loud with agreement and relief. It had been so long since she spoke, I was beginning to worry she might have lost her tongue. As much as I felt compelled to teach Annie good manners, hearing her flat, angry declaration made me feel that my little sister was a survivor, which was a good thing.

Just then, we heard Daddy's hoarse shout and the boom of his rifle. Staring past the fire, I saw his form materialize from the shadows and other, smaller figures hot on his tail.

Wolves! I thought, frantically, and scooted across the bench, fumbling for the reins. I remember feeling sorry for our draft horse, having realized the gelding had not been fed or watered since we came to a stop.

Too late now! I sighed, and shouted, "Daddy, jump into the wagon! Hurry!"

He turned around and took a wild shot, although the wolves had stopped just beyond the flames reach and were staring, balefully, at his fast-retreating form.

Then, he leaped into the wagon and yelled, "Go, go, go!"

I snapped the reins and the horse leapt against his traces, as anxious as we were to get out of harm's way. We flew down the hillside, minus a slab of bacon, a good frypan and a tasty loaf of bread and hit the road at a smart trot.

Daddy was heaving with left-over nerves and a sort of gleeful triumph. "Lord a mercy! That was close, but the good Lord provides a righteous man!"

I guess it hadn't occurred to him that his daughter made good his escape, but I wasn't about to argue the finer points of God's intervention. After a few miles I pulled on the reins and brought to gelding to a slow walk and then a full-stop.

"What are you doing, girl?" Daddy rasped.

"We gotta feed and water this horse or he'll be of no use to us!" I answered with all the patience and respect I could muster.

Daddy looked chagrined for a moment, but then he retorted, "Shoulda thought of that earlier, Sis, don't you think?"

I nodded, resentfully, and mumbled, "Yes sir! I'm sorry."

I jumped to the ground, found a bucket and some water in a keg and watered the horse, while Daddy fetched him a small container of feed-grain. While the horse drank water and munched his grain, Daddy stared ahead at the road and said, "The map I got says there is a town called Yankton, about forty miles from here."

He took a deep swallow of water from a canteen and handed it over to me. I drank as well and then shared the container with Annie as he continued to speak.

"I've been hearing a lot about gold, lately. The Dakota hills are full of it and, apparently, there are plenty of riverboats in that town willing to take folks upstream to dig. That's where I want us to go. It might take a while to get a good stake but we haven't got enough money to make it to the California territories yet, so we'll stop somewhere up ahead, do some panning and, hopefully, get our cash that way."

For the first time, I thought of the heavy bag of coin and paper money I had stashed in my skirt pocket. Averting my eyes from Daddy's keen gaze lest he suspect my secret, I realized it was unnecessary. His eyes were fixed on the road and some sort of vague future that might, or might not, include Annie and myself.

Dear Diary~ I am back to wishing, along with my little sister, that a hungry and avaricious Grizzly had chased Daddy back to the fire. And, instead of making a clean get-away, Frank Higgins had tripped and gone to his maker with that bear's teeth sunk into his neck!

Dear Diary,

Okay, I'm better now. I mean, my heart is broke in two but at least I can write about it without ruining the pages of this book with my own tears.

Let me think... Looking back I realize that the last time I wrote was on my birthday- the day before Mamma and Davey died. I could tell you about that, and I will, but first I want to talk about what happened at the church service, before I forget entirely.

We got ready for church that morning in our best clothes, except for Mamma, who would not budge from her bed. In fact, she grew increasingly frenzied, like a wild animal caught in a trap, when I asked her to get up and put on her Sunday best.

Daddy tried to help me, but Mamma was bucking around and baring her teeth at him so fiercely, he almost struck her again. Finally, he gave up and said, "Let her be,

Nellie. We'll have Davey stay home with her while we're gone. Won't be more than three or four hours, anyway."

I hated to leave her, but I knew better than to argue. We left Davey sitting by the side of mamma's bed and walked the mile and a half to the Church.

Daddy was in fine form that morning... for all that I know he's a brute, Frank Higgins is also a handsome man with brilliant blue eyes and a thick mane of salt and pepper hair. Every once in a while he *does* seem to be filled with glory and his sermon shook the pews that day.

Afterwards, although I hated to do it, I followed his orders and picked up one of the large, wooden tithing platters. I was as polite as can be and respectful but no one- not one soul- put a coin on my platter.

I was confused and worried, too. If I came back up to the alter with an empty plate, I just knew I was in for a beating, but short of shaking coins out of the parishioner's pockets, I was out of luck. And yes, my daddy was watching, and he frowned horribly when I placed the empty plate on the bench beneath the pulpit.

I sat on the back pew as father finished his sermon, wondering how much more abuse my poor bruised ribs could take when Gertrude McNab turned around on her pew and said, "Girl, I need to go to the privy as soon as this infernal sermon is done. Will you help me?"

Peter and Trudy McNab had glared at me when I tried to collect this morning's tithe but I attempted to turn the other cheek in a Christian manner and replied, "Yes Ma'am, I sure will."

A few minutes passed and then came the final AMEN. Mrs. McNab sprang to her feet in a decidedly un-infirm way and grasped my right arm with cold, crab-like fingers. "Let's go," she snapped.

I almost stopped in my tracks. It's accepted that the minister walks down the aisle first and his flock follows after him, but Trudy almost bowled my daddy over as she dragged me out the door.

I mumbled an apology as my father snarled in outrage but I followed in Trudy's wake as she made her way to the outhouse behind the church. Once there, she flung open the door, pulled a snowy white handkerchief from her pocket, placed it over the smelly hole on the bench and sat down without lifting her skirt.

"Stand in the doorway, girl, so if your father looks over here, it will look like you are guarding my privacy. Hurry up now!"

I did as she asked and peered inside as she fumbled in her pocket, pulled a heavy, leather bag of coins and dollar notes out and handed it to me.

"I know you were embarrassed, girl, when we refused your tithing plate but this is why we done it. This money is for you, your mamma and the little'uns. Don't let your father know you have it, alright?"

Dumbfounded, I nodded even as tears of gratitude pricked my eyes. I looked over my left shoulder and saw that a number of women had wandered up close. It was a long wagon ride back home for many of them and the privy was an absolute necessity but none of the women seemed in a particular hurry to get inside the out-house. In fact, I could tell that two or three of them were squatting, slightly, and letting their bladders go on the grass under the skirts.

Mrs. McNab spoke again. "I hear you and your family are headed out west?"

I nodded. "Yes Ma'am, We're going to the California territories. Daddy says the elders are sending us there to fight the Catholics."

She rolled her eyes. "The elders are not sending you there, girl, your daddy is. I know, for a fact, that Frank Higgins was fired as pastor here, because I was the one what made it happen!"

I stared at the old woman in shock but heard a ripple of feminine whispers behind me. One of the women stepped up close and said, "Better hurry up Trudy, Higgins is a comin' this way..."

Trudy stood up and tossed the hankie down the privy-hole. Glancing at me, she added, "Don't look so surprised, girl. Do you think we don't know what that man does to you kids and your mamma? Frank ain't no God-fearing man- he's a scoundrel, through and through. This parish and the good people in it deserve a man of God- not a thieving brute like yer pa!"

She took a step forward and put her arms around me in a brief hug. "Our advice to you... take the money we gathered up for you and run! Run away from that evil man before he does you all in. Now, step away and let me pass."

I stumbled backwards as Trudy stepped outside, groaning, "Oh... my rhumatiz... it's killing me, I swear! Henrietta, help me, please."

Suddenly, the hale and hearty little woman was as crippled as could be and leaning heavily on her daughter-in-law's left arm. My father *had* come to check on us, but the women were now moving, as one, toward the front of the church and the many horses and wagons in the driveway.

"What was the hold up?" Daddy snapped.

"Oh, Missus McNab was having some... lady trouble." I answered.

It looked as though he wanted more information but, luckily, an innate sense of common decency took over and he let it go. But that didn't stop him from adding, "You and I are going to have words about that tithing plate once we get home!"

I ducked my head and mumbled, "Yes sir," thinking about the heavy purse in my pocket and about how he was dragging us out west... not on a mission from God, but because he had just been run out of town by our own neighbors.

After the congregation left, Annie and I helped Daddy pick up the church- house pews and sweep the floors. Then we walked back home. My whole body tingled all over- every inch of it wondering where his nasty wooden paddle would land, and hoping it wouldn't land on my already bruised ribcage.

My punishment was put on hold, though, once we got back home. After what we found...

I just realized that I'm not ready to talk about that quite yet. I have to figure out how to get Annie's and my own worldly belongings into two, measly carpet-bags for our trip out west.

Good night, dear diary. Good night.

Dear Diary,

We stopped for a bit and ate a meal of cold jerk and buttered bread while the horse fed. Then, after ducking off the road to do our personal business we took off again and drove the wagon into a town called Yankton.

Unbeknownst to me, we had left Iowa behind sometime in the dark hours and now traveled in the Dakota Territories. It didn't look any different though... the river still muscled its way through the prairies and foothills and the landscape remained the same.

The sun was starting to lay its head down behind a high bluff when we headed down a long slope toward what I thought was a small town but turned out to be a tumultuous, thriving community. I guess Daddy was right. I found out later that huge deposits of gold and silver had been discovered in the Dakota Black Hills and it seemed like every Tom, Dick and Harry had come from all over the land to fetch some of that ore for themselves.

Peering down at the town and the long stretch of river that it sat next to, I saw a number of boats- some small and some, very big with paddle-wheels and tall smoke-stacks sticking up into the air. I also saw hundreds of men and woman, tiny from this distance, milling about the boats, docks, warehouses and ramshackle piers. They looked like ants swarming a honeypot.

I had lived close to a large town most of my life, but Sioux City seemed sedate by comparison. It was certainly quieter and as we rode into town, the roar of the crowd filled my ears and made my sister cringe back in alarm.

Bars and warehouses, municipal buildings, a mercan-tile, a doctor's office, a milliner, more bars, dress shops, solicitors, fish-mongers, stables and stockyards jostled one another for room and across the street the river teamed with activity. Boats, ferries, barges, fishermen, soldiers and passengers jostled one another in an effort to get to where they wanted to go.

The main street through town was nothing but a long mud-swamp, probably because of the spring thaws but also because there was simply too much traffic, both foot-traffic and that of the many horses, carriages and wagons loitering along the beach and docks.

A little ways down Main Street a handwritten road sign declared itself as 3rd and Broadway. A huge, wooden structure squatted on the road like a medieval fortress. Daddy said it was a stockade that had been built by the Yankton Militia as protection against marauding Indians.

Glancing to the right, I saw an Army barracks with soldiers- both young and old- marching to and fro across the parade grounds. And, across the street from the fort were a series of two-story houses with gaily painted porches and balconies festooned with scantily-clad women- both young and old.

It was a circus; a carnival and I felt like a fish out of water… half excited with the thrilling strangeness of it all and half scared, like the place might rear up and eat me whole if I wasn't careful. Looking over Annie's head, I saw my daddy gazing about with wide, hungry eyes.

His eyes lingered on the prostitutes in the near distance who stared right back at him, crooking their fingers and smiling lasciviously in welcome. He grinned and shrugged as if he was too good to be tempted but I knew better and my heart sank anew. How could he even entertain the thought of carnal relations after seeing my mamma- his own wife- laid out cold and bloody, just yesterday?

My excitement died as quickly as it had come and I hoped we could get away from this den of inequity before my father succumbed to his baser instincts. Looking down, I saw that Annie's thumb was tucked back in her mouth but when I tried to remove the offending digit, her pretty blue eyes filled with tears.

Sighing, I gave up and watched as daddy drove the wagon toward the front of a mercantile. The sign above the door read, **LAND OFFICE and MINERAL CLAIMS~**

He pulled the wagon to a stop, and looked me in the eye. "You stay here and feed the horse. Feed yourselves while you're at it… this might take a while." He stared up and down the street for a moment realizing, apparently, that the wagon was parked in the street between two bars and across from the whore-houses.

"Don't go wandering off, either." He grinned slightly. "I might not be able to find you if you go missing." With that, he stepped up onto a muddy boardwalk and walked into the land-office.

I looked around and saw a number of men watching me. Three grizzled old men gazed at me through the window of the saloon on my right. They were filthy, worn-out looking and exhausted. They seemed harmless enough, though, more wistful than threatening.

But another man gestured at me from a bench in front of the bar on my left. I don't know what he was doing by forking his fingers over his mouth and waggling his tongue at me the way he did but it made my skin crawl and my cheeks burn with shame.

I looked at Annie again and she stared up at me with wide eyes. Taking her thumb from her mouth she whispered, "Is Daddy leaving us here- alone?"

Swallowing, I nodded, "Just for a little while, sweetie. We'll be alright. Just don't look at the man, okay?"

Suddenly there was a commotion and I looked up to see two deputy sheriffs looming over the man with the sneer and busy tongue. "What the hell do you think you're doing, McCall, being disrespectful to little girls like that?"

One of the lawmen kicked the offender's feet out from under him and slammed his chair to an upright position on the tavern's porch. The man in question wasn't grinning anymore and he snarled, "Hey, God Dangit! This is public property... I was just a-setting here minding my own business. Why are you two pups rousting me?"

The other deputy answered, "You know Goddamn well why, Jack! Now, get the hell outta here before we haul your sorry ass off to jail!"

Picking his hat up off the floorboards, Jack McCall clapped the battered derby on his head. Then, after giving me a long and meaningful wink, he sauntered down the walk, turned a corner and was lost to view.

The deputies walked up to where I sat. One of them removed his hat and asked, "Are you two girls here alone?"

"No, Sir. Our daddy is in that land office. He'll be out in a minute or two." I replied.

"Well," the other one said. "Don't get out of this wagon, miss. Your pa picked a bad place to park if you ask me and we don't want to see you two come to any harm"

"Thank you, we won't, I promise" I answered with all sincerity.

The taller of the two young men said, "Our names are Steele and Caruthers, if you girls find you need any help. You can get ahold of us at the sheriff's office."

They wandered off down the street and Daddy returned about a half hour later. We drove around the block and pulled up in front of a rundown-looking boardinghouse, with pee-smelling rooms and a clerk who stared at me almost as nastily as that other man had.

Daddy hauled our bags up to the room, told us to go to bed and stated he would be back in a couple of hours. That was eight hours ago. There are unwholesome, scary sounds coming from the rooms on either side of us, and Annie has cried herself to sleep on a pallet on the floor.

I'm tired too, and am going to put you away in my hiding place. I'll crawl in under Annie's blanket- maybe she'll take some comfort from my presence- hopefully get some sleep and wake up to another- better day.

Good night, dear diary, until tomorrow.

Dear Diary,

I have a lot of news, but first I need to tell you about Mamma and Davey. I don't want to talk about it, or even think about it, but it needs to be done. Especially since our lives have changed so drastically in the last few days. Annie and I are moving on with our lives, whether we want to or not. More on that later...

Daddy, Annie and I stepped up on the porch after we got home from church that day. I was worried about the whipping I knew I was about to receive and Annie was fretful, too...thinking about Mamma, I'm sure, and scared for me.

It wasn't until we stepped inside, though, that I started to wonder about something other than my own silly self. The house was completely silent and I remember thinking, *Where's Davey? He should be at the top of the stairs, waiting to greet us.*

My father seemed to sense something out of the ordinary too, because his voice grew sharp as he called out, "Davey! Where are you, boy?"

His words echoed eerily and my heart started to pound with dread. "Stay here, Annie," I cried and ran up the stairs to check on my mother and brother.

I won't even try to describe what I saw as I entered the room. I only know that it was covered in red... pools, rivulets and sprays of red everywhere- the walls, the coverlet and all over the floorboards.

Mamma's body was crumpled up against the head-board. I couldn't see her face, which turned out to be a good thing since I found out later, she no longer had a face to look at.

I did get a good look at my brother, though, which was enough to send me into a fit of horror and grief. His little body was slumped over by the wall and his chest and belly were nothing more than a mess of blood, like puddles of strawberry jam.

A shotgun lay on the floor beside the bed and the smell of gunpowder, the copper stench of blood and fecal matter saturated the air like smoke, making me cough and sending what was left of my early breakfast up my throat and out onto the floorboards.

I heaved until I was empty and then looked up at my daddy who was standing by the door. His back was turned toward me- he was apparently trying to block the view from Annie's eyes- and I staggered to my feet.

That was when I spied a note on the table beside the bed. It was addressed to me, which I knew would make my father even angrier than he already was, so I snatched it up and crammed it in my skirt pocket.

Just in time, too. I heard him tell Annie to go downstairs and wait for us in the kitchen. Then he walked over to stand by my side. Staring down at what remained of my mother's face, he sighed and murmured, "So, she done herself in and took her son with her to hell..."

Although, I tried not to react to his words, fear of God's wrath for suicide and murder filled my heart and tears poured, afresh, from my eyes. *Could it really be true? I wondered. Was God so harsh and unforgiving he would punish my poor suffering mamma and even little Davey with ever-lasting hellfire?*

Filled with horror at the thought I started to shake, but Daddy put a heavy hand on my shoulder and said, "You need to pull yourself together, girl! What your mamma did was a sin- plain and simple- but now we need to pack up our belongings and get ready to leave. You won't be of any use to me and your little sister if you make yourself sick over the act of a demented sinner!"

His hand tightened and suddenly his grasp was hard enough to send me to my knees. Gasping out loud in pain, while the blood that had left my mother's body drenched the front of my skirt, Daddy hissed, "You get up, Nelly. Go downstairs right now and pack up you and your sister's belongings. Only two bags for each of you, mind. Then go outside and wait for me by that big oak tree. I'll be out shortly."

He let me go and I backed away as quickly as possible only stopping long enough to gaze, one last time, at my mamma and brother. Then I ran downstairs, grabbed my sister's hand and we crept back up to our rooms to pack what few belongings would fit into two small bags.

Within minutes Annie and I were standing under the giant oak tree that stood sentinel in the front yard.

Although my sister hadn't really seen the carnage (thank God!), she knew that something horrible had happened and she kept pulling on my hand and asking me, "What's wrong? What's happened? Where's Mamma? Where's Davey?"

I wanted to scream at her to stop. Although I knew exactly what had happened, I couldn't cope with it quite yet, much less answer Annie's questions. I knelt down so we were eye to eye and lied, "Annie, sweetie, Mamma and Davey are really sick right now. The catching kind, you know? The kind that makes all of us sick if we get too close!"

Her dark blue eyes clouded over and she gazed thoughtfully at the house. "You mean they got the typhoid?"

Where she had heard that term was beyond me but it sounded as good a lie as any so I nodded and said, "Yes, that's it. They have typhoid fever and Daddy sent us outside to wait for him so we can go fetch a doctor."

Although Annie seemed upset at the notion that her mamma and little brother were stricken with a catching sickness, she accepted my untruth at face-value and sat down on the grass to wait for Daddy to bring the wagon around.

While we were packing, I had hurriedly changed my bloody skirt when Annie's back was turned and I sat down on the grass beside her, overwhelmed and exhausted with sorrow.

Expecting my father to show up quickly we waited- and waited until Annie grew fretful. "Nelly, where's Daddy? Shouldn't we hurry so the doctor can come?"

Staring at the house, I also wondered what on earth

was taking him so long. Then I saw something out of the corner of my eye, just as Daddy flew out the front door and ran around the back of the house.

A horse whinnied and I knew Daddy was bringing the wagon around from the barn but my gaze was transfixed on the heavy, black smoke pouring from what I knew to be my mamma's bedroom.

My heart stopped or, at least, it felt like it... Daddy had fired the house! Annie noticed the smoke as well and suddenly she was screaming hysterically. "No!!!" she wailed, "Nellie, Mamma and Davey are in there! No, they'll burn up!" she howled.

The poor mite was unclear about the dangers of typhoid fever but she wasn't blind or stupid. She knew what fire was and her heart filled with terror. Jumping to her feet, Annie started running toward what was now a blazing inferno but I tackled her from behind and held her tight as she wailed in horror and grief.

Then Daddy was there and he plucked her from my arms, snarling, "You two get in the wagon. Now!"

Annie and I climbed up to the bench and our bags landed in the back. Just as Daddy stepped into the wagon and snapped his whip above the horse's rump the house groaned, almost like a person, and let out a huge sigh of smoke and flames. Fire licked out of every window and the air filled with tiny black pieces of soot.

We took off at a dead gallop. Annie buried her face in my chest and I could feel her body shiver and shake like a leaf in a gale. I tried to calm her with soft words of comfort but she was inconsolable. I knew then that I should have told her the truth in the beginning- that her mamma and little brother were not burning up in a fire but had already, mercifully, died.

But it was too late. I vowed to tell her what had really happened just as soon as possible- just as soon as daddy couldn't hear my words- but for now, she had stuck her thumb in her mouth, like an infant, and was staring blindly at the escaping landscape.

Strangely, Daddy turned the wagon right at the main road instead of left which was the way into town and the river docks. At this point, though, I couldn't have cared less. As the miles passed and Annie fell asleep in my arms all I could think about was that my mamma and little brother were gone and Annie and I were stuck with a man whose heart was as black as sin.

I glanced back once, right before we crested a hill that would obscure my view of the only life I had ever known, but all I could see was a tall column of smoke and the smudgy, dying embers of what was now nothing more than a nightmarish, burnt-out husk.

MARCH 22, 1876

Dear Diary,

Looking back, I see that it's been almost two weeks since I wrote to you, dear diary. There's a good reason for that, though, and while Annie and I are alone I'll try and fill you in on what's been happening.

The first night we arrived, Daddy didn't come back until the birds started singing the next morning. When he *did* finally arrive he was stinking, stupid drunk and as mean as a snake. I was not able to sleep- too many thoughts and sorrows ran through my mind and the noises coming from the rooms adjacent to ours were wild and filled with violence.

So much had happened over the last few days, I almost forgot about the blood-splattered note my mamma had addressed to me, but one particularly loud outburst from the room on my right startled me into wakefulness and I suddenly remembered.

I scrambled over to where my skirt was hung over a

chair and pulled the letter from an inside pocket. With shaking fingers, I lit a candle and studied the last words my mamma would ever speak to me;

Dear Eleanor,

I know what I'm about to do is a sin in the eyes of the Lord, but I can see no way out- for me nor for little Davey. That tiny sprout has been beaten so badly by that devil of a man, I doubt he will ever recover.

I am so sorry, honey, but I truly believe this is for the best.

One thing I DO know is that you are strong. Much stronger than I have ever been. So, I want you to take your little sister's hand and run away from your daddy just as soon as you can.

I've been squirreling away some money for quite a while now. It's hidden in an old sewing box under that big oak tree in the front yard. I think that there's about a hundred dollars in there by now, which isn't a whole lot but will help, in a small way, to start a new life.

Go to my sister's house- she will welcome you with open arms.

But, above all, get away from that evil, skunk of a man. I have no doubt that, given half a chance, he will beat the life out of you and your sister, both.

Pick your time, get away, and live your life to the fullest, dear Nelly. I love you- all of you- with all my heart.

I hope you can forgive me for what I'm about to do, but I cannot take anymore.

Affectionately;

Your loving Mamma

Tears stung my eyes as I folded the letter, paused and then passed it over the candle's flame. It would not do for

Daddy to find it and would only serve to enrage him more. It didn't matter anyway- her words would be written on my heart, until the day I died.

On one hand I was having a hard time forgiving her but on the other hand, well, I could hardly blame her for checking out. I also knew that she was right. I *am* stronger than she ever was. At least, I know that I am more of a fighter... I would rather die than let my father hurt me- or my little sister!

Which meant- since I had no intention of dying- I would rather Frank Higgins died than hurt Annie OR me!

That was the minute I started planning our escape. As the early morning sun started to paint the darkness in pallid shades of peach and cream, I plotted and schemed. I also took the time to actually count the coin and bills Daddy's old congregation had given me.

As I huddled over the money my heart was filled with gratitude, even after realizing $47.29 wasn't nearly enough to start anew. But what a sum! My neighbors had dug deep in their pockets to share such an amount.

I wondered how much a coach ticket to Chicago would cost and reckoned in the one hundred dollars Annie and I had practically sat on before Daddy whisked us away. I figured that the extra money would be more than enough to help support my sister and me at Aunt Chloe's, at least until I could find a job and pay our keep...

All these and other thoughts ran circles in my mind for the next couple of hours and then the door crashed open, followed by a raucous peal of laughter. Daddy stumbled into the room with a woman draped over his right arm. They both stunk to high heaven; the sickening stench of booze, sweat and flower-water.

"Shhh! The girls are sleeping," my father whispered.

"They are in here?" the floozy hiccupped. "I don't want to do the deed in here with them looking on, Frankie!"

"Aw, now," Frank replied, "They are sound asleep and won't hear a thing! Come on now, Darla, you promised!"

Darla let out a low chuckle and whispered, "Well, if you don't mind them listening in, then neither do I. Come on over here, big boy…"

The next twenty minutes were truly one of the most humiliating moments of my entire life. It wasn't as though I was ignorant of what went on between men and women, but Mamma and Daddy had always been pretty quiet about it.

Neither did I quite understand what was happening as the tart crouched over Daddy while he moaned and groaned like a dying man. I tried not to look, I promise you, but it was hard not to peek as they were only about four feet away from where Annie and I were lying on our pallet.

Rest assured, I learned more about the birds and the bees that night than I had gleaned in all my sixteen years! I tried covering Annie's ears and eyes but she watched anyway, and the next morning she could barely look me in the eye without blushing.

Oh! I hear somebody coming this way- it's either Daddy or his new girlfriend Darla, and I can't be seen writing in this book, so goodbye for now!

Dear Diary,

I have a job! I'm nervous and excited too, but I need to write about a few things before I forget so, I will fill you in on that later.

Daddy and Darla are gone again, thank God. That's the way things have been the last couple of weeks. They sleep until late morning or early afternoon and then stumble out into the light of day to carouse from one bar to the other.

It's a terrible situation, but one I can't figure how to get out of, especially since Darla stole most of my cash two days after she showed up. I could kill her really, I could, but she's twice as big as me and three times as mean.

Four days after she entered our lives, Annie and I had just come back from the mercantile with eggs, bacon and coffee- Daddy's orders. He had gone down the hall to use the bathroom and Darla was rooting through my bags. I opened the door to the room just in time to see the woman tuck a wad of my cash in her bodice.

"Hey!" I shouted. "Put that back, it's mine!"

She sneered and said, "Finders Keepers, darlin'. That's what you get for not hiding yer stuff better."

I remember balling up my fists in fury. I would have attacked her if I thought I could beat her but, sensing my intentions maybe, she stared at me with her mean gray eyes and smirked.

I saw the tension in her body as she squared off against me and rolled up her sleeves, and I knew she would beat me to a pulp if I tried to fight her. Realizing she would prevail, I started to think about Annie... what would happen to my little sis if I wasn't around to protect her?

Taking a deep, calming breath, I put the foodstuff on the table by the woodstove, took Annie's hand and murmured, "Let's step outside for a little while, Annie."

"Where do you think you're going, Eleanor?" Darla's southern twang rang in my ears as we stepped out into the hallway.

I stopped and looked back at her. Sunlight fell on a face that might have been pretty once but was now bloated and etched with lines of avarice and anger. Her blonde hair was stringy and needed a wash, and sweat stains had made permanent, smelly half-moon stains under her armpits.

Seeing the look on her face, I said, "Just tell my father that Annie and I are taking a walk. We'll be back later."

"Frankie ain't gonna like it..." she yelled as I slammed the door shut.

Annie's eyes were over-flowing tears. She knew, in her

own childish way, that the cash I carried was vitally important to our survival but she was also hungry. The two of us had been basically living off the crumbs and crusts of what was left of Frank and Darla's meals and both of us were losing weight from the lack of food in our bellies.

I shook her hand a little as we tramped down the stairs. "Don't worry, I still have a little cash in my pocket. How 'bout I buy you a nice breakfast?"

She stared up at me for a moment and then smiled. "Really? With eggs?"

"Yes!" I answered as gaily as I could. "Eggs and bacon and spuds. How does that sound?"

In truth, Darla hadn't got all of my cash- only the coin that I had traded for bills... about twenty dollar's, worth. Still, that meant I was down to a little under thirty dollars. I couldn't bear the fear and sorrow in Annie's eyes, though, and figured a good meal might perk her up.

And, it worked! Immediately, Annie started skipping down the staircase and I had to run to keep up with her. We headed outside and walked down the block to a nice little café. We had been in before and knew it to be a plain place with threadbare curtains and smoke-blackened ceilings but the food was good and plentiful.

I ordered up a big breakfast for Annie and settled for a hot-cross bun and strong coffee. Looking around at the patrons I saw many happy families smiling at one another, joking and eating their food with gusto.

I saw the old Chinese laundry man and his middle-aged daughter eating together in contented silence and the same two deputies who had stopped that rude young man from sticking his tongue out at me when we first arrived in town.

Everyone seemed so happy... so normal. Suddenly, the thrill of my unexpected (and probably unwise) gift of breakfast curdled in my stomach and I stared down at the tablecloth, blinking back tears.

"Nelly," Annie whispered, "What's wrong?" New moisture had sprung up in her wide blue eyes and her voice wobbled with fear.

I knew that the only thing keeping my little sister from falling to pieces was me and I shook my head. Then, I lifted my eyes and winked. "It's nothing, silly. I'm just mad at... you know who!"

She nodded in an exaggerated manner and exclaimed, "Me too! I hate her!"

Knowing I should talk to her about using the "Hate" word, I couldn't help but agree with her assessment, and grinned at her across the table. That was when a masculine voice interrupted our conversation.

"Hello, miss?"

I looked up and saw a young man standing next to our table, staring down at me with his hat in his hands.

Heart sinking, I wondered if those two young deputies, who had acknowledged my presence with a friendly tip of their hats, would have to come to our rescue again.

I stared up at the interloper and studied his face. He looked to be in his twenties with a pencil-thin mustache, dark brown eyes and curly black hair. He looked quite clean but seemed like bit of a dandy with his black derby hat and Seersucker suit.

"Yes, what is it?" My words came out sounding rude, but I was nervous.

The man rolled his hat in his hands and answered, "Well, it's kind of a long story, but I'm a photographer. My father, who is at home right now, is a painter." He glanced around at the customers and said, "Would you mind, terribly, if I sat down with you for a moment"

Seeing the doubt on my face, he added, "I promise you, I won't bite."

His eyes seemed so kind, I couldn't help but grin. Gesturing at Annie, I beckoned her over to my side of the table and told the man to take her chair. Once seated, he stuck his hand out to shake and announced, "My name is Martin, Martin Leibowitz. Pleased to meet you..."

"Eleanor Higgins, and this is my sister Annie," I replied.

He shook my hand and Annie's with a smile and then sat back as our breakfast plates arrived. As we ate, he explained himself. "My father has been given a commission for the finest, new bar and hotel in town... the River Queen. It's being built right now- two blocks over on Third Street."

He seemed moonstruck with admiration of the newest building in town. He took a deep breath and continued, "What the new owners want is a picture of a beautiful woman to hang on the back bar in the saloon area. What my father and I usually do is take a picture first and then render the photograph into an oil painting. The problem is there are not that many pretty women in town."

I think my mouth was hanging open in shock and I elbowed Annie as she giggled at the dumb expression on my face. Martin smiled too. "Well," he added, "there are quite a few pretty girls around the area but they're whor..." he stopped speaking and stared down at Annie's upturned face.

Blushing, he stammered, "What I meant to say is, I am not supposed to use a familiar face, if you get my drift, and most of the God-Fearing ladies about town wouldn't like their picture on the walls of a hotel- even if it *is* in high-repute."

Staring at my face, Martin grinned. "I've seen you a few times, you know, walking around town with your sister. Even my father saw you once, and he agreed, you would make a fine subject for a painting."

His voice dropped into a whisper. "I think you are one of the most beautiful girls I have ever seen. I promise, the only thing you would need to do is sit in my father's studio- in plain view of the street. You would wear one of the costumes we keep in the back... and you would stand to make a hundred dollars for the privilege of having your likeness in one of the nicest hotels west of the Mississippi!"

My heart was beating so fast, I felt faint.

"What do you say, Eleanor?" he asked again but I was already nodding yes, yes, yes!

March 24th, 1876
   Dear Diary,

As you can probably tell, Daddy and Darla are out again spending what little money they have (or, I should say, what I had) at the many bars in town. I have come to realize that my father's plan of buying mining equipment and heading up into the hills to pan for gold stalled out the moment we rode our wagon into town.

Anyway, I'm glad they're gone because the minute Annie and I got back to our squalid little room at the boarding house, Daddy picked a fight with me. I'm sure Darla instigated it, although I'm not sure how or why. I doubt she would have admitted to stealing from me... for all she knew, the cash she stole could have been Daddy's.

Still, for whatever reason, the second I stepped into the room, my father grabbed my arm and propelled me to the messy, unmade bed by the back wall.

"Ow!" I hollered as his fingers pinched my flesh. Then I saw stars as his palm smashed against my left cheek. Tasting blood and hearing Annie wail in fright from somewhere behind me, I stared up at him and said, "What's wrong Daddy? What did I do wrong?"

He took a step back and regarded my face before saying, "Darla told me you were disrespectful to her while I was in the bathroom this morning. Is that true?"

I was in a quandary now. I couldn't admit that the trollop had stolen money from me because then I would have to admit I had some cash to begin with- which would open up a whole new can of worms. I couldn't even say that his new girlfriend was going through my things, which I found morally offensive, because that was skating too close to the other issue so I gave up and said, "Yes, Daddy. I'm sorry."

Darla was standing by the stove watching the show with glee in her eyes. She held the upper hand in this debacle and obviously relished the sensation of power she had over me.

My father, on the other hand, seemed confused by my

easy capitulation and studied me with suspicious eyes. "So, what did you do, Nel?" He seemed genuinely curious, as apparently Darla had been vague in her accusations.

Thinking fast, I answered, "I took Annie out for a walk. Darla thought I should talk to you first but you were... busy, so I went out against her will. I'm sorry, Daddy."

He studied me for a moment. I couldn't help but notice that although he had cleaned himself up a bit from last night's party, his eyes were dull and seemed to crouch in the dark pouches that surrounded them like birds in a nest and his chin whiskers were more gray than black. He was looking old and used up- much older than the 38 years I knew him to be.

I felt something trickle down my chin and wiped a streak of blood away from my split lip with the back of my hand. He watched me for a second and then turned to face Darla. "Do you mean to tell me that you got mad because Nelly took her sister out for a walk?"

Darla's triumphant expression turned sour. "Why, Frankie darlin', I told her she'd better ask you first but she disobeyed me and went without a by-yer-leave anyway! She was being sassy!"

Frank Higgins advanced upon his new girlfriend with fury in his eyes. "Next time you got something to say about my daughters you better show some respect! You had me believing Nelly was the very devil and I punished her for it. Next time you will be the one on the receiving end, you hear me?"

Darla was all smiles by now, and phony apologies. She hastened over to the makeshift shelf sitting close to the woodstove and poured Daddy a healthy glass of whiskey.

"Here honey, I'm sorry too. I guess I over-reacted. Come on and drink up. You'll feel better for it, I promise!"

My father downed the glass in one long swallow and wiped his mouth off a rag-towel. Gazing over at me he said, "Clean your face off, Nel. I will cook us up some bacon sandwiches for lunch, okay?"

Some little shred of decency had suddenly surfaced in my Daddy's heart and I could see Darla glaring at me in furious silence from over his shoulder. I understood then, that battle-lines had just been drawn, whether I was a willing participant in her war- or not.

"Annie could use a wash too, Daddy. Can we both go to the bathroom?"

Frank shrugged and said, "Sure, why not. Hurry up though, Darla and I are going out in a little while."

So, Annie and I took soap, a towel, underwear and two clean blouses into the bathroom down the hall and cleaned up as best we could with the cold tap water. It felt like one of my front teeth was loose but I figured if I was careful it wouldn't fall out.

A while later, Daddy served Annie and me bacon sandwiches, which I ate carefully but happily while Annie only picked at hers. She had stuffed herself at breakfast earlier and couldn't fit in one more bite.

"What's wrong with you, Sis?" Daddy barked angrily.

"I got a stomach ache, Daddy," she complained (Bless her heart...she knew not to say anything about her bought breakfast).

"I'll take it, Frankie, if she don't want it," Darla generally ate twice as much as anyone else and was, in no way, ashamed of herself over it.

"Oh, I don't care," Daddy grumped and took another

gulp of whiskey straight out of the bottle. Darla snatched the sandwich off of Annie's plate with a self-satisfied grin and ate it in three large bites while I stared at her in disgust. Honestly, that sandwich would have been a pretty good supper for the two of us later on in the day.

About twenty minutes later, Daddy and Darla left, which meant that Annie and I had the rest of the day and evening alone. This wasn't guaranteed, of course. Every once in a while, one or the other of them would tuck into the room to pick something up or just to check on the two of us, but usually, once they were gone- they were gone for the rest of the day.

That was fine by me. I didn't want to see either one of them, my mouth hurt and I was just over-whelmed by unhappiness.

"Why don't you lie down while I wash the dishes, Nelly?" Annie volunteered.

I stared at her. "Really? That would be so nice of you."

Annie shrugged. "I can wash a dish as good as anybody, Sissy. Just... could we go to that little park after a while?"

Annie and I had stumbled across a piece of unattended lawn a couple of days earlier, three blocks away and close to where some of the bigger, nicer houses in town had been built. We had only peered through the fencing but what we saw was beautiful.

It was a small enclosure, about a quarter of a block square with high, fancy wrought iron surrounding it and a couple of stone benches placed alongside the fence. Mature willow trees seemed to lean towards one another in leafy friendship and a family of bluebirds had taken up residence there, sparking about on the green grass like two-legged sapphires.

I closed my eyes, and mumbled, "Sure, honey. Just give me an hour or two to catch up on some sleep, okay?"

My jaw throbbed, my tooth ached and I wondered if I would be black and blue by tomorrow morning. I also wondered if my face was too marred now to take a picture of so I could get my hands on that promised money. I wondered if Darla would try and kill me when Daddy wasn't looking on...

Pulling my birthday locket from my pocket, I stared at it and wept until I fell asleep.

Dear Diary,

As you can probably tell, Daddy and Darla are out again spending what little money they have (or, I should say, what I had) at the many bars in town. I have come to realize that my father's plan of buying mining equipment and heading up into the hills to pan for gold stalled out the moment we rode our wagon into town.

Anyway, I'm glad they're gone because the minute Annie and I got back to our squalid little room at the boarding house, Daddy picked a fight with me. I'm sure Darla instigated it, although I'm not sure how or why. I doubt she would have admitted to stealing from me... for all she knew, the cash she stole could have been Daddy's.

Still, for whatever reason, the second I stepped into the room, my father grabbed my arm and propelled me to the messy, unmade bed by the back wall.

"Ow!" I hollered as his fingers pinched my flesh. Then I saw stars as his palm smashed against my left cheek.

Tasting blood and hearing Annie wail in fright from somewhere behind me, I stared up at him and said, "What's wrong Daddy? What did I do wrong?"

He took a step back and regarded my face before saying, "Darla told me you were disrespectful to her while I was in the bathroom this morning. Is that true?"

I was in a quandary now. I couldn't admit that the trollop had stolen money from me because then I would have to admit I had some cash to begin with- which would open up a whole new can of worms. I couldn't even say that his new girlfriend was going through my things, which I found morally offensive, because that was skating too close to the other issue so I gave up and said, "Yes, Daddy. I'm sorry."

Darla was standing by the stove watching the show with glee in her eyes. She held the upper hand in this debacle and obviously relished the sensation of power she had over me.

My father, on the other hand, seemed confused by my easy capitulation and studied me with suspicious eyes. "So, what did you do, Nel?" He seemed genuinely curious, as apparently Darla had been vague in her accusations.

Thinking fast, I answered, "I took Annie out for a walk. Darla thought I should talk to you first but you were... busy, so I went out against her will. I'm sorry, Daddy."

He studied me for a moment. I couldn't help but notice that although he had cleaned himself up a bit from last night's party, his eyes were dull and seemed to crouch in the dark pouches that surrounded them like birds in a nest and his chin whiskers were more gray than black. He was looking old and used up- much older than the 38 years I knew him to be.

I felt something trickle down my chin and wiped a streak of blood away from my split lip with the back of my hand. He watched me for a second and then turned to face Darla. "Do you mean to tell me that you got mad because Nelly took her sister out for a walk?"

Darla's triumphant expression turned sour. "Why, Frankie darlin', I told her she'd better ask you first but she disobeyed me and went without a by-yer-leave anyway! She was being sassy!"

Frank Higgins advanced upon his new girlfriend with fury in his eyes. "Next time you got something to say about my daughters you better show some respect! You had me believing Nelly was the very devil and I punished her for it. Next time you will be the one on the receiving end, you hear me?"

Darla was all smiles by now, and phony apologies. She hastened over to the makeshift shelf sitting close to the woodstove and poured Daddy a healthy glass of whiskey. "Here honey, I'm sorry too. I guess I over-reacted. Come on and drink up. You'll feel better for it, I promise!"

My father downed the glass in one long swallow and wiped his mouth off a rag-towel. Gazing over at me he said, "Clean your face off, Nel. I will cook us up some bacon sandwiches for lunch, okay?"

Some little shred of decency had suddenly surfaced in my Daddy's heart and I could see Darla glaring at me in furious silence from over his shoulder. I understood then, that battle-lines had just been drawn, whether I was a willing participant in her war- or not.

"Annie could use a wash too, Daddy. Can we both go

to the bathroom?"

Frank shrugged and said, "Sure, why not. Hurry up though, Darla and I are going out in a little while."

So, Annie and I took soap, a towel, underwear and two clean blouses into the bathroom down the hall and cleaned up as best we could with the cold tap water. It felt like one of my front teeth was loose but I figured if I was careful it wouldn't fall out.

A while later, Daddy served Annie and me bacon sandwiches, which I ate carefully but happily while Annie only picked at hers. She had stuffed herself at breakfast earlier and couldn't fit in one more bite.

"What's wrong with you, Sis?" Daddy barked angrily.

"I got a stomach ache, Daddy," she complained (Bless her heart...she knew not to say anything about her bought breakfast).

"I'll take it, Frankie, if she don't want it," Darla generally ate twice as much as anyone else and was, in no way, ashamed of herself over it.

"Oh, I don't care," Daddy grumped and took another gulp of whiskey straight out of the bottle. Darla snatched the sandwich off of Annie's plate with a self-satisfied grin and ate it in three large bites while I stared at her in disgust. Honestly, that sandwich would have been a pretty good supper for the two of us later on in the day.

About twenty minutes later, Daddy and Darla left, which meant that Annie and I had the rest of the day and evening alone. This wasn't guaranteed, of course. Every once in a while, one or the other of them would tuck into the room to pick something up or just to check on the two of us, but usually, once they were gone- they were gone for the rest of the day.

That was fine by me. I didn't want to see either one of them, my mouth hurt and I was just over-whelmed by unhappiness.

"Why don't you lie down while I wash the dishes, Nelly?" Annie volunteered.

I stared at her. "Really? That would be so nice of you."

Annie shrugged. "I can wash a dish as good as anybody, Sissy. Just... could we go to that little park after a while?"

Annie and I had stumbled across a piece of unattended lawn a couple of days earlier, three blocks away and close to where some of the bigger, nicer houses in town had been built. We had only peered through the fencing but what we saw was beautiful.

It was a small enclosure, about a quarter of a block square with high, fancy wrought iron surrounding it and a couple of stone benches placed alongside the fence. Mature willow trees seemed to lean towards one another in leafy friendship and a family of bluebirds had taken up residence there, sparking about on the green grass like two-legged sapphires.

I closed my eyes, and mumbled, "Sure, honey. Just give me an hour or two to catch up on some sleep, okay?"

My jaw throbbed, my tooth ached and I wondered if I would be black and blue by tomorrow morning. I also wondered if my face was too marred now to take a picture of so I could get my hands on that promised money. I wondered if Darla would try and kill me when Daddy wasn't looking on...

Pulling my birthday locket from my pocket, I stared at it and wept until I fell asleep.

Dear Diary,

I awoke a couple of hours later with the sun in my eyes and my sister huddled over me, tapping my cheeks and crooning, "Nelly, wake up! Wake up, sis, it's been hours and hours!"

I groaned and glared up at her. "Stop that Annie! It hurts!"

She scooted backwards and whispered, "I'm sorry, Nel. I forgot…"

Staring across the room at the large, untidy pile of belongings we had brought up from the wagon, I saw my mother's pretty little mantle clock perched on a box of lard. I really *had* slept for quite a while- it was almost 3:00 in the afternoon.

Sitting up, I winced at the spear of pain lancing through my head. I wasn't particularly prone to headache but I sure did have one now! Wishing with all my might that I hadn't promised Annie a walk to the park, I stared up at her pinched face and hopeful expression.

Sighing, I stood up and stumbled over to the wash-basin to splash my face with cool water. "Here, Nelly," Annie said, handing me a cup of lukewarm coffee.

I swallowed it in one big gulp and ran a brush through my hair. Staring into the cracked mirror above the basin I saw that there was some slight bruising where Daddy had smacked me but *that*, so far, was the extent of the damage.

I smiled at my reflection. Martin Leibowitz had asked me to meet up with him at his father's studio in two days, and it looked like my face would pass muster unless Daddy or, more likely, Darla took another shot at me before then.

Wide awake, suddenly, and inordinately pleased, I grabbed my day-bag and Annie's hand. "Sorry I snapped at you, sweetie. Let's go!"

Grinning, she practically dragged me out the door. We skipped down the stairs and headed east. I wanted to see the new hotel being built on Third Street and knew that the park was close by.

The day was bright and beautiful, rich with the promise of spring. Stylish men and women strolled slowly along the thoroughfare. Ladies spun gaily colored para-sols and tiny feathers on the gentlemen's hats danced back and forth in the warm breeze.

It was as though a completely different town, affluent and elegant, hid modestly behind the raucous façade of Main Street. Luckily, both Annie and I had donned our bonnets, which was the only affectation we could afford in this more rarified society.

Three blocks away from our boarding house, we

found the new hotel... the River Queen. It wasn't hard to spot. Saws screeched, hammer blows fell and the grunts and shouts of, at least, fifty men reached our ears long before we arrived.

Annie and I stood across the street and stared in awe. It looked like a castle! It would end up being almost a block long with high turrets rising on either end of the building. I could tell that the rooms would be upstairs and staring through the many un-glassed windows downstairs, I figured the lobby would be in the middle with a restaurant on one side and... possibly, a saloon on the other. It would be so grand!

Imagining my likeness taking a place on the walls of that magnificent establishment made me blush with both pride and embarrassment. I hoped that Daddy, Annie and I would be long gone before the hotel opened for business.

Looking to my left and trying to spot the street on which our little park resided, I caught the eye of an older gentleman. He was tall and quite fat and wore a purple and black-striped satin vest which fairly gleamed in the sunlight.

Another man stood next to him. He was as short as the other man was tall, and he held a sheaf of papers in a hand that was missing a number of its digits. They were both staring at me intently.

Grabbing Annie's hand, I muttered, "Let's go, sis. I think the park is this way."

That was a lie. I actually thought the area we sought was just behind the two men but there was no way I wanted to walk their way. I don't know why, but their attention scared me.

Annie was no fool. She knew, exactly, where the park was but she followed my convoluted trail willingly enough until we came upon the place by the back way. The fence was not quite as high here and when we saw no gate, we hiked our skirts and climbed over. Instantly, it was as if we had entered an enchanted woods.

The dell was hushed and green with a tiny brook that tinkled between two big willows. The bluebirds were there again, industriously searching for bugs and tiny twigs with which to line their new nests.

I could feel the tension leave my body as we walked along the fence-line, searching for the benches we had spied a couple of days earlier. I bent over to study a crocus that had heaved up through the soil when I heard Annie squeal in alarm. Standing up, I saw her getting to her feet and rubbing a place on her shin.

She looked up at me and, pointing downward, declared, "I tripped over this rock, Nelly. I'm bleeding!" Her face was red and she blinked back tears of pain.

Running to catch up, I saw a bloody gash right below her left knee and what was obviously a tombstone, leaning haphazardly from the ground. I realized that we were not in a park at all, but were trespassing in a cemetery! Grabbing my sister's hand, I hissed, "Come on- we got to get out of here!"

"But- what about my leg, sis? I'm bl-leeding all over!" she howled.

I don't know if it was the pain of her stumble or the fact that her much anticipated jaunt was suddenly being cancelled, but suddenly I had a bleeding, screaming wreck on my hands.

Kneeling down, I wrapped her in my arms. "Sssh,

honey. Let me put a kerchief on your leg, okay? I know you don't want to leave but this is a graveyard, not a park. I'm sure we are trespassing, so as soon as I wrap your leg, we gotta get out of here!"

Annie's eyes grew as big and round as saucers and she promptly stuck her thumb in her mouth, staring about in horror as I wrapped a blue bandana around her cut leg. Murmuring around the obstacle in her mouth, she asked, "Is there ghosts, sis?"

Feeling a prickle of alarm, I glanced up at her and said, "No! That's nonsense, Annie. It's just a nice place where folks lay their dead to rest, that's all."

That information seemed to upset my sister even more, and she trembled as I took her hand and back-tracked to where we had climbed in over the fence.

I was just helping Annie over when I heard a harsh, feminine voice. "Who are you and what are you doing in my family's graveyard?"

I froze and set my little sister down on the grass. Turning around, I saw two people standing behind us. One was a tall, extremely handsome young man in a soldier's uniform and the other was an older woman in widow's weeds who was staring at me with an offended look on her face.

"Answer me!" she snapped.

And I blurted out the truth. "My sister and I are new to town and we thought this was a park. I am so sorry ma'am! It wasn't until my sis tripped over a gravestone that I realized we were in a cemetery! We were just leaving..."

"Mamma, look at the little girl's leg," the young man said.

The woman's face seemed to soften as she stared at Annie. My sister's leg was a bloody mess, her cheeks were red and stained with tears of fear and pain and her thumb was stuck as deep as it would go in her mouth.

Gathering herself up, the woman said, "Well, we can't have that, can we?"

The young man gave a slight smile and shook his head in agreement.

Looking me in the eye, the lady said, "My name is Mrs. Burrows and this is my son, Adam. Our house is just there, behind those big trees. If you will come with us, I'll have my lady's maid tend to your sister's leg."

I hesitated for a moment, undecided, and she growled, "Well, what are you waiting for? I, for one, am ready for my tea!"

The young man winked and said, "You might as well come with us, miss. My mother is now on a mission and will not give up until your little sister is bandaged up and the four of us have afternoon tea..."

So, throwing caution to the wind, Annie and I followed Lieutenant Burrows and his mamma back to one of the biggest and nicest houses I have ever seen.

Same Day
   Dear Diary,

I had been giving some thought to my father's fall from grace. Was he ever a real preacher? A genuine man of God? Or was his vocation merely a job... an easy way out of having to do any *real* work? I knew, although he didn't know I knew, that he had been run out on a rail by his own parishioners.

Good thing too- his behavior outside the pulpit was as far from God's teachings as the human race from the moon. Still, I was shocked, frankly, at how easy it had been for him to fall into the depths of depravity after we left Sioux Falls. His descent was quick and complete, akin to Lucifer's fall from the vasty fields of heaven, straight down into the fiery pits of hell.

These thoughts ran through my brain as I sat and listened to Mrs. Burrows in her opulent parlor while her son, Adam, tended to Annie's bloody leg. The minute I stepped inside the Burrow's mansion, I knew that the people who owned this house were deeply religious- at a fundamental level.

The Burrows were of the Catholic persuasion (a fact which would have given my father an apoplectic fit had he found out). At the far end of the great hall, a gorgeous statue of the Lord Jesus sat in a niche of its own. A small but elaborate stained-glass window behind the statue cast the wooden figure in shades of blue, gold and red.

The minute Mrs. Burrows stepped inside, she walked up to the figure, bowed her head and fingered a long necklace of wooden beads that wrapped around her waist like a belt. Then she turned around and said, "Come along, girls. Mrs. Henderson is bringing tea in now."

I was standing, in awe by the front door and as I took a step forward I practically fell over a neat pile of luggage. Cheeks blazing, I felt awkward and clumsy, like a filthy, godless heathen in a chapel but once seated, the lady was as kind as could be.

An old woman came into the room seconds after we both took seats, carrying a wide silver tray with coffee, tea, little pointy sandwiches and tiny cakes. I had never

seen anything so fancy... or so casual. These folks must
have come from old, old money. The kind of money that
made high tea on silver platters as common-place as back-
strap in a cast-iron skillet.

I was tongue-tied at first as Mrs. Burrows asked me
one question after another but once Annie and Adam
came into the room, I realized the lady was just being
polite, and my answers came easier. Yes, we are new to
town... No, my Mamma has passed on... Yes, my Daddy is
a preacher.

I didn't exactly lie but I couldn't make myself tell the
full truth either. Besides, I would probably never see this
woman again, much less the stunningly handsome boy
who was her son.

I also realized that Mrs. Burrows was giving as good as
she got. Even while grilling me for information, she
volunteered that she was a widow- four years gone and
her oldest boy, Stephen, had been killed in the war (I
assumed the Civil War, although she didn't clarify).

Her heart was broken, just broken because now her
youngest son was heading into another war, this one
against hostile Indians in the Yellowstone area.

Staring into my face, Mrs. Burrows sighed. "I always
wanted a girl, you know, but the good Lord denied me
that pleasure." She glared at Adam, who looked as if he
wanted to flee for his life.

"Instead, I was given sons, so they could go off and get
themselves killed!"

"Mother, please!" Adam objected.

Tears suddenly rimmed the woman's eyes. "Oh
darling, I'm sorry, truly I am. It's just that I know you'll be
leaving soon and I can hardly bear it!"

Adam swallowed the tepid tea in his cup and set it down on its saucer. Standing up, he said, "Speaking of which, I really need to talk to the stable-master." Turning towards Annie and me he bowed slightly and murmured, "Ladies, it was wonderful to have made your acquaintance." Then he clicked his heels together in military fashion and left the room.

Some of the air in the room seemed to leave with him and I took a deep, shuddery breath. I was never one to moon over boys, even though I had been kissed more than once by some of the saucier young men around our old parish.

There was something about Adam Burrows, though, that set my heart to beating hard. He was very tall, for one thing, with wide shoulders and hard, calloused hands, attesting to a life of activity and labor. He also had golden hair and the greenest eyes I had ever seen. Hmmm…

Taking myself firmly in hand, I said, "Ma'am, I want to thank you for the nice tea and for fixing up my sister's leg. Also, I apologize for trespassing in your graveyard. It won't happen again, I promise!"

Mrs. Burrows had been sitting in contemplative silence and she jumped slightly at hearing my voice. "Oh! That's alright, my dear. Please excuse my absentmindedness. Adam will be leaving quite soon, on a riverboat, and I really *do* fear for his life up in that wild country."

I had gestured to Annie that it was time to take our leave, and we stood in awkward silence as the older woman climbed to her feet, looking much older and sadder than when she had first sat down. I offered her my arm to lean on but she waved it away with a small smile.

As we walked toward the front door, she said, "Girls,

perhaps once you've become established, you could send me your address? I will be awfully lonely once my boy leaves and since your dear Mamma has passed over, maybe I could sponsor you as a sort of Auntie? We could have luncheon... just us girls. What do you say?"

Annie gave a slight hop of excitement and my heart was filled with joy as well. I thanked her and said that I would send over our address just as soon as we were settled- knowing full-well that I would do no such thing.

It wasn't like I didn't want to spend time with this sweet and lonely lady, but I knew that as long as my father acted like a gutter-rat, along with his gutter-rat girlfriend, Annie and I would not prevail upon her, or bring shame down upon her generous nature.

We had just reached the front door when a howling cacophony filled the air. It was the blast of an air-horn- the loudest one I had ever heard. Annie and I almost jumped out of our shoes and I exclaimed, "What on earth was that?"

"Oh! That would be the Far West, coming in ahead of schedule, as usual."

"The Far West?" I echoed stupidly.

Mrs. Burrows nodded. "Yes. It is one of the biggest and fastest riverboats west of the Mississippi. It's 190 ft. long and has a beam of 33ft. It will dock here for the next week or two, taking on supplies and troops for that dust-up in Montana."

She sighed and dabbed at her eyes. *"That* is the monster that wi

Dear Diary,

Once Annie and I got back to our room, we fixed dinner-beans and meat with some store-bought biscuits- and I watched as she practiced her letters- U through Z and did some arithmetic's. As usual, both our ears were pinned backwards, listening for the sounds of my father and Darla's rowdy arrival.

It grew later and later. Still waiting, Annie put away her school work and said, "That is a fine boat, isn't it, Nel?"

She was referring to the Far West, which was just pulling into dock as we arrived on Main Street from the Burrow's house. We had stood stock still and gazed in awe at the huge, lumbering beauty with her double smoke-stacks, giant paddle-wheel and the ungainly steam-powered spars that rose like a grasshopper's legs from the front end of the boat.

It looked as though half of the town's population had

turned out to watch the Far West's arrival and as it blew its air-horn many of the spectator's threw their hats in the air and waved their handkerchiefs in greeting. Caught up in the spirit of the moment, Annie and I jumped up and down and waved as well.

Then I heard, "Pardon me, ladies. May I pass?"

Turning around, I saw Adam Burrows standing behind us on the side of the road we were effectively blocking. The small pile of luggage I had almost tripped over in the great hall was now in his arms and slung over his shoulders.

Blushing in embarrassment, I stammered, "S...sorry! Annie step aside, please, so Mr. Burrows can pass!"

The young man smiled. "It's Lieutenant Burrows, Miss. I need to report to duty right now, but I don't think we are shipping out for a few days. Perhaps we will meet again before the boat leaves?"

I nodded and watched as the young man made his way past us, crossed the street and was lost in the crowd by the docks. I knew we needed to get back to our room at the boarding house before my father and his girlfriend got home but I wanted to get a closer peek at the boat.

Grabbing Annie's hand firmly in my own, I said, "Let's take a look, okay?"

Annie smiled and pulled me into the busy street. Up close to the boat, you could see just how scarred the prow was... probably from plowing through the rivers shallows with its rough rocks, dead wood and sandbars.

The rest of the boat, however, was smartly outfitted with giant steam engines, three decks, and a cupola-type pilot-house, a number of small cabins along the top and a tangle of ropes, gear and mysterious machinery all along the bottom. Even as Annie and I stood and ogled the boat, the engines stuttered and died, leaving a silence that rang in the ears.

Cheer from the spectators arose into the sudden silence and an older, fierce-looking man with a mane of gray hair and a wide walrus moustache stepped toward a metal rail and raised his hand in a slight salute.

Another series of hoots and hollers filled the air and it occurred to me that this boat and the man who piloted it were viewed as heroes to the folk in the Dakota territories.

Wondering why, I heard another familiar voice say, "That is Captain Grant Marsh. He is the pilot for this boat and has been known to go where no other man has dared go- and at record speed!"

Looking up, I saw Martin Leibowitz setting up a large, ungainly-looking camera. He grinned, adding, "I'm taking a picture of the boat for the newspaper, but I'm glad I saw you. Are you still willing to sit for a portrait?"

I nodded. "Yes, but…" I blushed.

He frowned. "What is it, Eleanor?"

I swallowed. "I don't have to take off my clothes or anything like that, do I?"

He smiled. "No, we have costumes that are designed to go right over whatever you're wearing." He paused. "Besides, neither my father nor I would dream of hurting you, okay?"

Something about his wide, dark eyes convinced me of his sincerity and I nodded in agreement. Thinking for a moment, I said, "Say, could we do it about 2:00 or so? Any earlier and I might not be able to make it…"

He agreed. "Done! I'll tell my father to expect you and Annie tomorrow about 2:00."

He turned away and started to fiddle with his machinery so I said, "Let's go, sis."

I looked up one last time and noticed that, for some reason, the captain's eyes had fallen on me. He gave a slight smile before turning away to consult with young Lt. Burrows who had just climbed the stairs with an older military man and was, apparently, reporting for duty.

Feeling a chill run through my body, I shivered and thought about the goose that sometimes walks on a person's future grave. Thinking that the chill was just my mind's way of reminding me to get back to the boarding-house, I took Annie's hand and said, "Come on..."

She groaned but came along with me as we stopped by the small grocer and bought a half a dozen biscuits. Late that night, we were well on the way to falling asleep when Daddy came barging in the door, alone, and in a rage.

"Where is it?" he roared.

Although some instinct told me he knew about my hidden stash, I played possum and asked, "What Daddy? What are you talking about?"

In answer, he hauled off and kicked Annie, where she lay snugged up against me on the pallet, as hard as he could. She screamed in pain but, luckily for her, my father was so drunk he lost his balance and kicking high, fell backwards half-on and half-off the bed.

"Argh!" he bellowed and groaned.

Annie and I sprang up from the floor and flew toward the door. I knew that fleeing into the night without proper clothes or money was a grave mistake but I was not about to let Daddy beat the tar out of me or my little sister. Pausing for a moment in indecision, I glanced down at where my father still lay sprawled on the floor.

"Sssh, listen!" I spoke to Annie who was sobbing at my side and trying to pull me out into the hallway.

She quieted down and we both heard my father's snores rattle up from the floorboards. Knowing that he was probably down for the count, I pulled the door shut and sat my sister down at the little kitchen table.

Taking her by the shoulders, I whispered, "We can't leave Annie- not until we get a little more money. Sleep here, on these two chairs, and I'll find a little cash to appease Father."

Darla didn't know just exactly how much cash I had so, if she *had* spilled the beans about my secret stash I figured a ten dollar note would buy time until I got paid from the photographer and his father.

Then, I swore to myself, that Annie and I would take a stagecoach back to Sioux City and leave Daddy behind to fend for himself.

I'd better try to get some sleep, dear diary. I'll try and write again tomorrow.

Dear Diary,

I barely slept last night what with keeping one eye on my father and worry about the photography session I had set up. I wondered if the portrait would come to haunt me in the days to come but I honestly couldn't see any other way to get my sister and myself out of the situation we found ourselves in.

When Father finally did awaken he was morose and ill from too much hard living over the last couple of weeks. He sat up, blinking at me from his place on the floor and said, "What happened, Nelly?"

Annie and I stared down at him in consternation and I couldn't help but wonder if he had actually forgotten about his accusations- and the powerful kick he had aimed at his youngest daughter, but no such luck.

A moment later, he cradled his aching head and growled, "Never mind, I remember." Grimacing, he added,

"Darla told me you have money stashed around here somewhere. Where is it?

Stalling for time, and fingering the ten dollar note I had stashed in my skirt pocket, I said, "Where is Darla, Daddy?"

He glared at me for a second, but then his shoulders fell and he mumbled, "She left me for a young cow-poke... and good riddance to bad rubbish!"

He looked sad enough, though, I figured the time was right to volunteer my cash (or a portion of it, anyway) and try to talk him into a different course of action. "Daddy, I have saved up a little over twenty dollars since I was born. When we packed up, I brought my savings along with us."

I pulled the ten dollar note out of my pocket and handed it to him.

"Darla stole half of that amount from me, yesterday when you weren't looking but here's what I have left. I was hoping that now she's gone and left, this money will help us on our way to pan for gold?"

Daddy gazed at the money in his hand and then stared up at Annie who stood a little behind me with her thumb in her mouth. Poor thing, she was as white as a spook with dark circles under her eyes and I could tell that he remembered his actions from the night before.

Clearing his throat, my father murmured, "Aw, Annie, I'm sorry for what I done. Are you hurt real bad? That, that... whore got me all spun up last night and I wasn't thinking straight!"

Annie's eyes got big and she seemed torn between taking her thumb- her life-line- out of her mouth and answering Frank's question. Fearing Daddy's quick temper, I bumped her elbow and hissed, "Annie, answer your father!"

She glanced at me and pulled her hand away from her mouth long enough to mutter, "It's okay, Daddy. I'm not hurt bad."

Nodding, my father said, "Nel, bring me a cup of coffee. My head's splitting in two, here."

The rest of the morning went pretty well, although I began to wonder if I was going to make my appointment at 2:00. After drinking coffee and eating a large stack of hotcakes, Daddy crawled back into bed and didn't wake until well after noon.

Feeling much better by that time, he tucked my ten dollars into his pocket and said he was heading to the mercantile to buy a few necessaries for mining. Adding that he might stop for a quick toot, he advised us to have a nice dinner waiting for him by 7:00 that evening.

Mentally kissing my money goodbye and knowing that his first stop would probably be at one of the town's many saloons, I just wished he would leave so I could make that cash back- ten times over.

After he left, Annie and I tucked into the boarding house bathroom and washed up as best we could. I brushed my hair until it shone and made one more appraisal of Annie's upper belly.

She really *was* lucky. It looked like just the tip of Daddy's boot clipped her lower ribs and there was a small but livid bruise on her pale, white skin. Asking her, again, if she was sure she was all right, she nodded and tugged on my arm.

"Let's go and see Martin, Nel. He's nice!" she pleaded.

I laughed and answered, "Now, you behave yourself

when we go there, okay? Don't go talking the man's ear off and remember, "What we're doing is a *big* secret! No telling *anybody, ever!*"

She nodded in agreement and we took our leave. Looking both ways up and down the street, we saw no sign of our father, so we walked three blocks down the road and found a neat little shop with a sign above the door that read, **LEIBOWITZ AND SON~ PHOTOG-RAPHY AND ART**.

Stepping inside, we were greeted by a tinkling brass bell and a little old man who scurried out from behind a canvas curtain. He was ancient! Not even as tall as me, he had a wild mane of wispy, white hair like dandelion fluff and brown button eyes that peered out from a million wrinkles.

Those eyes were kind, though, and his soft hands warm as he shook my hand and hollered, "Welcome young ladies, welcome!"

Both Annie and I winced as he yelled at us, but then we heard Martin say, "Father! You're shouting again!"

"Oh!" Mr. Leibowitz stammered, "Here, let me get my ear-horn!"

As the older gentleman scurried back behind the curtain, Martin sighed. "Meet my father, Solomon Leibowitz. He is a spry old goat but as deaf as a post. Sorry…"

"That's okay, he seems really nice," I said.

"Oh, he is a good man… and quite a talented artist," Martin replied with a rueful grin. "Speaking of art, I wanted to show you the costumes he picked out for you."

Gesturing toward a number of seats by the back wall, he said, "Take a seat, and I'll be right back."

Annie and I sat down and listened as Martin and Solomon argued over costumes behind the curtain. "But this one is too dull!" Solomon exclaimed while Martin retorted, "And this one makes her look like a tart!"

"Well, never mind that," the old man replied. "Now that I've seen up close, I think this is the one we want!"

Annie giggled and poked me in the ribs. "You're a tart, sis!"

"No, I'm not. You shush, now!" I answered, heatedly.

Finally, the two men came around the canvas screen, each carrying his idea of the prettiest costume for their prize subject. One was a vivid green satin with frills, flounces and lace... Martin's choice. But my eyes were drawn to the dress Solomon carried in his arms.

It wasn't a real dress- the whole back was wide-open, only held together by a series of strings which could be loosened or pulled taut. But the color and texture of that costume made me gasp with delight.

It was a deep, blush pink like a rose in first bloom and it was velvet- the type of material I had only ever seen and yearned for from a distance. I pointed at the old man's offering, and he smiled in triumph. "See, son?" he crowed. "Like most beautiful women, this girl knows, instinctively, what she is supposed to wear!"

Martin grinned in agreement. "Yes, Father. You are correct, as usual. Drape it over her and let's see how the color reflects her skin..."

That done and approved, I sat for two hours, fully-clothed under a pink velvet, imitation dress with a dusty bunch of paper roses under my nose while Martin took a series of photographs.

Thinking about it now, I know that, somehow, father

and son worked a sort of magic this afternoon, one I still don't quite understand. As Annie sat and watched, transfixed, they powdered my nose, fixed my hair and put enough kohl around my eyes to transform me, Nelly Higgins, from a fairly plain sixteen year-old preacher's daughter into an exotic and famous (if fictional), French courtesan named, Monique La Fleur.

Dear Diary,

Well, three days have passed since I've had a chance to write and, as usual, this sort of thing happens whenever our circumstances change. This time it's because Daddy decided to give up on Yankton.

The day I sat for the portrait, he came home early. He had taken a few drinks, I could tell, but he wasn't too inebriated. What's more, he had come back home armed with three gold-pans, two small picks and two pairs of tough, rubberized boots.

"We're leaving for the Black Hills, tomorrow!" he announced.

Annie and I were in the process of making dinner. It was only about 5:30 in the afternoon, so we were right on time, but my heart flew into my throat at Daddy's early arrival. I had just finished fashioning myself a soft, cloth money-belt in which to stash the five twenty dollar notes the Leibowitz' had given me.

Annie was helping me tie it around my waist and we had just let my dress fall down over it when he barged into the room. Feeling my cheeks blush with nerves, I stammered, "Where, Daddy?"

He shrugged. "I bought the mining rights to 100 ft. of sandbar alongside a river by the town of Lead, South Dakota. It's west of here, so we'll be going up river on the "LaBeque" as far as Chamberlain. Then, we'll take the horse and wagon the rest of the way."

The more he talked, with his eyes wide-open and his lips twisted into a manic grin, the more scared I got. I went over to one of my bags and pulled out the territorial maps I had brought along for Annie's studies. Opening it up, I traced my fingers along the blue pen-lines denoting waterways in the Dakotas and finally found the town of Chamberlain to the north.

Then, I traced from there to the small town called Lead which was close to the town of Deadwood. Even I had heard of *that* town and my heart skipped a beat. *What is Daddy thinking of,* I wondered frantically, *taking his two young daughters to such a wild and unholy place?*

"Watcha got there, Eleanor?" Frank demanded.

I glanced up at him and replied, "I'm just looking at Annie's school maps, Daddy. Looking at where we're heading."

"Well, let me in on the secret, why don't you?"

Apparently, Daddy had no real clue about where he and his girls were actually going, so I scooted over on my chair and traced the lines for him.

Nodding, he smiled in satisfaction. "I guess that broker knew what he was talkin' about. Looks like a pretty straight shot to me."

To me, it looked like over 500 miles of rough travel through hostile Indian Territory! As I looked up at him, something in my face- perhaps the fear I was trying to hide- made him puff up in anger. "He came highly recommended, you know, *and* I got a good deal from him on a nice stretch of real estate, too!"

Not wanting to rouse his temper, I put on a brave face. "I bet you did, Daddy! When does this boat- The LaBeque- leave?

"Tomorrow about noon or, at least, that's what the pilot said," my father answered, adding, "I already paid the fare."

Swallowing my dread, I looked up at Annie and said, "See, honey? We're going to go and pan for gold! Maybe we'll get rich!"

I had put as much enthusiasm into my voice as humanly possible but Annie knew me well. Something of my fear must have shown because her face fell and she came to my side, sticking to me like a burr.

Daddy went over and sat down on the edge of the bed. "Wake me up when supper is ready. Then, we need to pack up our stuff nice and tight. This pilot charges by weight rather than size, so we need to go as light as a feather."

Then he closed his eyes and fell into a deep slumber. I tried waking him when the stew-meat was tender but he kept snoring away so I pulled the pan to the back of the stove and started rearranging our worldly possessions into as few boxes as possible.

Annie tried helping me but got upset whenever I decided to leave this thing or that behind. Each discarded item gained so much significance in her mind, by eight o'clock tears were pouring down her cheeks.

I ordered her into bed and finished my work just as daddy woke up with a mighty yawn. "Thought you were going to wake me up when supper was ready..." he snapped.

"I tried, Daddy, but you were sleeping really hard!" I defended myself. "It's still warm, though, and there's two biscuits left over from last night."

He sat and stared at the much smaller pile of possessions I had organized into a pile by the front door. Shrugging, he said, "Better make it smaller, Nel. That pilot is a stickler."

My cheeks flushed in anger and I had to bite my lip to hold back an angry outburst. Most of what I had discarded were Annie's and my own personal items, including most of her school primers, many of the maps, our nicest dresses, Mamma's china tea-set, and her pretty, checkered curtains.

The rest of the things were absolutely essential- like pots, pans, tin-ware and food. Daddy must have sensed my frustration and was, surprisingly, gentle. "Sorry, sis, but I got a good deal by renting out the back of our wagon to carry a load of fresh vegetables up north. The good news is, we'll have an eight of a share of those veggies once we get to Chamberlain."

Nodding, mutely, I started unpacking again and barely responded when he stepped out the door saying, "I'm just going for one more nip, Nel, and to say goodbye to some of the friends I made here in town. Be back soon..." He waited a moment for my response, and then the door shut behind him as he made his way down the stairs.

I laid down, soon after, and wondered about the strange and frightening turn our lives were about to take. Feeling an almost suffocating sense of dread, I finally fell asleep.

Daddy came back to the room sometime in the middle of the night. I was so weary from my labors I barely stirred until I heard Annie scream and felt her body being pulled from my arms.

I awoke fully and saw my father hurl my sister onto the bed. Then he fell upon her with an inarticulate bellow.

Galvanized, I screamed as well. "Daddy, stop it! Daddy, what are you doing?"

Annie was weeping with fear but Frank seemed oblivious to anything beyond his own set of inebriated initiatives. I ran to the bed and tried pulling on him but he was far stronger than me and swatted me away with a backward sweep of his hand.

Somehow, his flying fist connected with the tip of my chin and, for a moment, I saw stars and felt my knees grow weak. Then, I shook my head and ran to the cookstove, grabbing the first heavy thing I could find in the rooms dim light.

It was one of our oldest and heaviest cast-iron pans; cleaned, oiled and ready to pack after last night's dinner. Hesitating for a second, I remember thinking, *this could kill him!* Then I heard the sound of material tearing and my sister's muffled cry.

Rage filled my heart as I realized in horror that my father had gone mad and was actually trying to rape my seven-year-old sister!

Too much had happened lately; his violent rages had

killed my Mamma and little brother- his intemperate needs had brought an evil, conniving minx into our lives- and he had, in the space of only a couple of weeks, turned into a drunk and rapist...

Something twanged in my chest. Perhaps a heart-string broke, I don't know, but I lifted that heavy old skillet over my shoulder and hit him on the back of the head as hard as I could.

Daddy fell forward with a grunt and effectively pinned Annie under him. I let the pan drop to the bed and pushed my father's dead weight off of her, until she popped up with a cry and hurled herself into my arms.

I carried her to the far side of the room and lit a lantern. "Stay here for a minute, while I check on him." I whispered. Her face was white and her eyes as wide as saucers but she nodded as I backed away.

Leaning over, I saw my father's body draped half-on and half-off the bed. A large pool of blood was spreading like pond water over the dingy sheets and his eyes were fixed and staring at nothing.

Heart pounding hard and fast in my chest, I realized that my life, which had seemed so dangerous- so frighten-ingly uncertain had just taken a turn for the worse. Whereas before I was a victim caught up and trapped on someone else's crooked path, now I was the victimizer... a murderer guilty of patricide!

Still, my heart beat just as strongly as before- maybe even more so. Although I would have to live with what I had just done, I knew that in my own way, I had done what was right. It would have been a hundred times harder to live with myself had I stood back and let Daddy do to my sister what he had wanted to do!

Finally, I turned away and faced Annie. "I think I killed him, sis, so you need to put on your clothes, okay? We're leaving, right now!"

Dear Diary,

My mind was blank as I grabbed our two small satchels and flew out the door of the boarding house. Annie and I ran down the stairs and stepped out into the early morning dawn, where I blinked in confusion.

The sun was well on its way to peeking over a high bluff to the east and early-bird vendors were trudging into the small flea market down by the docks, placing shabby cloths over their splintered tables and hanging FOR SALE signs on small hooks in front of their sundry offerings.

Realizing it was far later (or earlier) than I had thought, I looked up and down the street, not knowing what to do or where to go from here. Spying the same pair of young deputies that seemed, more often than not, to work together as a team, my heart skipped a beat.

I understood that, realistically, they wouldn't have heard yet of my father's murder but that didn't stop me from feeling a thrill of paranoia. We had to get out of this town, just as soon as possible! Thinking fast, I grabbed Annie's hand and turned away from the lawmen and up the adjacent street toward the Burrow's private graveyard.

Praying that Mrs. Burrow's was not visiting her son and husband's graves this early, my sister and I hurried to the wrought iron fence and climbed over. Ducking under one of the big willow trees and behind a row of rose bushes, we huddled together on the damp ground.

Tears filled my eyes as the ramifications of what I had done dawned on me, anew. What if the police ran us down? What would become of Annie then? Would she, an innocent, be allowed to return to her Auntie's house or... would she be swept away to an orphanage or workhouse in a tide of miscarried justice?

I started shaking with the aftermath of my own violence, fear over the future and what it might have in store for us. Suddenly, Annie said, "Nelly, thank you for saving me." Her thin arms reached up and enveloped my body in a surprisingly fierce hug.

"I don't know what happened to our daddy," she added, "but he was a bad man and I know he would have burnt me up, just like Mamma and Davey, if you hadn't stopped him!"

Her voice, which had started out strong, broke down into a series of gasps as she spoke and I knew she was trying her best to comfort me and give me what little strength she possessed, despite her own terror.

I hugged her back and whispered. "I'm so sorry about what's happened but I'll do my best to keep both of us safe, okay?" She nodded and I continued, "Try and get a little sleep. In an hour or two, we'll go to Martin's shop. Maybe he and his father will help us get away from here."

She must have been terribly weary because she fell asleep almost instantly and snored in my arms for the next couple of hours as I peered through a tangle of leafless rose branches, watching as more and more people stirred awake.

The crew for the new hotel arrived and set to work on the building that would, eventually, host my portrait on one of its walls. Folks stepped out onto their front porches and greeted the day- some by feeding their chickens, others picking newspapers up off their lawns and sipping coffee while reading the local news.

Fatigue made my eyes feel gritty and a couple of times I almost nodded off as the sun's warmth dried the dew on the grass. Finally, I startled awake when a couple of children squealed with laughter and decided to leave before I fell asleep completely.

Shaking Annie's shoulder, I murmured, "Come on, sweetie, it's time to go."

She grumbled but awoke and sat staring at the light of a new day. Her wide blue eyes looked dazed and she shivered with nerves. My heart heaved with sympathy. What a burden for such a young girl to endure!

First her mamma and brother had left their mortal coil behind and now her daddy had gone to make peace with his Lord. All she had left in the whole, wide world was me and now my savage actions last had put her in peril-again.

Sighing, I said, "Let's go to Martin's shop, shall we? I think that he might be able to help us."

She nodded, silently, and we scaled the fence. Keeping

to alleyways and lesser used roads we made our way to Main Street and the Leibowitz' shop. As we walked, I wondered whether Martin and his father could be trusted- or not.

Ours had been a working relationship, after all, not a friendship and they could just as easily turn us into the law than help me and my sister escape. Still, there had been something in Martin's soft brown eyes... something that told me he wanted to be my friend... and maybe even more.

It was still pretty early and I hoped-against hope- that the business was open. When I tried the door, though, it was still locked. Heart sinking, I started to turn away but then I heard the little bell as the door was flung open.

Martin stood in the doorway in an undershirt and shaving cream on his face. "Eleanor? Hello! What are you two doing here so early?"

Something about his face- bony and thin rather than handsome like Lt. Burrows –with his large brown eyes, long inquisitive nose and swarthy skin suddenly seemed so kind, so dear, my eyes welled over in tears. Knowing that I was putting me and my sister's fate in the hands of a virtual stranger didn't stop me... I started sobbing out loud like a child.

He led us inside, closed and locked the door behind us and said, "What's going on, Eleanor? Whatever has happened, I will try to help, I promise."

After he wiped the shaving soap from his face and put on a clean shirt, I told him everything... from our lives in Sioux City to what had befallen us over the last few weeks. I also admitted to killing my father and I wailed in fright at what I had done and renewed fear of entrusting this young man with a truth that could get me hanged in the town square.

He sat and listened to me cry and seemed sympathetic to our plight. When I finally fell into a fit of hiccups, he stood up and fetched Annie and I a glass of water.

Handing the drinks to us he sat back down with a sigh. "I get around a lot, Eleanor. More than I want to, actually, but it's a part of my job… being where the news is as often as possible."

Looking up at his father who was just now coming down a rickety set of stairs from their living quarters on the second floor, he smiled and shouted, "Good morning, Father! Eleanor and her sister have come to call. Isn't that nice?"

The old man started, slightly, at seeing unexpected guests in the shop so early but he smiled and said, "I will visit with you just as soon as I get a cup of coffee. You *did* make our morning coffee, didn't you, Son?"

Martin smiled and pointed at the pot on the stove. Turning back to me he said, "My father will go back upstairs to drink his coffee and get dressed for the day. He probably won't be back down for a couple of hours, so we still have plenty of time to make a plan."

I nodded, my fear having rendered me temporarily mute. I looked over at Annie who had curled up in her chair and fallen back to sleep. Wishing I could do the same thing I knew there was too much at stake for dozing the day away.

Martin watched Simon climb the stairs and then he said, "I knew your father, you know. Unfortunately, a lot of my work takes place in the taverns around town… it's where most of the news takes place. In the short time your father was here, he made quite a name for himself."

He stared me in the eye, apparently judging whether he should elaborate. I said, "Go on, please. I want to know everything."

Shaking his head, Martin replied, "I suppose you already know about his... engagement with Darla Hopkins?"

I nodded and something in my eyes made him grin. "Yes, well she is one of the worst and hardest used whor... prostitutes in Yankton. She has made a career out of fleecing every man she sets her eyes on and I'm sure that one of these days her games are going to end very badly for her. For sure, more than one man has come to a bad end because of her proclivities."

My blood ran cold. How could my father have been so blind- so stupid? Not only did he pick a rotten apple to spend time with, he picked one who was practically famous for fleecing her customers! I got mad at him all over again and then I remembered I had put his foolishness down for good.

It wasn't Darla Hopkins who had spelled Frank Higgins' end, was it? It was me who had done it... his oldest daughter that murdered him in cold blood! Tears started to flow as I realized- again- the seriousness of my crime.

"Hey! Hey, it's alright, Nel." Martin exclaimed. "I don't blame you for what you did, I really don't. If my father had done what Frank did I probably would have reacted the same way! Still, the law is rigid- especially against women."

His face, inexplicably, turned beet red and I watched in

surprise as he stood up and left the room. Wondering what had just happened, I squirmed in my chair thinking that, at the last minute, he must have decided to turn me in to the local constables for killing my father.

I was just about to shake my sister awake again and flee when Martin entered the room, got down on one knee and held a small box up in the air. "This was my mother's wedding ring, Eleanor. I want you to have it, if you will agree to be my wife."

My mouth dropped opened in shock and I stared back and forth between his worried face and the pretty blue-stone in the white-gold wedding band. "Wha...?" I sputtered.

He nodded, as if making up his mind for once and for all. "I know this must come as a shock to you but I think we're stuck. I could send you on a coach or by riverboat- somewhere- but you would be all alone and at the mercy of bounty hunters and lawmen- alike. I can't bear the thought of it, honestly."

He set the little box on a nearby table and took my hands in his. Looking into my eyes, he said. "I wasn't lying to you when I said I thought you were the prettiest girl I had ever laid eyes on, you know. I would be honored to have you as my wife, and I could also protect you- you and your sister- from prosecution."

He looked upward as if deep in thought and contin-ued, "All I would have to say, if asked, is that you and Annie were home here with me when your father met his end. Most of the lawmen in this town have no fond feel-ings for your dad- I'm sure if I stood as witness to your innocence, we would be left alone in peace."

Giving my fingers a gentle squeeze, he asked. "What

do you say, Nel? I will be gentle with you, I promise, and patient. Can you, somehow, find it in your heart to become the wife of a Jewish photographer?"

I could feel that same, silly heart trying to pound itself out of my chest, but I told it to be still. Picturing Lt. Burrow's handsome face one last time and knowing that agreeing to Martin's proposal would banish my girlish dreams forever, I took a deep breath, smiled and said, "Thank you, Martin. Yes, I would be proud to be your wife."

Dear Diary,

If a gypsy fortune-teller had rolled into Sioux City a couple of months ago and told me that within two months' time I would be a happily married woman but minus my mother, father and little brother, I would have laughed and told her to throw away her crystal ball.

Still, that is what's happened and I can hardly believe my good fortune. The day Annie and I stumbled into the Leibowitz's shop, fearful and heart-broken, was the same day Simon donned his frayed yarmulke and performed a Jewish wedding ceremony.

It took place upstairs in their sitting room. It was a nice little apartment with burgundy horse-hair furniture, doilies and fussy lamp-shades, a decent kitchen and two small bedrooms- one of which would be mine and Martins. I gulped, nervously, at the thought.

Simon sang the wedding vows in a language I didn't understand and Martin and I jumped onto a small, cloth-covered crystal wine-glass (which seemed like a waste of a perfectly good glass to me). Then the old man put his cap away and burst into a noisy gust of tears.

Martin and I spent the next five minutes comforting him while Annie served slices of a white confection cake Martin had bought from the local bakery.

It felt so strange, like I was a spectator at someone else's stage-play and yet it was all too real. Martin, who was normally confident and self-assured seemed stiff with nerves, and as I caught him gazing at me with shy eyes, I realized that he was as scared of me as I was of him.

Knowing that every new husband had a right to his bride's body, I felt timid, suddenly, and self-conscious. Sneaking a sniff under my own arms I realized that I was none too clean... it had been a number of days since I'd taken a bath.

Blushing, I sat down and nibbled my cake as far away from Martin as possible without giving offense. His feelings were on high alert, though, and after studying my down-cast face, he sat on the end of the small couch I was perched on and whispered, "Nel, are you unhappy?"

I shook my head. "No! No, actually I'm happy. It's just..."

He frowned, "Just?"

I studied him out of the corner of my eye. Then I looked over at where Simon was nodding off in his armchair and Annie was studying her atlas at the kitchen table. It was evening time by now and the day's events were catching up with me.

Clearing my throat in embarrassment, I blurted, "It's just that I'm dirty! I... I haven't taken a bath in days and I don't want you to- to..."

Martin grinned. "Nel! I thought I'd shown you... come on!"

He got up and walked to the far end of the room where he stood in front of a door I hadn't noticed before. Opening it, he gestured and I stepped past him into a modern-looking water-closet. There was a large, porcelain bathtub, a pretty wash-stand and even a commode-type affair. I walked over to it and peered into a hole that had been cut into a bench.

"What happens here is, once a week, the offal-wagon stops by and empties the bin underneath this commode. It will help, though, if you and Annie remember to use the lime-powder after every use."

I smiled with pleasure. Our old house had an outhouse only and so did the boardinghouse. This was quite a modern convenience for me. "Thank you, Martin," I whispered.

My new husband smiled. "Go over to the tub and run a little cold water, okay? Not too much, though, or the hot water won't catch up. I'll start it now."

He left the room and I could see him filling a large metal bucket of water in the kitchen sink to heat on the wood-stove. Annie came into the bathroom to investigate and told me she wanted a bath too but generously offered to wait until I was finished.

With a bit of huffing and puffing, Martin (with Annie's help) eventually filled the bathtub with steaming hot water, brought in a bar of rose-scented soap and a large towel. Then he said he would sit and help Annie study while I took my bath.

Sinking into the warm water I smiled with profound pleasure. The water caressed my skin and I could feel myself blushing. My senses were alive and tingling with anticipation. I had felt Martin's hot gaze on me all day long and for the first time in my life, my body was warming in eager response.

I ran my fingertips over my nipples and gasped as they rose up and puckered like tiny pink rosebuds. My womanhood, that dark triangle of throbbing, monthly discomfort, suddenly throbbed in a different way- a slow, intense pulse of heat that sent shock waves from the top of my head to the tips of my toes.

Groaning softly, I shook myself out of it. Sitting up, I seized the soap and washcloth and scrubbed my skin until it tingled. Then I washed my hair and used the last of the hot water in the bucket to rinse it clean.

Finally, figuring I was as clean as I was likely to get, I stepped out of the tub and studied myself in the steamy mirror. A tall, slender girl gazed back at me; one with dark, auburn hair, high full breasts and large blue eyes. A young woman who, somehow, had come into great beauty.

Satisfied by what I saw, I grabbed the toothbrush and paste Martin had left by the wash-stand and combed out my wet hair. Then, I donned my cotton flannel night-gown and opened the bathroom door a crack. "Annie, the water is still warm. Why don't you take advantage of it?"

My sister grinned and said, "Okay, I will," taking no notice of the hot, sexual gaze that passed over her head between me and my new husband.

I helped Annie get into the bathtub, warned her to not make a mess, and reminded her to wash behind her ears. Then I stepped out into the living room. Simon was fast asleep, but his son was standing by the couch, staring at me like a starving man gazing at a side of beef.

Feeling beautiful, suddenly, and bold, I walked over to where he stood, took his right hand and placed it on my left breast. Gasping as my nipple stirred under his palm, he glanced over at his sleeping father. "Not- not here!" he stammered.

Grabbing my hand, he pulled me into our bedroom, closed the door and kissed me. I had kissed a couple of boys before in my life, but that was nothing like this! Martin's mouth covered mine and the tip of his tongue explored my teeth until they opened in submission. Then our tongues met and danced a waltz of passion as old as time.

Next thing I knew I was on the bed and my nightgown was being pulled over my head. I sat up in a daze as Martin gazed at me with such longing my heart sped up in my chest. "My God, Nel... my good God."

He fell forward and licked my sensitive nipples and then sucked on them until I gasped and trembled. Then he moved south and I felt his warm lips trace a hot line of desire from my bellybutton to my most secret place. I cried out, panting like an animal as my need grew almost painful in its intensity.

Somehow, Martin had managed to shed his clothes, and now he was poised between my legs. I could just make out his manhod in the shadows and I stroked its silken length until he cried out. Whispering through gritted teeth he said, "Are you ready? Oh Nel, let me in!"

I nodded, straining against him and then... Awwwww!

We moved against each other like a well-oiled machine, groaning and gasping as quietly as possible and then, despite the tiny throb of pain that must have been my maidenhead tearing, we rose up as one and cried out in release.

A little later, we tiptoed out of the room and saw that Annie was sound asleep on the couch and Simon, still in his easy chair, had not moved a muscle since the earth moved and shook beneath us.

Smiling at each other, we took a sip of water from the kitchen faucet and a couple of slices of our wedding cake and crept back to the bedroom to start another earthquake.

PART II
PART TWO

Dear Diary,

Well, Annie was right... *I am* a tart! Ever since Martin touched a flame to my wick, I've been on fire with passion... insatiably hungry for sex. Day and night I dream about it, desire it, demand it... much to my new husband's delight. It's as though I've come alive for the first time in my life and I bless my lucky stars that Martin was the man who woke me from my dull slumber.

Now, when my gaze falls upon him, I am shocked to realize that Martin is quite handsome in his own dark manner. He is always scrupulously clean and his curly hair is as black and shiny as a raven's wing. His warm brown eyes are bright with intelligence and his teeth are strong and white. I don't know what first blinded me to his looks except, perhaps, the golden head of hair and smart uniform of a certain Lt. Burrows.

Still, there is more to marriage than passion. Now, I hungered to learn more about his heart. So, when we weren't sneaking off to be alone, Martin told me about himself, his family and what had transpired in his life, so far, to bring him here to Yankton.

Solomon Leibowitz and his young wife, Rebecca, had come to New York three years before Martin was born from a town called Warsaw after Russian troops invaded the area and put down a series of peasant uprisings in a most brutal manner.

Solomon worked as a tailor's assistant, when he wasn't perfecting his craft as an artist. By being frugal, he was able to support his new bride but only minimally. He despaired when revolts rocked his city, and was aware that the soldier's ire seemed especially focused upon the countries Jewish population. He feared that he and his wife might be swept up in the wholesale slaughter but, as chance would have it, one of his paintings came to completion at approximately the same time.

The commissioner of the painting, a magistrate, was so thrilled by the quality of his family's portrait he paid a handsome tip to the earnest, young artist- enough for Solomon and Rebecca to set sail for the Americas. Martin was born two years after they arrived.

He could remember many happy days of his youth. Days when he and his mamma would take long walks in Central Park and the two of them would stand by his father's side and pitch in to help when he offered to take a picture portrait of passers-by.

Then came the dark time when his mother became ill. He was too young to really comprehend what was making her so sick, but she suddenly went from being a pretty, dark-haired, vibrant woman of twenty-seven, to a stick-thin, gray-haired, haggard ghost who couldn't eat or even get out of bed.

"It is a cancer, my son," his father explained but Martin didn't understand what that meant. He was frustrated and angry.

"Well," the eight-year-old exclaimed indignantly. "We must kill it! It is making Mamma sick!" Solomon only smiled and patted his heart-broken son on the head.

Six months later, they stood together by her graveside. Martin still could not fathom the foul, malevolent beast that had stolen his mother away but he listened, carefully, as his father explained, "It's just us two, now, my boy. We must work harder than ever to make our way in this land, so I think I will teach you to work the camera while I take up the art of painting, again."

And so, that's what they did. Luckily, Martin had an artist's aptitude for capturing a subject's likeness in the most flattering way. Not for him- the standard stance of sitting still and staring, grim-faced into the camera's eye... he liked to see laughter and movement, at least the sense of movement, in his pictures.

Since his type of photography was so far from the norm, it took a while for high-paying clients to commission his work, but finally his- and his father's- hard work paid off. By the time he turned fourteen many government officials, socialites and political figureheads were clamoring at Solomon's door to have their likeness photographed and painted.

Solomon and Son Photography enjoyed modest success, despite the fact their shop was in the heart of Jew Town, better known as Yonkers. In 1860, a certain Jewish Union officer commissioned Solomon Leibowitz to photograph and then paint a portrait of himself in full-dress uniform. He was preparing to engage his troops in the War Between the States and desired a reasonable likeness of himself done before he and his men left Ohio.

Solomon and Martin left their shop and home behind to fulfill the colonel's wishes and afterward, followed the officer and his regiment south to commemorate the Civil War in all of its gruesome glory. They took pictures of officers, soldiers and fields of battle. They painted those same pictures and heard that many of them were being placed in the country's capital buildings.

They stuck with it for two years, made a name for themselves and earned enough money to catch a wagon train west. Heartsick and filled by then with a life-long distaste for man's violence against his fellow man, Solomon and Martin would become sworn pacifists- bent on capturing all the beauty life had to offer rather than the horror of bloodshed and war.

"And that's when we came here, opened this business and have been pretty happy ever since…" Martin stroked my dark curls away from my cheeks. "At least, I thought I was satisfied until you came along," he smiled. "Now, my happiness is complete."

We made love again and then I heard my sister call from the living room. "They're here!" she shouted, and I knew that she and I would have to talk, again, about the good manners of proper young ladies, which included not shouting their fool-head's off.

Martin hopped out of bed and dressed quickly. Going to the window that opened out onto Main Street, he called out, "Hallo! I'll be down in just a minute!"

I was bored stiff and wished like anything I could go down and help him with his customers but we had agreed that, until my father's body was found and it was determined whether, or not, I would be held responsible for his untimely death, Annie and I should remain hidden indoors.

Martin had also sworn that, no matter the outcome, he and Solomon would die before letting anything bad happen to us. This loyalty and fierce protection did as much as anything to tie me to my new family with the strongest of laces.

Solomon was in his bedroom working on his painting of me. I had heard him and his son arguing about it, more than once, over the last couple of days. Martin didn't want his father to sell it, now that the subject of the portrait was his wife but Solomon insisted that, by the time he was finished with it, the girl in the painting would barely resemble me at all.

"Besides," Solomon said, "we could really use the cash now that we have two more mouths to feed…" That argument seemed to win the day, and I longed for a way to help add to my new family's coffers.

Those words had stung me until I remembered that I still had the one hundred dollars in my makeshift money-belt. Now that Martin was busy, I thought, *now is as good a time as any* so I knocked on my father-in-law's door.

"Come!" Solomon called out and I opened the door. I couldn't help but notice the canvas he was working on as I walked up to stand by his side. It was huge but, so far, there wasn't much there… just a rich swell of background color surrounding a vaguely feminine clear space in the middle.

Still, Solomon hastily covered the canvas from my eyes. "Mustn't peek, my dear... it brings bad luck."

"I'm sorry, sir. I didn't mean to look..."

He held up a liver-spotted hand, "Ach, that's alright. Only old scratchers like me know about that curse." Smiling, he asked, "What can I do for you, Nel?"

I knew that my new father-in-law disliked being disturbed while painting and I made it quick. "Here, sir. I want you to have this!" I thrust the notes at him, smiling at the surprise I saw in his eyes.

He stared at the bills for a moment and then his hands folded over mine as he pushed the cash back in my direction. "You must have heard Martin and me talking, yes?"

I nodded, "Yes sir, and I agree. Annie and I should pay our way, at least until I can be a proper helper and earn money for the family."

He shook his head with a small smile. "The truth of the matter is... well, it's not the money. I just used that as an excuse to finish this painting. I believe with all my heart that this might be a masterpiece- and, perhaps, the last painting I ever do... these old hands are getting too stiff and shaky to wield a brush and spade for much longer."

"But!" I protested.

He shook his head. "Have no fear, dear girl. Martin and I are not hurting for cash and I want you to keep your little nest egg. One never knows when the tide may turn and I like to think that if something bad ever happened you would have something to fall back on."

Filled with a rush of affection for the little old man I thanked him, kissed his whiskery cheek and backed out of the room.

Dear Diary,

Three days have passed since Martin and I got married and it's time for him to step outside and go back to work catching photographs of news stories, and the people involved.

If there is a fly in the ointment of my newfound joy it's worry about my father's murder and whether, or not, I would soon be facing justice. We read the paper every day, searching for an obituary about Frank Higgins but nothing has caught our eye. Still, I was as strung up as an alley cat and Martin had promised to look into things while he was at work today.

Worry and frustration made me pace the room until, finally, I decided to go downstairs and do some dusting. Although Solomon and Martin kept their shop tidy, I couldn't help but notice the dust-bunnies that tumbled and romped along the windowsills and floorboards and two rather large spider webs (one occupied) hanging from the ceiling.

Armed with a broom, rags and a bucket of vinegar-water, Annie and I headed downstairs. I set to work bringing down the spider webs while Annie swept the floor, squealing as a large, brown spider landed on the floor by her feet.

As she broomed the corners and behind the counter I cleaned the numerous framed pictures hanging on the walls and the dusty countertop. Noticing as an errant beam of sunlight illuminated numerous finger and nose smudges on the shop's one window, I plunged a rag into the vinegar water and stepped outside to wash the window.

As luck would have it, the familiar young faces of Deputies Steel and Caruthers stared at me with a certain amount of surprise as I stepped out onto the boardwalk. They both tipped their hats, and murmured, "Good day, Miss," as they sauntered by, despite the fact that my face had turned beet red with alarm.

They didn't seem to notice, though, and I finished my work fast and headed back inside. Heart still slamming in my chest, I locked the door and fled back upstairs with Annie in tow. Once there, we decided to carry on with our cleaning and did a nice job of dusting the furniture, sweeping and beating the dirt out of a pretty, Turkey rug by dangling it out the window above the alley way.

The whole time we worked, I thought about the deputy's nonchalant manner and hoped, against hope that meant I was not under suspicion of man-slaughter. Still, my whole body crawled with nerves and I glanced, continuously, at the stairwell hoping that Martin would come home soon and tell me what, if anything, he had found out.

A couple of hours passed and I started dinner. Knowing that Solomon liked his supper served about 5:00, I put a chicken in a pot and added some potatoes, onions and turnips. Then I went in to wash my face and arms and change my frock as I was covered head to toe in dust and dirt. Ordering my little sister to do the same, we had just come back into the living area when Martin ran up the stairs with an anxious look on his face. "I have news!" he blurted.

My heart started to pound with dread and he must have understood the look in my eyes for he stepped up to me with a small smile. "Not to worry, Nel. There have been no reports, yet, of your father's death and you are, as far as I can tell, under no suspicion of wrong-doing."

But," I stammered, "What happened, I wonder?"

He shook his head, "I have no idea, except that, perhaps, he ended up in a pauper's grave. There are a lot of people who pass through these parts- people who never make themselves known. Sometimes, when they die and no one steps up to claim them they just get carted off to the Potter's Field. Maybe that's what happened."

I nodded, thoughtfully. On the one hand it seemed a pity that my father would go, unclaimed, to some pauper's grave, but on the other hand, although what I had done sickened me still and probably always would, I didn't want to hang for simply defending my sister from harm.

Feeling the noose around my neck loosen for the first time in days, I smiled slightly and Martin gave my shoulders a light squeeze. "I do have news, though. News that concerns you and your sister." He stared over his shoulder at his father's bedroom door. "Have you talked to him today?"

"Oh yes! He says he'll be coming out for dinner at 5:00."

"That's good. Do you mind if I wait until then to share my news? It's something we should discuss together as a family."

Pleased at being included as family, I nodded and smiled.

He stepped toward the water-closet saying, "I want to clean-up... be back in a minute." Then he turned around and said, "Nel, I want to thank you for all the work you did around here today. I noticed, but almost forgot to mention it."

"I did it too!" Annie piped up from her place at the kitchen table and Martin grinned. "I'm sure you did, Annie, and you both did it proud!" Then he stepped into the washroom and closed the door.

Smiling, I asked Annie to put her schoolbooks away and help set the table, while I sliced bread to go with our stewed chicken and vegetables. I couldn't have been happier had I tried, especially now that the threat of the law seemed to be diminishing.

"So, when I went to the newspaper office," Martin told us at dinner, "I learned that Mr. Holmsworth won't be commissioned as the Army's photographer after all, since he has come down with pneumonia. That's when the Colonel asked me if *I* was interested in accompanying Custer's troops into the Montana Territories."

Solomon, who had seemed quite happy when he first sat down at the table and who had complimented me on my fine cooking, suddenly turned white and set his spoon down on his plate with shaking fingers.

He picked his napkin up and wiped his mouth, keeping his eyes firmly fixed on his dinner. "And, what was your response?" he asked his son.

Martin had been studying his father's face and some of the enthusiasm left his voice as he answered, "I told him that I would have an answer to his proposal by tomorrow, noon."

Solomon looked up at Martin's worried face. "You are twenty-six years old, my son, and must do what you think best for yourself and your family. I don't want you to leave here where you are safe and travel to a land that is still as wild as the people who call it home, but I will not try to stop you if that's what you desire."

Martin sat up straight in his chair. "Father, the money they are offering is staggering, and it has been promised that many of the photographs will end up in the White House and the Library of Congress. Just think what that would do for my... our careers!"

"Besides," he continued, "I would rather Nel and Annie left this area as quickly as possible. You know what she did was justified but you also know that women seldom get a fair shake in this world. The wrong word dropped in the right ear could see her swinging." Martin's words sent another jolt of fear through me.

Solomon sighed. "Yes, there is that. But, Martin, has so much time passed that you have already forgotten the evils of war? And, make no mistake, this is a war you're so keen to head into."

Martin nodded his head, "Yes sir, I know, but the Colonel has told me they intend to make it as safe as can be. While Nel and Annie will stay on board the Far West, I will accompany the Brevet General and, as you know, the higher-ranked officers usually stay far back from the action. In truth, it was Custer who asked for a good photographer. He apparently wants a series of flattering photos sent back to his wife, Elizabeth."

"So, you're going, then?" Solomon asked.

"Yes, Father. With your blessings, that is."

"And when will the boat leave?"

"In three days-time, sir."

Solomon tossed his napkin on the table and said, "Very well. God be with you- with all of you," Then he stood and made his way slowly into his bedroom/studio.

Watching Solomon leave the room, Martin took my hand. "I knew Father wouldn't be happy with this plan, but *you* haven't said a word. How do you feel about it?"

I had been listening and feeling a strange sense of... familiarity. I remembered the strange thrill of doom I had felt when I caught Grant Marsh's eyes and I wondered, uneasily, what that great boat had in store for my sister and me.

Dear Diary,

We are on board the Far West! After a couple of days of frantic packing, Martin, my sister and I are ensconced in a small but fairly tidy cabin on the second deck. There is a smallish bed tucked up under a window and a trundle was brought in to accommodate my sister, who thinks this is a grand adventure.

So do I, really, but I'm trying to curb the natural exuberance of all children that causes her to shout out loud and make a nuisance of herself. Still, as the giant engines rumbled to life, shaking the deck under my feet, and the two looming smokestacks belched out black plumes of smoke as the boat was poled away from the shoreline, I jumped up and down with excitement right along with Annie.

Many people had come to the docks to see us off. They seemed to think that the boat, along with the soldiers, armaments and the red, white and blue bunting strung along the gunnels spelled an end to the troublesome native population in the Dakota, Wyoming and Montana territories.

I didn't know, or particularly care, about that. All I knew was that I was with my new husband on a great quest to capture images of the final fall of the indigenous peoples who had made the frontier such a dangerous place in which to settle.

Annie and I waved gaily to the people below as the boat backed away from the docks and then I heard a voice speak my name. "Why, Miss Eleanor, fancy meeting you here. I thought that this boat was closed to everyone but military personnel!"

My heart skipped a beat. Lt. Burrows was standing close by and staring down at me with bright, inquisitive eyes. He was as handsome as ever and my face flushed with the carnal knowledge of men I had only recently acquired.

"Oh!" I stammered. "Hello, Lieutenant! Yes, I heard that as well, but Annie and I were invited along because my husband will be photographing the coming engagement."

His eyebrows lowered in a frown. "Your hus... do you mean to say you've gotten married in the last week since I saw you last?" His voice echoed his incredulity and he looked past my shoulder as if searching for the mysterious man who had suddenly made me his wife.

Blushing miserably, I realized how outlandish I must sound. Of course, it was shocking news and quite unheard of for a young girl to marry so quickly and without legal notice. I understood, as his eyes grew chill, that he must think me very loose.

I also knew there was a perfectly good reason I had done what I did but that I could not blab about it, as I could still be caught and brought down by the law.

Defensive, suddenly, and somewhat offended by the look in his eyes, which seemed half angry and half-disgusted, I shrugged and murmured, "It was sudden, yes, but I am very happy, sir. Thank you." I muttered.

He crowded in a little closer and his voice throbbed with emotion. "Tell me, who is this lucky man?"

Glancing up, I saw the look in his eyes and realized he wasn't really angry but hurt and the heat in his gaze spoke of honest jealousy rather than disgust toward me and my actions. "His name is Martin Leibowitz. He and his father…"

Adam's eyes got big and he hissed, "I know perfectly well who he is, Nel. Do you mean to tell me you married a Jew? How did your dear father, the Lutheran pastor, react to this?"

He had, apparently, quizzed his mother for information about me or else how would he know about my daddy and what he once was? Thinking how close I was coming to being caught out, and offended anew at Adam's disparaging comments about Martin and his father's religion, I snapped, "My father didn't care one way or the other, sir. Now, if you'll excuse me, there's my husband now."

Adam followed my gaze and his green eyes glinted as Martin approached. He had been on the main deck taking pictures of the rows upon rows of shiny new Army Gatling guns the president had commissioned for the upcoming engagement.

He looked dusty and slightly sweaty from hauling his

heavy camera up and down the stairs but he smiled radiantly when he caught my gaze. Then his eyes landed on the lieutenant and a look of worry came over his face.

Stepping up to Annie and me, he set his camera next to the railing and bowed toward the Army officer. "Good day, sir. May I introduce my new wife, Eleanor and her sister Annie?"

Adam looked like he wanted to say something nasty in reply, but good manners prevailed and he bowed stiffly at the waist. "We are already acquainted, sir, and I offer my congratulations. Truly, though, I'm in shock because the last time I saw these young ladies they were caught trespassing on my family's private estate."

Martin's dusky skin flushed a deep, brick color and he returned the officer's glare. "Yes, Nel and her sister were in a rather vulnerable state at that time, but you will be happy to know that they are well looked after now."

My husband's voice was trembling with outrage but somehow he managed to thwart Adam's aggression because, after a breathless pause, the lieutenant clicked his heels together and backed away, saying, "Well, it is my honor to meet you again. Good day to you." His swept his hat off his head, bowed once more and walked away.

Martin and I stared after the lieutenant's retreating figure for a moment, and then Martin turned toward me. "I thought you said you didn't know anyone in town..."

"I really don't-didn't!" I exclaimed quickly. "But what he said was true. Annie and I visited what we thought was a little park, but we were caught out by Adam and his mother, Mrs. Burrows."

"I fell and hurt my leg!" Annie offered, "And the nice lady fixed me up and gave me some cake!"

Looking down, Martin said, "Well, that was very good of her, wasn't it?"

Annie nodded and turned back around to watch the slowly receding shoreline. Turning toward me again, Martin sighed. "Well, unfortunately, Lt. Burrows knows something about your father, which complicates things a bit."

I bowed my head. "Yes, and I'm so sorry, Martin. I had forgotten all about the lieutenant and his mother until he walked up to me (a lie but just a small one)."

Thinking for a moment, I added, "He seems so angry!"

Martin shook his head. "Yes, he does, doesn't he?" Turning sideways to gaze down into my eyes, he continued, "I think he's quite jealous of me, Nel. Apparently, you made more of an impression on him than you realized. Plus, don't forget, Catholics and Jews don't cohabitate well- never have and probably never will."

Taking my hands in his he said, "Nel, why don't you and Annie go up to the stateroom for a little while. This is a busy time for the crew, and I don't want any one of us getting underfoot or becoming a nuisance while on board."

Feeling strangely nervous, I agreed to Martin's request. I was shocked to see such open hostility in Adam's eyes as he gazed back and forth between me and my new husband and I knew I had come perilously close to the subject of my murdered father.

Shaken, I kissed Martin's cheek, grabbed Annie's hand (although she wanted nothing more than to linger on deck) and fled upstairs.

Dear Diary,

The one thing I *was* able to do before we boarded the Far West, (with Martin's help), was send a telegraph to my sister and auntie in Chicago. I hardly knew what to say... although I was happier now than I had been for a while, the fact remained that my mother, brother and father were all dead- a fact that haunted me every minute of every day.

Not knowing how to tell her everything, word by expensive word, in a telegraph, I ended up saying that I had a lot of news to share but I would be sending a letter very soon.

Now that we are rumbling slowly northward on the Missouri River in route to a number of Army forts such as Fort Randall, Fort Pierre and further into North Dakota and on to Fort Lincoln to meet up with Custer and his troops, I figured it was time to write my letter to Patsy and Chloe.

I hardly knew how to start, so I ended up telling them the good news first. I told her that I am now a happily married woman and my husband's name is Martin Leibowitz. I informed her that Annie and I are on board the famous riverboat, the Far West, and that it's Martin's privilege to take photographs of General Custer's campaign against the high plains Indians in the Montana territories.

I wrote that both Annie and I are well… and then I ran out of happy news. Taking a deep breath, I penned what had happened to us and to Patsy's family as a whole over the last couple of months.

I knew the news was harsh…horrible in fact, but she had a right to know what had happened and why. By the time I finished, I was filled with fresh tears and remembered sorrow for all that had gone wrong.

Headachy and tired, I folded the two pieces of paper in two and laid down on the small cot for a nap. I could see Annie sitting and talking to a young crew-mate just outside the open doorway of our cabin. He was coiling long ropes together with elaborate knots and seemed pleased enough to have an eight-year-old girl peppering him with questions.

I knew Martin was in the pilot's cabin. He had been asked the night before at dinner to take a few pictures of Grant Marsh and his shipmates for posterity's sake, and Martin was happy to oblige.

Head pounding, I also remembered the foul gaze Lt. Burrows had leveled upon my husband all throughout the dinner party. Many of the Army officers noticed, as well, and some even joined in the scornful tribute, but Martin seemed unperturbed.

Finally, to my relief, Captain Marsh took notice and asked if the Lieutenant had been taken ill, at which point, Adam's superior officer- Colonel Fremont- told Adam and his fellow soldiers to please take themselves off to the soldier's quarters which were located at the other end of the boat.

Sighing with relief, I watched the soldiers file out of the room and felt an almost over-whelming sense of dread. I couldn't imagine what had ruffled Adam's feathers so violently besides his apparent hatred of Jews. Thinking about how handsome I had thought he was before marrying Martin, I wanted to hang my head in shame.

How could I have even entertained the thought of his kisses when his eyes glinted, oh so dangerously as he sneered, sideways, at Martin? And to think, I had even caught myself, once or twice, comparing the two men with wanton speculation- me, a pampered married woman filled with the power of my own sexuality!

Martin took it in stride, though. Later on that night as we tucked Annie into her trundle-bed, he glanced at me and murmured, "I think that more than heredity has tinted the lieutenant's eyes green, don't you?"

I stared up at him and blurted, "Oh, it's not me, Martin, at least I don't think so. I think he just hates Jews!"

He nodded. "Perhaps, although that young man has always been most civil to me- his mother, too. No, I think the green-eyed dragon has seized ahold of him."

Martin, I realized, is twenty-six years old and, of course, had seen Adam and his mother about town many times over the ten years they had lived in Yankton. Biting my lip, I wondered, *Could that be true? Are Adam's bad manners merely reflective of his jealousy over my new husband?*

Martin grinned. "Try not to let it bother you, Nel. But remember, we'll all be stuck together for the next few weeks, so it might be best if you avoid too much of his company, at least until we meet up with General Custer and the troops go their separate ways."

Sighing, I agreed, and we cuddled up together on the bed. We made love as slowly and quietly as possible. But, once or twice, as Martin racked my body with pleasure, Adam's face seemed to loom over me in the darkness like a ghost. Annoyed at my over-active imagination, I sternly shooed it away and gasped with passion at our lovemaking.

Now, as I stared at the back of Annie's head, admiring the rich, golden waves of hair that fell down her back, I thought of Martin's hands on my body and smiled. The sun was out and the air warm with the first true hint of spring.

The river's waters glinted and spangled and my eyes closed drowsily when, suddenly, I heard a high-pitched scream. Sitting up in alarm, I could make out a strange drumming noise, an unsteady but increasing thump of something hitting the side of the boat.

Looking over at my sister, I saw the young boy next to her writhing in silence on the upper-story deck. A steady stream of blood was coming from two holes in his neck where an Indian arrow had found its mark from right to left. Realizing that the drumming sounds were actually arrows hitting the boat, I understood we were under attack.

I grabbed Annie's shoulders and pulled her bodily into

the safety of our cabin, and then I went back to drag the young man inside as well, although I could tell he was already dead. Weeping, I pulled him past the doorway and heard the thunderous sounds of our soldier's guns returning fire.

Looking down in sorrow at the dead boy at my feet, I closed his eyelids and took Annie in my arms as she screamed in fear and horror. The guns roared and a frenzy of panic seemed to fill the whole world. Even the boat's engines seemed louder and the floorboards trembled and shook. It dawned on me that Captain Marsh had sped up in order to flee the native attack.

The Far West moved north at breakneck speed for a couple of hours and then, finally, she slowed down. Martin, who had carefully crept up the stairs to watch out for me and my sister, stepped outside the cabin and disappeared.

He returned a few minutes later, and stepped back inside. Sighing, he said, "The river has grown quite wide now, perhaps as much as a mile across, so Captain Marsh says we're safe."

Speaking softly so as not to alarm my sister more than she already was, I asked, "Are any others hurt?"

"Unbelievably, only one. One of the soldiers caught an arrow in his ankle but it has already been removed and the doctor is patching him up now." Staring down at the dead boy at his feet, he added, "Some of the soldiers will be in in a minute to fetch this young'un."

I stepped outside and peered over the railing. Everything seemed to be tidy enough, although I could still see arrows pin-cushioning the boat's sides and double decks. Grant Marsh stood with his co-pilot, watching as his own men helped the soldiers clean and put away the many rifles they had used to drive the Indians away.

My nose was filled with the odor of gunpowder, smoke and blood and my heart felt like it was broken in two.

Dear Diary,

The Far West reached Chamberlain late this afternoon. We would have kept going but the sudden death of young Ethan Cline and the painful ankle injury of Private Marvin Heckler forced us to stop in town rather than head straight up to Fort Thompson, which was originally planned. Apparently, the boat is ahead of schedule, though, so Grant Marsh thought docking for a day, letting the dead and wounded off the boat and patching up the numerous arrow holes... and crew morale a good idea.

I did too, although for purely selfish reasons. Annie had been thoroughly terrorized by her young acquaintances' sudden death- in fact, she had been drenched in the boy's blood when the arrow struck his neck. She tossed and turned with nightmares all last night and refused to eat this morning. Both Martin and I thought it would be best to get her off the boat, at least for a day.

Annie and I stood earlier today, shivering, by the

railing as the boat chugged up the river toward the town of Chamberlain. It seemed that the full force of spring had delayed its arrival in these more northern climes. But it was pretty country. I pointed out a large herd of big-horned sheep grazing on new tufts of grass on a stony bluff and we saw an arrow of geese land with a splash in the river ahead of us.

Here and there, we could see the tall peaks of the Rocky Mountains to the west. The mountain range loomed purple, gray and white in the distance and I could have sworn that hidden eyes within the glittering snow peaks were watching our progress with a chill and forbidding demeanor.

Writing this now, I also understand that my dour feelings of fear and apprehension are residual feelings left over from the Indian's assault upon our boat. I have nothing against the natives who attacked us... I would probably fight us too if our positions were reversed. Still, my sense of fun and adventure has been supplanted by doubts and trepidations.

And, for the first time, I fear for my husband's safety. I know what he said- and what he was promised. That he would be kept as far back from the action as possible in the upcoming engagement. But... if the natives can get to us here, on this riverboat, without warning or provocation what will Custer's troops be in for when they finally meet in battle?

Martin must have sensed my fear because he pulled me to the side a couple of hours later. Placing one of his greatcoats over my shoulders after draping Annie's body in a quilt from our bed, he said, "Captain Marsh was saying that this has happened more than once over the last year or two. Mainly it's because the Indians are losing more and more ground in the region since Custer sent word of that big gold strike in and around Rapid City."

He frowned. "Thousands of people have poured into the area over the last year or so to mine for gold. Also, more than one land treaty has been broken since the first gold strike." Sighing, he added, "The native people take a broken promise seriously... much more seriously than our federal government, I guess."

I didn't want to add to his worry but I couldn't help myself. "But, what about you? I'm not sure if taking pictures of the battle will be safe! Are you sure you'll only be expected to stay by the general's side? What if they send you right into the middle of the battle? That boy... he died in seconds!"

He pulled me to his side and kissed the top of my head. "The colonel I spoke to assured me that-in all likelihood- I will be as safe as can be."

Giving me a slight squeeze, he continued, "Besides, it's too early to be worrying about that quite yet. Custer, from what I've heard, is heading to Washington and won't even be joining the troops until the beginning of June. That gives me...us time to line our coffers. I already have five photos lined up and two of those will be painted by my father once we get back home."

I looked up into his face- already familiar and dear to my heart. "Okay, Martin, if you're sure."

He grinned. "I'm sure as shooting, Nel. Say, I've been meaning to tell you something. There is apparently a rather nice hotel in Chamberlain and I thought that you and Annie might be able to pick up a couple of new dresses and maybe a couple of warmer coats while we lay over. What do you think?"

Remembering the dresses and petticoats we had been forced to abandon when we fled the boardinghouse, I felt a thrill of excitement. "Could we really?" I exclaimed.

Martin nodded. "Absolutely, dear. Maybe one new dress, each, and two new coats. How are your shoes?"

We stared down at my feet. "Oh, I am fine with what I've got, but Annie is growing out of her boots. I don't want to be a burden, though."

"Nonsense!" he snorted. "My father and I have done pretty well, financially, and I have never really had occasion to spend my earnings, until now that is… hey, look!"

He stood up and I followed his gaze toward the river ahead. The town of Chamberlain was coming into view, and I could see Annie's natural exuberance take over as she glanced back at me with a small smile.

The town, at first glance, seemed to be smaller than Yankton but I could see the spires of two separate churches on the skyline and the outline of a large building that must have been the hotel. Thinking, *thank goodness, maybe I can get Annie to settle down a bit,* I linked arms with Martin, watching as the first stop on our journey came into view.

Chamberlain was, indeed, a smaller town but quite nice with a few stately homes and more houses of God than saloons. Martin got Annie and I settled in the hotel and then rushed off to be handy if a photographical opportunity presented itself. Before he left, though, he gave me twenty dollars to spend on new clothing.

I was thrilled. My dress was shabby and my underclothes threadbare. Annie's toes were pinched and starting to swell from shoes that were far too small for her so we set out to the nearest mercantile. Knowing that we would have to buy ready-made, rather than made-to-fit, I hoped that there were plenty of clothes in stock and, maybe a bolt of material I could fashion into something while on board the boat.

We walked down the boardwalk to the store and saw a dress-shop on the far side of the street. Looking both ways, I took my sister's hand and we crossed over and stood, staring into the shop window. There was a beautiful gold satin dress on a mannequin just inside the window that made me almost drool with desire but I knew it would be far too expensive. I saw other, plainer gowns as well and decided to step inside to see if any of them were affordable.

Once inside the shop I saw a couple of dresses I thought would do- one was a pretty yellow with black piping along the bodice and sleeves and the other was a pale blue cotton with tiny pink flowers I knew would suit Annie's coloring. I purchased both of them and then picked out a sturdy pair of boots for my sister. They were a tad big but I figured she could wear two pairs of socks while they broke in.

Running low, by now, on cash, I decided to spend the rest of my money on a bolt of heavy felt for two cloaks. They would be easy enough to make while on board and would help keep us warm for the next few weeks on our trek north.

Pleased by our purchases, Annie and I stepped outside just in time to see some sort of fight brewing in the street.

APRIL 13, 1876

Dear Diary,

By the time Annie and I got home from our shopping spree we were both so exhausted and emotionally spent, we went straight to bed. At one point, I heard my husband enter the room but he knew that both of us needed rest and he stayed as quiet as a mouse until he finally joined me on the bed.

This morning as I awoke, I saw Martin staring down at me. The sympathy I saw in his eyes made my own well up in tears again. "Shhh!" he whispered. "I'm so sorry you had to witness that but there's no helping it now and we don't want to upset Annie again, do we?"

I shook my head and swiped away the moisture from my cheeks. Martin was right- if anything, she needed a happy day today. We needed to do something fun, just to wipe away the horror of yesterday's events. "Martin, do you have time today to maybe take Annie and me on a picnic, or something?" I asked.

He nodded. "Yes, of course. That's a great idea. Captain Marsh is having a memorial for young Ethan today, at four o' clock. I'll pick something up to eat from the café and we'll picnic before the service, okay?"

Nodding, I said, "Thanks… maybe that will help."

He kissed me on the cheek and got up out of bed. "I need to be going now, but shall I have the staff bring water up for a bath?"

Grateful, I said, "Yes, that would do wonders!"

He left the room and I walked over to the one window that looked out over the town square. From where I stood, I could see the tall platform where the town fathers had hanged a whole Negro family in front of me and Annie's eyes.

Glancing down at where Annie was curled up on her pallet, I could see her pale face and I wondered about how much one child could take before her sanity was affected.

We had just stepped out of the dress-shop when we saw a number of deputies wrestling a Negro man, woman and three young children down the middle of Main Street toward the gallows.

"We didn't steal nuthin' boss! Nuthin! Fact is 'twas the other way round… those men done stole from us! Listen, y'all gotta listen!"

The poor man was trying to explain what had happened but his pleas for mercy fell on deaf ears. Seeing the two slouchy-looking characters who followed close behind… apparently the victims… I couldn't help but think they were probably the culprits rather than the injured parties.

It didn't matter, though. The whole family was marched down the street and, in a matter of minutes, were standing high on the hanging platform with nooses strung around their necks. I remember how my heart had started hammering in my chest.

I also remember thinking: *what about due process? What about a trial? They can't mean to hang this whole family right in front of our eyes?* It's not like Annie and I had never seen justice carried out in the town square before but *never* had we seen tiny children swing!

I stood there, dumbfounded, as those lawmen dispatched that whole family to the after-life. It wasn't until Martin came running up to us that I realized I hadn't possessed the presence of mind to hide my sister's gaze from the horrible spectacle.

Too late, I tried to cover Annie's eyes even as Martin picked her up in his arms and hustled her across the street and into the hotel. Following, I heard a number of spectators clapping and cheering with delight at the impromptu entertainment. Veering into the water-closet just off the main lobby, I threw up until there was nothing left in my belly.

My mind is clearer today but my confusion is worse than ever. I had thought that when the North beat the South in the Great War, the Negro was granted freedom. Then why were those poor folks hanged yesterday, without proof of guilt and paraded on the street to the delight of onlookers, as if some sort of justice had been done?

Could no one, besides me, see the horror of it? And, when did it become all right to hang little children?

Annie woke up a little later and she seemed much better today than last night. I fed her some hot cereal and tried talking to her about what had happened, but she seemed to have shut down. Apparently, in her mind, if lawmen had done the deed, the Negro family must have deserved it. I let her think what she wanted, at least until I could figure out how to justify my own bewilderment.

Finally our hot water arrived and we both bathed, relishing the idea that we had new dresses to wear to a picnic and later, to Ethan's funeral. Getting dressed in our new clothes, Annie begged me to put her hair up in a bun, like a big girl, and I complied, twisting her honey-colored locks into a braided coil and pinning it up on top of her head.

Pulling a few moist ringlets down around her cheeks she stared into the mirror, in awe. I was staring as well. I could tell, suddenly, that little Annie would grow into a great beauty with her pale skin, tawny hair and wide blue eyes. I smiled at the expression on her face and said, "Now, don't get too puffed up, this fancy business is just for today, okay?"

She grinned. "Yes, I know, Nelly. But… I might be as pretty as you someday, right?"

Nodding, I agreed. "Oh yes, I'm sure you will."

There was a light knock at the door and Martin stuck his head partially inside. "May I come in?"

"Yes, we're ready!" I called out.

He walked in with two large parcels in his hands. "Oh, don't you both look fresh and pretty as daisies?' He grinned. "Here are two more dresses- one for each of you."

I gasped but Annie grabbed hers with a cry of delight. As the paper came off I saw a light green chiffon dress with a lavender sash- one of the more expensive party dresses in the store we had visited yesterday. "Oh!" Annie whispered. "This looks like a princess' dress!"

I stared, awestruck, and Martin grinned. "Aren't you going to open yours, Nel?"

"Yeah, Nelly, open yours!" Annie cried.

"Oh," I breathed. "You shouldn't have, Martin."

He looked at the parcel in my hands. "We have been invited to a formal dinner tonight at the mayor's house and I wanted my girls to look beautiful. Go on, sweetie, open it!"

I tore the paper and sighed. It was the evening gown I had seen on display at the dress-shop yesterday. Gold, with an over-skirt of silver-starred tulle, it was a dress fit for a queen and my eyes filled with tears of gratitude.

I already felt pretty in my new yellow and black dress, this... well, I was overjoyed and filled with the promise of better things to come in this new life with my handsome and generous new husband.

Our picnic was nice. Martin had picked up a half a fried chicken, some hard-boiled eggs and three apple turnovers for our lunch and we ate on a blanket by a small stream while Annie flew a paper kite in an adjacent meadow.

Although the breeze plucked at my sleeves and ruffled my bonnet with icy fingers, the sun was warm on my back and I was lulled by the soft cooing of mourning doves in the near distance.

My eyes started to drift shut but opened wide again as the image of the Negro children flashed through my mind. I gasped slightly and sat up with a sudden chill.

I felt Martin's gentle hands on my back. "Hey, what's wrong?"

I sighed. "Martin, did I miss something? Did that Negro family receive a fair trial before they were hanged?"

He said nothing and when I turned around to study his face, I saw his sad eyes watching as a few people started walking up to the town's graveyard. Apparently, Ethan Cline's funeral was about to begin.

He shook his head. "No, I don't think so, Nel. I think we were witness to nothing more than a common lynching. I'm so sorry you had to see that."

Indignant, I replied, "That's not what matters, Martin! What really matters is that those people were hanged for no good reason, and I'm almost certain that those two scoundrels following behind were the guilty ones!" Tears leaked from my eyes again.

Martin nodded. "You're probably right, Nel. But... you've got to remember that not all people agree with Lincoln's emancipation proclamation. Black folk will always be considered by some no better than pack animals. Besides, I believe this particular area has mainly been colonized by Southern sympathizers."

"So?" I snapped, resentfully.

"So," he smiled, "although the war was declared officially over years ago, folks on both sides of that conflict have long memories. Fathers, brothers and sons, both Northern and Southern, were killed over the slave issue."

He stopped speaking for a second and continued with a small shake of his head. "Well, actually, the war was fought over money but right or wrong- in some people's minds the Negro will always be held accountable for those losses. I'm sorry but you must know I'm right."

I wanted to argue with Martin's logic but I knew, deep

inside, that he was probably correct. It didn't really matter whether the Negro family from yesterday was guilty of theft or not, in someone's mind those poor folks had stood as scapegoat for all the injustices of society as a whole.

Dear Diary,

Let's see, it's been three days since I last wrote. Not too much has happened, except we are back on board the boat and chugging slowly toward Fort Thompson where we will pick up more guns, ammunition and soldiers.

Before I forget entirely, though, I thought I would tell you a little about Ethan's funeral and the dinner party Martin, Annie and I attended later on that night.

The funeral was wonderful, really. The whole crew showed up to honor the young orphan, and although Annie and I both wept at the site of the small wooden coffin, something about seeing it lowered into the ground and the Bible phrases spoken both by the local minister and Grant Marsh seemed to emphasize the importance of life, all together, whether ye be great or small.

Captain Marsh spoke of the young boy who had made a study of knots and how Ethan had confided that his greatest ambition was to become a famous riverboat pilot like Marsh. The preacher talked about green pastures and right on time- a rainbow broke through the fitful clouds overhead and seemed to lay its pot of gold in the meadow in which we stood.

I couldn't help but notice Adam Burrows staring, more than once, in my direction. I figured it was because of my new yellow dress. (I actually felt a little ashamed at showing up in something other than black, but Martin assured me that no one of any social importance would be in attendance to cast judgement upon my attire.)

It was nice receiving manly attention but the lieutenant's face was still gloomy with jealousy and resentment. I breathed a sigh of relief when he and a number of soldiers left right after the service. Afterwards, Annie looked up at me with a smile on her face. "That was nice, Sis, wasn't it? I betcha Ethan woulda been proud."

I squeezed her shoulder. "Yes, it was a very nice service, Annie."

The crowd ambled back toward town which was about a quarter mile away. At one point, Captain Marsh called out, "Mr. Leibowitz, I trust you and your lovely wife will be joining us later?"

Martin smiled. "Yes, sir. We would be honored."

Marsh nodded his head and his fierce walrus mustache shone silver in the afternoon sunshine. "If I were you, I would bring your camera contraption. Word has it that two important Army officers, Major Reno and Captain Benteen will make an appearance tonight."

"Will do, thank you for the invitation."

Marsh's eyes fell on me for a moment, and he tipped his cap. "A pleasure, Ma'am."

I gave a small curtsy and belatedly murmured, "...pleasure, Sir!" but Marsh and his co-pilot had moved ahead.

Cheeks burning, I muttered, "Oh Martin, do I have to go? I don't know the manners of high society. I don't want to embarrass you..."

He grinned. "You could never embarrass me, Nel, but if you're nervous about how to act at the party, just don't say too much. I have found that it's hard to step on a trapped tongue."

Smiling at the image, I put my arm through his and we followed the rest of the people back into town.

Later that evening we walked up the road to a big, beautiful house that blazed brightly with lanterns and candlelight. Many fine carriages were parked in front of the house and my heart pounded with nerves... and, a certain amount of pride. I looked quite pretty, I though, in my golden gown, at least as nice as many of the ladies I saw making their way up the porch steps.

I entered the house and tried to keep from gawking at the heavy oak furniture, the china and the crystal glassware which seemed to glitter and twinkle with a life of their own. I saw the backs of ladies and military officers, many of them in full-dress uniforms, the beautiful women in their best clothes.

The gowns they wore were all colors of the rainbow, and cut quite low in the bodice making my own dress seem spinsterish. Still, I was proud that I could present myself in any kind of formal wear until I heard one young lady hiss to another, "Oh, look, Myrna. That gown hung in the dress store for ages! It must be heavy with dust. Honestly, I wouldn't be caught dead in such a get-up!"

Suddenly, I felt as gauche as the lowest gutter-tramp

and wanted to hide my face in shame, especially since the girl had spoken loud enough for everyone in the foyer to hear. Of course, human nature being what it is, practically everyone queuing up to enter what I assumed to be the dining area, turned around to stare.

I heard Annie gasp and felt Martin's grip tighten on my arm. Glancing up, I also saw the deep blush of embarrassment rising on his neck and cheeks. Although I wanted to sink through the floorboards in humiliation, I grasped his hand and smiled. At that point, Captain Marsh turned around and shouldered his way through the staring crowd. "Ah, there you are!" he said loudly. "The evening would not have been complete without you."

Stepping behind us, the man somehow managed to propel the bunch of us to the front of the line to where a stout older gentleman and his wife stood by the doorway. "Mr. Mayor, may I present one of the finest photographers in the country, Martin Leibowitz, his beautiful wife Eleanor and her little sister, Annie?"

I heard the crowd behind us stir with excitement and then fall into a hush as the mayor bowed toward Martin and murmured, "I have heard of you, Mr. Leibowitz. Congratulations on your upcoming engagement. I look forward to seeing photographs of our great victory over the heathen population…" Turning toward me and Annie, he continued, "And, welcome to you and your charming sister, Eleanor. Martin seems to be a very lucky man!"

I looked sideways in gratitude at Captain Marsh and saw his eyes gleam with mirth. Giving me a slight wink, he moved forward into the dining room and we followed, finding our names on place-settings close to where

Marsh, Lt. Burrows and many other resplendent officers were sitting.

I found out, through the course of the evening, that two of the officers were none other than Major Marcus Reno, a rather handsome younger man with rich brown hair and wide dark eyes and an older man named Captain Frederick Benteen, who said very little but sat in a cloud of pipe tobacco smoke listening to the conversations around him.

It seemed that these fellows would be playing a rather large role in Custer's campaign and, according to Reno anyway, the Brevet General couldn't hope to succeed without them. "Old Iron Butt won't have a snowball's chance in hell without our help!" he declared more than once.

There was plenty of talk about the Far West and what was expected of her as support and news exchanged about how many more soldiers and weapons needed to be picked up before our rendezvous with Custer in Bismarck.

I said nothing but, "Please, could you pass the butter?" but watched all those great men and women with a certain amount of pride. I found it hard to believe that Annie and I were sitting amongst such august persons and were a part of something that would surely go down in history as one of our finest hours.

APRIL 18, 1876

Dear Diary,

The river remained as wide and blue as a lady's satin sash for a couple of days after we left Chamberlain with thick green forests stretching down toward the shoreline as far as the eye could see. After the Indian's attack a few days ago, I was nervous and ever-watchful lest more arrows pierce our boat and our bodies when the river grew narrower.

Annie was growing more and more resentful of my protection, however, especially since two young children came come aboard when we stopped at Fort Thompson. That was a quick lay-over; only about four hours- as four soldiers disembarked along with seven Gatling guns and a dozen boxes of military supplies.

I saw a small crowd of people waiting below on the dock. There was a family with kids, two uniformed soldiers and, unfortunately, the same two men who had accused the Negro family of theft and laughed while they were hanged. I could feel my face flush with anger as the men stared up at the boat and I wished with all my might that they would board a different boat than the one I was on.

And, finally, there were two wild Indians! I had never seen a native up close and I couldn't help but admire both men. One was dressed, more or less, like an Army Private with the same dark trousers and matching jacket. Instead of a shirt underneath the coat, though, he sported an elaborate beaded chest-plate and wore high, leather moccasins that were as black as night and shiny with tar.

The other young man made no concession to White Man's apparel, but wore beautiful buckskin pants and a matching knee-length overcoat. His shiny black hair was coiled into an elaborate knot on top of his head and spiked with a number of eagle feathers. He was a magnificent specimen and Annie crowed with excitement.

"Lookit, sis, real live Injuns!" she shouted.

To my mortification, the two natives along with the rest of the passengers were just then climbing the gangplank and heard my sister's hollers. The Indians glanced in our direction as I lightly boxed Annie's ears.

"That was rude of you, Annie, and I am ashamed by your behavior!" I cried as she clapped her hands over her ringing ears and howled, "Ouch, Nel! That hurts!"

"Well," I sniffed. "That's what happens when you open your mouth once too often. Just think about what you said, Annie! Do you think your hasty words didn't hurt *their* feelings?"

Tears of shock and dismay leaked from the corners of her eyes and she bit her lips as she studied the backs of the two natives who were, thankfully, heading toward the opposite end of the boat. I noticed the younger Indian frowning as he tapped his companion on the shoulder with a questioning look in Annie's direction.

The taller Indian with his patched together Army uniform grinned and whispered something into the other man's ear. Turning beet red, Annie spun toward me and whispered, "Oh, sis, they heard me! I didn't mean to be rude. I thought they were handsome!"

I grabbed her gently and held her tight. Sinking to my knees, I looked her in the eyes and whispered, "I know you're not a mean person, honey, and that you meant no harm, but you *have* to curb your tongue. Not everyone will be as patient with you as Martin and I... you could get all of us in terrible trouble!"

It had been a long time since I disciplined my little sister, and I felt horrible about it. She really is a sweet-natured child and has been through so much... still, her big mouth will get the best of her if she doesn't learn to be more careful!

"What's wrong?" Martin was standing next to us and looking down at Annie with a small smile.

"I... I was mean but I didn't mean it!" Annie blurted and more tears ran down her cheeks.

My husband fell to his knees as well and took Annie's hand in his. "Well, I'm sure you didn't mean it that way, but everyone on the boat heard you. Just remember to be more careful- like your sister said- and you won't get into any more trouble, okay?"

She nodded and said, "Nelly, I'm tired. Can I go to our cabin for a little while?"

I knew that she was humiliated by the unwanted attention she had brought upon herself, and I murmured,

"Sure, we'll go up now if you like…" when I heard another little girl say,

"Hi! My name is Mary and this is my brother Percy. Do you wanna play?"

We turned around and saw the young family standing behind us on the deck. The man and his wife were probably about the same age as Martin and the kids looked to be more or less Annie's age. They were dressed rather nicely and the man had a large leather sack slung over his left shoulder with rolls of paper stuffed inside it.

'The name is McDonald… Trevor McDonald and this is my wife, Natalie and my two young 'uns, Mary and Percival. We are heading to Bismarck to do some land surveys. Pleased to meet you." He had stuck his hand out to shake and I liked him and his whole family immediately.

Trevor was quite plump with very short red hair, freckles and small blue eyes. His grin was infectious, though, and although his wife was rather plain, her brown eyes were warm and bright with intelligence. The children were much like their parents with wide smiles and numerous freckles. The little girl, Mary, was holding out a large rag-doll for Annie to inspect.

"My mamma made her for me. Do you want to comb her hair?" she offered.

Annie looked up at me for permission and I nodded, saying, "Stay back by the cannons, all right?" Instantly, the two girls skipped away, holding hands and for all intents and purposes, already the best of friends.

Martin was grinning as well, and the five of us (including little Percy, who seemed ready for a nap) walked toward a large cabin on the lower deck that had been set aside as a general meeting place for the many passengers on board. There was a small woodstove and a number of benches along the walls for sitting. A pot of coffee had been started on the stove and Martin poured fresh cups for the McDonald's.

We sat together for quite a while and learned that Trevor and Natalie had been hired by the Great Northern railroad to help survey the Dakota territories for the best possible rail-routes either over or around the Rocky Mountains. Also, as it turned out, they would be traveling most of the way with us to the Bismarck area, since General Custer desired more accurate maps of the region than he currently owned.

Gesturing toward his large, overstuffed, leather satchel he added, "That's what I'm carrying now. Hopefully, the General will get these before he sends his troops into the region. Many of the older maps are corrupted or highly inaccurate."

We spent over an hour chatting about everything under the sun and simply getting to know one another. Martin and Trevor seemed to hit it off right away and by the end of our meeting I couldn't help but feel the same toward Natalie. Although she's quite a lot older than me she seems very sweet and had shown me four skeins of yarn her husband had given her as a present.

Smiling she offered, "I would be more than happy to share some of this with you, if you would like to make your sister her own little rag doll..."

My heart soared with delight. *Maybe,* I thought, *now that I have a lady friend, she can help me with some of the questions that are plaguing me like, why have my monthly courses stopped and why are my breasts so tender all the time?*

Dear Diary,

I know it's been quite a while since I wrote but that's only because I'm happy and rather busy. Every day, while Martin either visits with the land surveyor- and new friend- Trevor McDonald or takes photographs of the boat and crew, I spend equal time with his wife Natalie. She is a wonderful person, and although she is a few years older than my sister Patsy, she reminds me of her in many ways.

Natalie has confirmed my suspicions about being pregnant, and Martin is ecstatic, although overly-worried now about my safety and comfort. I have assured him, though, my health has never been better...in fact, I feel like the cat that ate the cream. Languid and ripe with sensation, I drift through each day with a small, self-satisfied smile on my face.

A couple of times, the smell of food cooking or the

odor of unwashed bodies has sent me, retching, to the side of the boat but for the most part, I have never felt happier. Most days, Natalie and I sit in the main passenger cabin sewing or playing cards while Annie and the other kids play with their toys at our feet. Lessons have resumed for Annie, but she's having far more fun now than before since Mary and Percy have joined her in learning their sums and letters.

The only flies in the ointment are the two horrible men that came aboard at Fort Thompson and Adam Burrow's continuing attitude. No one in charge seems to mind that the women and children on this trip have, more or less, taken over the great cabin on the main deck. Indeed, Captain Marsh seems relieved that we are not underfoot during the daily Army drills, shooting practice and general running of the boat.

But, we are almost always in there when a passenger comes inside to warm up by the fire or grab a cup of coffee. Most of the soldiers and crew nod in a friendly manner, grab a cup of water or coffee and leave again. A few times, Adam and his fellow soldiers have come inside and although the lieutenant is always extremely polite, he is also as cold as ice. It has really begun to sting because, for the life of me, I can't understand why we can't remain friends despite my marriage vows. Still, those visits are brief and easily forgotten.

What is much harder to accept is the almost constant attention Natalie and I are receiving from the two scouts (the same two men that had accused the Negro family) that climbed onboard at Fort Thompson after signing up for Custer's campaign.

I already hated them for what had happened in Chamberlain, and it doesn't help that neither one of them ever bathe. Now, I know it's not easy to stay as fresh as a peach while onboard the riverboat but most of us try, at least. Martin, Annie and I don't leave our tight quarters in the morning without brushing our teeth with soda and sharing the last of our bathing water, which is doled out on a daily basis.

It's harder for most of the men to stay clean... for one thing the crew are working hard and sweating with the efforts of their assorted tasks. The soldiers also sweat and grunt with their labors, but I have seen the whole regiment line up at the far end of the boat every day while they scrub their bodies with harsh lye soap and are then thoroughly doused with cold river water.

The two rascals that are haunting Natalie and my every waking moment are a different breed, however, and they stink to high heaven. Their sour body odor and stale breath have sent me running to the gunnels more than once and I have even seen some of the crew wrinkle their noses and sneer as they stroll by.

I asked Martin a couple of days ago if he knew their names and he had said no, but had promised to find out. Meanwhile, the two, rude skunks have taken to malingering in the main cabin while Natalie, the children and I are there. They creep in and stand by the walls watching us with strange, lascivious eyes. Their body odor fills the room with eye-watering intensity until even the children, normally rather immune to strong odors, beg to be set free.

This morning, Martin told me their names are Jack

Williamson and Pierre LaFontaine... well-known trap-
pers and guides for many of the pilgrims and settlers that
have come to the western territories over the last decade
or so. Apparently, although they are well-respected for
their knowledge of the land, they are not particularly
popular, especially since it's rumored that these same men
have recently been caught trading tainted blankets to
some of the Northern tribes.

A horrible practice; even some of the fiercer settlers
who would like nothing more than to see their native
competition for land rights blow away like dust off the
face of the earth, feel that infecting whole tribes with
Cholera and Small Pox is dealing a cheating hand and
want no part in it.

Well, the two disease-agents came into the passenger
cabin again this morning. Natalie and I watched in disgust
as the men sauntered inside and had just decided to take
our leave when we heard a panicked shout. For the most
part, we have enjoyed mild weather on this trip and
although it's much cooler here than it was further south,
the waters have remained steady and calm... until now.

As Natalie, the children and I rushed out onto the deck
to see what the fuss was about, I was amazed to notice
that the egg-shell blue sky of dawn had been replaced by
huge thunder clouds. Raindrops as hard as shot-gun
pellets poured down in sheets, soaking the decks and
great zig-zags of lightning were lighting up the thunder-
heads with a greenish glow.

The sound of thunder crashed through the air like
giant kettle drums and I heard the livestock at the far-end
of the boat screaming in terror. All of that was bad

enough, but what had caught the captain and crew's attention was the towering, teaming wall of black, foamy water that had risen up out of the northern waters and seemed to be rushing toward us now like a run-away mule-train!

Dear Diary,

I stood and stared for a moment, wondering what on earth the captain was going to do, and then he leaned over the rail of the wheel house and started barking orders. "All passengers- line up in the middle of the boat and grab something to hold on to. Crew... batten the hatches- we're heading in!"

And then I heard the great engines roar to life and the floorboards shuddered under my feet. Unbelievably, Grant Marsh was speeding up to meet the maelstrom of water head-on! Grabbing my little sister, I staggered over to one of the posts that held up the top-deck. Understanding now why there was a built-in hand hold on the post I grabbed on tight and pinned my sister to the upright with my body.

Looking over my shoulder, I could see Natalie and her kids doing the same thing about six feet behind me and further back, both Martin and Trevor were fighting their way toward us. A few moments later, as the clouds ripped apart with a roar of protest overhead and rain pounded down on us from the broken sky, I felt Martin come up behind me as he grabbed the post, trying to shelter both me and Annie from the tempest.

If we leaned a little to the right, or starboard, side we could see the seething hump of rubble-filled, ice-laden water heading our way. Apparently, the sudden rainstorm had torn loose an ice dam that had held broken tree branches, mud, dirt, leaves and a winter's worth of deadfall. The water didn't rise significantly but the whole mess was approaching rapidly and my heart started to thud in fear.

I just couldn't imagine how this large but fairly shallow-draft riverboat would avoid capsizing under the impact. Even as I watched, I saw what looked like a whole tree suddenly rise up out of the water, cartwheel and go under again.

I felt Martin's warm breath on my neck as he spoke into my ear. "Hold on tight, Nelly. Marsh has been through this before and he knows what he's doing but this looks like a bad one. Whatever happens don't look toward the wave when we hit!"

The Far West was still picking up speed and I knew that in a few seconds the bow would meet the oncoming waters. I reached down with a free hand and pressed Annie's face into my sodden skirt and felt Martin's arms clamp down hard on my body and the post we clung to.

Then, with a jolt and a mighty groan of the ship's timbers, the wave of debris-strewn water washed over the front of the boat and split off, harmlessly, to either side.

We slid over the top of the maelstrom but the worst wasn't quite over...

As Martin, Annie and I clung tightly to the post, we could see rotten logs, whole trees, broken branches and mud sweeping across the deck and out the back. We heard a series of crashes and thumps as the rubble hit the giant paddle-wheel behind us. Over the roar of water and the raging storm overhead, I could hear screams and cries as people were swept off their feet or hit by the flying debris.

I even saw a small group of beaver, swimming madly past our knees and heard as one of the horses in the live-stock pen lost its footing and sailed, squealing, over the starboard railing. And then, thank God, it was over. The boat had decreased speed and now stood still in the water as the rest of the ice dam swept past us.

Shaking, I peeled my fingers off the post and fell to my knees to see if Annie was hurt. Other than a red weal on her cheek where I had pressed her into the post, she seemed fine and wide-eyed with curiosity. "Lookit!" she pointed past me to where a sow and her litter were trying to escape from a pile of roping by the port railing.

I asked, "Annie, are you hurt?"

She shook her head. "No, I'm fine. I want to go and help the pigs!"

"No!" I shook my head. "You stay right here until the captain says it's okay to move. We don't want to get in the way..."

She rolled her eyes in exasperation but stayed still as Martin gave me a quick hug and said, "I have to go see what needs to be done. Are you all right?"

I smiled and wiped the rain and mud from my face with shaking fingers. "I'm fine, Martin, just a little shook up is all. Let us know when we can head up to the cabin, okay? Or... let us know if we can help with anything."

He nodded and dashed away. Natalie and her children walked over to us and we exchanged wide-eyed hugs. "Did you see the beavers?" little Percy cried in glee.

We nodded, watching as a couple of deck hands freed the sow and her piglets from the hemp and they ran back to their pen. A few moments later the captain walked downstairs from the wheelhouse and tipped his hat. "Ladies, the worst is over for now. We are going to drop anchor, however, and do some repairs and clean-up before getting underway again."

I hated to question such an impressive person but I cleared my throat and asked, "Is there anything we can do to help?"

He shrugged. "Well, although I would rather you and the children were not on deck during the clean-up, I'm sure the crew and soldiers would appreciate some hot coffee while we undergo repairs. I will have my men bring in dry wood and fresh water. Also, some of the men have bumps and bruises... nothing serious, mind you, but if you ladies could help with a little doctoring I would appreciate it. "

"Thank you, sir. We'll be happy to help," I replied. Smiling, he turned away and started issuing orders as Natalie, the kids and I stepped inside the main downstairs cabin.

Someone had doused the woodstove with water (probably to keep flames and hot coals from catching the boat on fire) and we needed to clean that up but, eventually, we got a new fire burning and put on the first of many pots of coffee while the crew, passengers and soldiers cleared the lower deck of debris and extra water and fetched the swimming horse back to shore.

Three men came in with scrapes and cuts but, as the captain had promised, there were no serious injuries. Regardless, Natalie and I were kept quite busy serving water, hot coffee, some hastily-made sandwiches and comfort to the rattled crew and soldiers.

Clean-up and repairs took the rest of the day and at about 4:30 the captain announced that the boat would remain at anchor for the night. Some of the crew had seen elk grazing along the far shore and wanted to do a little hunting before we cast off again.

Also, Marsh thought that the tall, steam-powered spars should be uncased and ready for some "Grass-Hopper" maneuvers. Not only did the river, at this point, begin to narrow drastically, he thought that there might be some additional flooding further upstream which meant the boat might need to hop over sandbars and piles of deadfall.

Meanwhile, he suggested that the civilians might like to row ashore for some much-needed rest and relaxation. He promised a feast of either elk meat or venison and offered to uncork some of his best brandy in celebration of our close call.

There was a smattering of applause and in short order, two small rowboats were lowered to the muddy water. About half of the soldiers rode with us toward the shore-line and I was grateful that they were fully-armed. Although I couldn't see any Indians, of course, I hadn't forgotten the swiftness of their previous, surprise attack.

Martin sat close by my side as we approached a sandy beach and whispered in my ear, "Stay close to me, Nelly.

I'm sure we'll be safe, but I don't want you or Annie to wander off where I can't see you."

So, the civilian passengers were able to relax and roast a young buck on an open fire while Grant Marsh and his crew repaired the boat from spring's sudden, violent run-off.

Dear Diary,

We are underway again but, as suspected, it's slow going. The river has gone from being wide and deep into a series of narrow washed-out switchbacks. The storm that caused the river to swell also made the waters over-flow their banks so that the shoreline is littered with small mountains of deadfall and shallow lakes.

Three times in the last couple of days, Captain Marsh has shut down the main engines and deployed the steam-driven spars, so that the whole boat rises up and over piles of river rubble. It's amazing to watch, albeit a bit nerve-wracking.

It's also a lot of work. The water, although fairly sluggish is still active and works against the boat and crew with steady pressure. This means that the crew has to attach the boat to a tree or "Deadman", sink the spars into the river bottom and winch the boat up and over the numerous sandbars.

There has been more than one injury the last few days... pinched fingers and toes, one broken arm and a cracked noggin. Ever since Natalie and I played nurse during the thunderstorm, Captain Marsh sends anyone with an injury our way, which is fine by me as this whole "grasshoppering" business makes me nauseous.

We are on our way to Pierre and should be there within the next couple of days- if we can fight ourselves free of these infernal sandbars, anyway. I am excited about that- for a couple of reasons. First, my former friend, Lt. Adam Burrows will be disembarking at Fort Pierre along with five men from his battalion. He and the other soldiers will, apparently, be heading into Wyoming to join Crook's forces.

I have always been as sweet and polite as can be with the young man but he has not forgiven me for marrying and never fails to meet my good manners with chilly reserve. I am sad about it but, at this point, tired of it as well. I wish him and his fellow soldiers luck but am happy enough to see them go.

I also heard that Williamson and LaFontaine will disembark in Pierre and, for that, I am extremely grateful. Those two men have been Natalie and my constant, smelly shadows for the better part of a week now and we are sick of it. They are everywhere- constantly dogging us- lurking just out of sight.

Twice, I have caught Williamson, the bigger and dirtier of the two men, standing just outside of our cabin door waiting eagerly for a glimpse of me or my sister when Martin leaves every morning for work. And, Natalie has reported the same thing, only it's LaFontaine who snoops her and her children.

Finally, yesterday morning, we told our husbands about our feelings of being preyed upon, and late last night we heard the captain bellowing in anger. Although Marsh could certainly bark orders with sharp authority, I had never before heard him speak to anyone in this way. Curious, I stepped out onto the upper deck and, looking up, saw the two skunks in the wheelhouse being dressed down by the captain while Martin and Trevor looked on.

Both of the scouts looked somewhat cowed but as I watched, Williamson gazed past the angry captain and met my eyes with his. Rage glittered within those brown, murky depths and I stepped back inside my cabin with a thrill of foreboding. I knew, without a doubt, that if he could have put his greasy hands around my neck at that moment, he would have squeezed and squeezed until I was dead.

I have never before felt such hate and I sank onto our small bed with a sigh.

"What's wrong, Nelly?" Annie asked with a worried expression on her face. Ever since she learned I am going to have a baby she's hovered over me like a fussy nursemaid.

"Oh, it's nothing, sis," I answered with a tired smile. "I'm weary though… why don't we make ready for bed?"

It was almost eight o' clock and I knew Martin would be up soon. As I heard Annie start to snore lightly, Martin opened the door and stepped inside the cabin. "Are you still awake, sweetheart?" he whispered.

"Yes," I answered. "Come to bed…" I opened the covers for him and he snuggled up against me in the twilight. Both of us stared, for a moment, through the filmy curtains at the moonlit sky.

"You spoke to Captain Marsh about Williamson and LaFontaine?" I asked.

He nodded and pressed his lips against my neck. "Yes, dear. I only wish you would have told me about your suspicions sooner."

I shrugged. "It's only just occurred to Natalie and me that they are trouble, Martin. I wasn't trying to keep it secret."

He sighed. "I know. It's just that some men are wild at heart... truly as wild as beasts of prey with no sense of right and wrong and no moral compass. I think that those men would rape and kill you, both of you, and think nothing of it at all." His voice was hushed and I could feel a light sweat break out on his body.

Scooting around, I faced him on the bed. "Well, thank God you told the captain. Has he asked the men to leave the boat?"

Martin said, "Yes. They'll be leaving once we get to Pierre. Still, you need to take care, Nel. Even if everything goes smoothly, which is unlikely, we won't arrive for two more days and that's plenty of time for those men to do their worst." His right arm slipped around me as he shifted position.

Shaking his head, he continued, "Marsh actually threatened to put them ashore if they misbehave in any way but he is, after all, a civilian captain under contract to the military... he could get in trouble with the Army if something bad happened to their two hired scouts. Even if they are nothing but criminal trash."

I whispered, "I'll be careful, Martin, I promise."

He replied, "Okay, I know. But, if at all possible, I would appreciate it if you stayed in the cabin as much as possible, at least until we hit Pierre. I know that Trevor is asking the same of Natalie and his kids. Both of us sensed murder in those men as the captain laid down the law..."

I kissed his cheek and agreed to lay low, at least for the time-being. It made me angry to be jailed in our tight little cabin while those rascals were allowed to roam free but I knew Martin was scared for me and I didn't want to add to his fear.

Staring out the window again as the moon rode up over the tree-tops and seemed to sail through the sky with invisible wings, I heard my husband's breath deepen as he fell asleep.

Turning over so my bottom spooned into Martin's belly, I drifted off to sleep as well, but the last image that filled my mind was the dull and bitter hatred in Williamson's small, dark eyes.

MAY 2, 1876

Dear Diary,

A horrible thing has happened- just as I feared it might. My poor friend Natalie has been violated and the man who did it has escaped. The Captain, crew and soldiers are subdued by this afternoons events and, in order to put an end to the unpleasant experience, the ship is making high speed-almost 30 miles an hour- toward Pierre and its docks.

The morning started out nice enough. When Annie and I stepped onto the deck from our cabin the skies were as blue and clear as the finest sapphire. Song-birds twittered busily from the trees along the shoreline and the temperatures were warm and balmy. I remember putting my face up to the sun and smiling as the world quickened around me, just like the life that was quickening in my womb.

A small body rushed past me with a childish giggle and turning around to look, I saw young Percy dash off to his favorite place... the make-shift livestock corral by the bow. He had, over the last few days, fallen in love with the piglets and sought every opportunity to caress their floppy ears and squirmy, silken bodies. The sow has been surprisingly tolerant but usually, either Natalie or I try to keep an eye on things as a mature hog can kill a full-grown man, much less a small boy, if provoked.

Looking toward the McDonald's cabin I watched for Natalie or Mary to appear in chase but neither one dashed out after the boy. Turning to Annie, I said, "Sis, go and make sure Percy keeps out of the pen, okay? I'm going to go and check on his sister and mother."

She nodded and started after Percy while I walked fifteen feet, or so, down the deck to my friend's cabin. The boat had stopped, briefly, to fix a couple of broken boards on the paddle-wheel and many of the men onboard, including Martin and Trevor were on the shore fishing for pike and trout. Seeing the men lined up with their poles and nets, I gave them a little wave and went to fetch Natalie.

The door was closed tight. Worried, suddenly, I approached the cabin door and knocked. It was strange to me that the door was closed so far into the morning. I was the one who could hardly be roused from my slumbers in the morning- not Natalie, who was usually up at the crack of dawn cooking breakfast and chasing after her kids.

Hearing nothing and wondering, briefly, if Natalie and Mary had left to go fishing with Trevor, I realized that the idea was absurd... she wouldn't have left Percy behind on his own- at least not without informing me or Captain Marsh. Knocking again, I called out, "Natalie? Are you in there? Hello..."

I don't know if I've mentioned this before, but this boat is *loud*! At rest even, it rumbles and purrs, as the thirty or more daily cords of wood that keep the steam engines running roar and whoosh. It was fairly quiet at the moment with half the men and crew on shore but I still had to strain my ears to hear Natalie's reply.

None was forthcoming, but I did hear what sounded like a series of thumps and a thin, high-pitched wail. Realizing that *something* was wrong, I started pounding on the cabin door and shouted as loudly as I could, "Natalie, what's wrong? Open the door! Natalie!"

My panicked shouts drew the attention of two sailors who ran quickly to where I stood screaming and trying to wrench the door open. They gazed down at me, and one of them asked, "What's the matter, Mrs.?"

Not knowing myself but sensing that something was amiss, I said, "Its Mrs. McDonald... Natalie. Something's wrong, I know it. Please, unlock the door or knock it down!"

Looking aghast, the sailor stared at me and then stepped backward toward the railing. Looking up at the wheelhouse, he shouted. "Sir! Permission to unlock one of the passenger cabins?"

I couldn't hear the co-pilot's response, (Captain Marsh was onshore, fishing with the other men) but a couple of minutes later a younger sailor ran up with a large ring of keys. In short order the door was opened and I saw my friend, Natalie, curled up on the small bed under the portal window. She was sobbing and shaking with shock. Something or someone was knocking on the stowage cupboard.

Gesturing weakly, she pointed toward the bulkhead

and whispered, "Mary is tied up in there. Help her, please?"

One of the men ran to the cupboard as I flew to the side of the bed and tried putting my arms around her but she shied away, cringing in revulsion. Staring at me, her small, round eyes as wide as an owl's, she whispered, "Oh, Nel... it was LaFontaine... he r-raped me!" Then she gulped, buried her face in my shoulder and howled like her heart had been ripped out of her chest.

Next thing I knew the small cabin was filled with men- all asking questions of Natalie who could only stare at them with mute shame. I heard the boat's whistle- a particular tone that would signal an emergency to the captain's ears, and holding my friend's shaking body in my arms as tightly as I could, I asked the men to please leave.

They stopped what they were doing and stared at me but, one by one, they stepped out the door. The only one who stayed behind was Lt. Burrows. The soldiers had been denied the pleasure of fishing and had been doing drills on the boat instead.

"Nel, does your friend know who did the deed?" he asked softly.

I nodded. "Yes. She said it was that Army scout, LaFontaine. You should try and catch him before he escapes."

He gave me a slight bow and stepped outside. At once, Natalie began to weep again. "My husband, my darling Trevvie, will never want to touch me again!"

I shook my head in denial. Although there was no way of knowing how Mr. McDonald would react, I couldn't believe that he would shun his bride over something that was no fault of hers. "Shush," I crooned. "He will too! He adores you and the children.

Mary, Percy and Annie had been collected and were, even now, being entertained in the third-story wheelhouse while the captain and crew were heading swiftly back to the boat. Mary was inconsolable. After being let out of the cupboard, she couldn't imagine what was making her mother cry. She had thought that she, Natalie and that stinky scout were playing some sort of hide and seek game. Now the poor mite thought that she had done something to make her mamma cry.

Not sure whether I should ask or not, I whispered, "Natalie, did he hurt you... I mean, are you okay besides... you know..." I trailed off in embarrassment, knowing I wasn't helping matters any.

Natalie just shook her head. "No. Well, he was terribly rough but I think I'm okay. It's just that, oh God! He was so dirty! I probably have lice now and fleas!" She squirmed away from me saying, "Nel, get away from me! You'll catch them!"

Sure enough, I immediately felt my skin crawl, but I knew that a good hot bath and some close inspection would cure me. What I really worried about was the possibility of some sort of venereal disease the scout might have transmitted to my sweet friend. Judging by Natalie's expression, I knew she was afraid of that, too.

Before long, the captain, Martin and Trevor crowded into the room. Trevor was white and shaking with rage but he fell to his knees and cradled his weeping wife in his arms. This gave Martin and me a chance to slip away and, once in our own room, I quickly removed my dress and asked him to inspect my body for lice and fleas.

First, after shaking his head in anger, he stepped outside the cabin and asked for a hot tub of water for the ladies. Then he stepped back inside and inspected me from head to toe. Announcing me as pure as the driven snow, Martin gathered me in his arms and rocked me back and forth while I wept for my hurt friend.

MAY 3, 1876

Dear Diary,

Yesterday, after Martin and Trevor saw to our needs and made sure there were men guarding our cabin doors, they joined the soldiers and crew who were fruitlessly searching for the two white scouts. Some of the crew reported seeing Williamson fishing on the shore, others thought they had seen LaFontaine fishing by himself some thirty feet, or so, upwind of the other men.

Regardless, by the time the rape was reported and the manhunt was underway, both men had vanished into thin air. Although Martin and Trevor were enraged that the two white scouts had evaded justice, I was simply glad that they were gone.

Poor Natalie has recovered her composure by now but yesterday was a different story. She seemed shocked to the bone by what had happened and would only come out of her bath after bleach and vinegar were added to the bathwater and she had cut almost all of her hair off.

Which is a pure pity. Natalie, frankly, is not a very attractive woman (although there is beauty in her kind eyes and sweet smile) but her hair is very pretty... or at least it was. Thick and wavy, her chestnut curls swept past her hips in luxuriant splendor. Now, it is sailing down the Missouri river. She was convinced, though, that it was crawling with lice and fleas, despite evidence to the contrary, and was determined to rid herself of the whole infected mess.

Unfortunately, at least for Mr. McDonald, justice will be denied as the culprits have, somehow, escaped his clutches. Inexplicably, the two Indian scouts have disappeared as well, which is surprising... to us, at least.

Captain Marsh is not a bit surprised, however, and told us this morning that Indian motivation seemed to ebb and flow with its own mysterious imperatives.

In addition, he thinks that since we are close to the Cheyenne River Indian reservation the two scouts might have swam ashore to meet up with family and friends before their scheduled rendezvous with General Terry's troops in Bismarck. Whatever the circumstances, Annie is saddened.

She has grown fond of the two Indians since they came aboard. Although the natives usually keep to themselves, the younger of the two men, Three Bull-Man, (apparently, when he was a little boy, his parents had seen three young buffalo calves following him from a large herd to a water-spring.) had become absolutely fascinated by Mary's ragdoll.

When he first spied the girl's doll, Three Bull had stood stock-still and stared in wonder at the bright-orange toy. Annie's doll is only partially finished, although she's working hard to finish it before the family gets off the boat in Bismarck.

Pulling at his companion's coat sleeve, he had gestured at the dolls and demanded to know what manner of medicine the two girls held in their small arms. The older man, whose name is Little Owl, smiled at the children and explained. "My friend wants to know if your dolls hold good magic, or bad?"

Mary had blushed to the roots of her hair and remained silent, but Annie said, "Oh, they're good dolls! Does he want to hold mine… it's not finished yet, but he can touch it if he wants to…?"

Flabbergasted, Three Bull took Annie's almost finished dolly in his hands and traced the yarn gently with his fingers, stared into its flat, wooly face and silently held the ragdoll up in the air as if in prayer. Finally, he handed it back to Annie and whispered, "Nea ese meno…" Annie wasn't sure what the young man had said, although she thought he had thanked her.

Since then, although the two Indians kept a respectful distance from the white passengers, Annie, Mary and Percy have hollered hello and waved at them from across the deck. Also, a number of times, as either Natalie or I circulate the deck with a fresh pot of coffee, we have stopped to fill the Indian scout's tin cups.

And always, the natives puff on their tobacco pipes and bow their heads in polite greeting. Now, although the horrid white scouts who had hurt Mary's mamma were gone- so were the Indians, whom Annie had grown to respect and trust.

It has been a gloomy time for all of us and the only thing that helps is the almost stunning speed at which the riverboat is now sailing. The wind whips at our faces and ears as we cut down the middle of the river- no longer blue but wide, flat and mud-brown. The scenery has changed, as well. Before, there were hundreds of bluffs and coulees, vast high hills and millions of trees, both evergreens and deciduous.

Now, what few trees there are have become stunted and gnarled and low, grassy plains stretch as far as the eye can see on either side of the river. About four hours ago, the boat came around a bend in the river. For quite a while, everyone on board had been keeping an eye on a huge plume of either dust or smoke rising up into the northern sky.

When the Far West nosed around the bend, I couldn't help but gasp at the spectacle that met my wondering eyes. Thousands upon thousands of buffalo milled around on the right side of the river. Hundreds of the animals were lined up on the shoreline, shoulder to shoulder, drinking the river's liquid bounty.

Thousands more filled the land as far as the horizon. It was like looking at an enormous, brown carpet that seethed with a life of its own and I understood, at that moment, that I had been given a gift.

Hearing, more and more lately, that the great herds of bison that used to fill the western territories are disappearing, I was overjoyed- and humbled. Here was one, right in front of my eyes and tears pricked my lashes at the creature's rough, unadulterated splendor.

"What do you think about that, Nel?" Martin stood by

my side, setting his camera up on its long legs to take pictures of the great herd.

"It's beautiful," I answered, "Beautiful and… sad."

Martin stared at me for a moment, and winked. "Well put, my dear. I don't think that herds of this size will be a common sight from now on… at least you and Annie can say you've seen them, in the wild, before they fade from history altogether."

A tear leaked from my eye and I wiped it away in frustration. Recently, my emotions were overblown and tender to the touch- much like my swollen breasts.

Martin frowned and put his arms around me. "What's wrong, Nel? Are you feeling okay?"

Looking around for my sister, I saw her standing next to Trevor and his children. Natalie was alone in her family's cabin. Turning back to Martin, I asked, "Do you think that Mr. McDonald will hate Natalie now?"

My husband stared at me in shock. "Why would you ask such a thing, Nel?"

Fresh tears welled up in my eyes and ran in two little streams down either side of my nose. My voice rose in terror, "Natalie said that she didn't think Trevor would want anything to do with her now that she… well you know- after what has happened!"

He squeezed my shoulders and whispered in my ear. "Nel… Nel, shush! You mustn't worry about such things! Trevor loves his wife and will continue to do so. It's true that he wants to give her all the time she needs but that's only until the two of them can find out if she's become pregnant and if that God-awful man gave her some sort of disease." He sighed, adding, "Whatever happens, I'm sure that he will not reject his wife's embrace."

Just then, the wind shifted slightly and a heavy, powerful odor overwhelmed my senses. I broke away from Martin's arms and ran to the starboard rail to vomit. It was the herd, I knew. Their stench was not unpleasant but rather so raw and primal, musky and oppressive in intensity I felt, for a moment, as if I would suffocate.

Hearing a shout, I looked up from the muddy water and saw the captain and crew members pointing toward the front of the boat. Martin had come to hold my hair away from my face and he said, "Something has grabbed Captain Marsh's attention. Do you want to go and see what's happened?"

Feeling much better, I nodded and grabbed his outstretched hand. We made our way past a number of people, including Annie who was sitting with Mary now, stitching button eyes onto her new dollies face. Looking up, she grinned as I walked past. Then we came to stand a little ways behind a number of other men and listened as Marsh said, "It looks like the Indian scouts have bagged us some supper, lads!"

Then, I heard the men utter a collective gasp. "Oh…" they whispered and the awe in their voices was plain to hear.

Martin and I ran to the rail and peered at the shoreline. Sure enough, the missing Indian scouts were standing on the beach. Two buffalo were lying dead at their feet and we could see the men's lances still sticking up from the beast's hides.

More importantly, though, were the decapitated heads each man held up in the air for all of us to see. We were leaving the large herd behind and now that the loud thunder of their hooves, their giant seething bodies, and their very breath no longer filled the air, we could clearly hear the Indian's cries.

Three Bull Man and Little Owl held the severed heads of the two white scouts, LaFontaine and Williamson, up high and hollered, "Oo xo e eh! Oo xo e eh, Natlie!"

Dear Diary,

I have never fainted in my life... I think I am made of starchier stuff than that. Still, the sight of those two, still dripping trophies sent me swooning into Martin's arms and I woke up a few minutes later in our cabin with a cold, wet rag pressed to my forehead.

"What happened?" I murmured, groggily.

Martin smiled and said, "You fainted, dearest. Don't you remember?"

I did recall, suddenly, and my stomach roiled again with nausea. Groping for the bucket I kept handy by the side of our bed I retched but my belly was empty. Exhausted, I lay back on the pillow and stared up at my husband's face.

"Guess those men got what was coming to them," I said. "Does Natalie know?"

Martin nodded. "Oh yes, she knows and let me tell you, she took it quite well."

"Are the Indian scouts and the men's... bodies onboard?"

He shook his head. "No. The captain is heading ashore now and it's my understanding he will ask Three Bull Man and Little Owl to make themselves scarce. As for Williamson and LaFontaine, I think they are bound for an un-marked grave."

I sighed. "It seems a pity that the Indians should be cast away when they were only trying to help. I think that, given half a chance, Trevor would have done the same."

He replied, "Yes, as would I in his place. But, what they did was against the law. Never mind that the white scouts injured and ruined a sweet, innocent woman- and this probably isn't the first time. Still, Three Bull and Little Owl would probably hang if they were caught and accused of murder. There are men on this boat right now-men who hold such hatred for the native population- they would make sure of it."

I looked away and stared out the little porthole window at the ice-blue sky. Although some small piece of me applauded the Indian scout's actions, I realized that the native men simply did not regard things... life the way most white folk did.

I also can't help but feel glad, now, that the scouts are leaving us. I'm not sure I would want Annie to spend time with them anymore. It would feel as dangerous to me as tossing her into the pig's pen without supervision or letting her play with a pack of wild wolf cubs.

I felt my eyelids drift shut and was almost asleep when Martin murmured, "There's one more thing, sweetheart, and then I'll let you get some rest while I watch over Annie."

I looked up at his dark, handsome face and realized, with a start, that Martin could easily pass for an Indian. His coal-black hair is quite long and since he never finds time to visit a barber, he holds it back from his high-cheek boned face with a leather cord. His eyes are every bit as brown as an Indian's and his body smooth and virtually hairless- again, like a native.

Martin is Jewish but I suddenly realized that the wrong person, with any kind of wrong agenda, could easily mistake my husband for a hostile. Determined, for safety's sake, to coax him to a barber's shop once we reach Pierre, I smiled and asked him what he wanted to tell me.

"Trevor told me a few minutes ago," Martin said, "that he and his family are leaving for good in Pierre. Natalie wants off this boat and away from the people who witnessed her shame." He studied my face with worried eyes as I processed this latest news.

I didn't blame her- at all- but my heart sank, never-the-less. I had grown so fond of her and her kids since they came aboard that she had begun to feel like a sister to me. I had counted on her companionship all the way to Bismarck and had hoped, against hope, that she would be close by my side once Martin left with the brevet general, Custer, and his 7th Cavalry.

Oh yes- I guess I forgot to mention that. Martin told me, a few days ago, that the captain has asked that the ladies and children disembark in Bismarck- we will not be allowed to follow the troops into Montana. Not even Elizabeth Custer, who is accustomed to following her gallant husband from one fort to the next, will be allowed on this campaign.

Apparently, the Far West will not only be an Army

supply depot for the troops, it will also serve as command headquarters for General Terry and the other officers. There is simply no room for us.

I am not happy about it, having originally thought that Annie and I would be staying onboard as the troops went to work rounding up the Indians for transport back to their reservations and my husband documented the whole process in a series of photographs.

I had even imagined, after hearing Marsh's orders, that Natalie and her family would keep me and my sister company until Martin returned to my arms. Now, hearing that the McDonalds will be disembarking hundreds of miles earlier than anticipated, feelings of worry and abandonment filled my heart.

A fresh wave of tears fell from my eyes. I rubbed them away and muttered, "I'm so sorry, Martin. I don't know what's gotten into me lately!"

He grinned. "I have a good guess, Nel, but still, I know that this news comes as a blow. Why don't you take a little nap so you're fresh and happy when we reach Pierre? Marsh says we'll make port in about five hours." He brushed my messy hair away from my feverish cheeks.

Continuing, he added, "That way you can say goodbye to your friend without making her sadder than she already is, okay?"

I nodded. "Yes, of course. I'm sorry I'm such a mess today."

He kissed my cheek and whispered, "You're entitled, Nel. We live in a rough part of the world- a place where life is cheap. Just know that you are loved... you and Annie both, and I will do everything in my power to keep you safe."

He stepped out the door and I rolled over to face the window again. Presently, I closed my eyes and slept until the boat's whistle sounded. We had reached the town of Pierre and its attendant Army fort.

Everything I had taken for granted was about to change... the McDonalds were leaving and Lt. Burrows and his fellow soldiers were going, as well, in route to Fort Fetterman, in eastern Wyoming.

The Indian scouts who had exacted rough justice for my friend were also only a memory now and Annie and I would soon be alone in a wild frontier town while my new husband sought to record the unfolding events for public consumption.

Rising from my bed, I splashed water on my face, brushed my hair and scrubbed my teeth. Then, I plastered a wide, false smile on my lips and headed out the door of the cabin to say goodbye.

I was determined to send Natalie and her family off with a warm smile and fond wishes rather than show them how I really felt- forsaken and abandoned in this wild, fearful land.

PART III
PART THREE

MAY 12, 1876

Dear Diary,

Well, we are on our way again and making good time. Captain Marsh seems quite impatient now and is worried that his boat will come late to the party in Bismarck and Fort Abraham Lincoln. He has heard that, after some political maneuverings in Washington DC, Custer and General Terry are even now on a Northern Pacific train heading west to Fort Lincoln and Marsh wants to be on hand when they arrive.

I heard that the captain will be paid almost 360 dollars a day to provide forage, ammunitions and transportation to the cavalry, so it's no wonder he is driving his steamboat- and his men- hard to arrive in a timely fashion.

For my part, I am relieved to be underway. We left Pierre two days ago and, despite my best efforts, parting with Natalie and her family in that small, frontier town was a sad affair. I had lost her friendship, I knew, although she meant me and mine no harm.

I think that when LaFontaine assaulted Natalie that day, everything she was *before* then had run away and hidden in a small private place in her soul and probably won't emerge again until she has had sufficient time to heal.

There's no place for me- for us- in her heart anymore... not until time has cured her broken feelings. Still, although I understand why she had shuddered and stepped away from my fond embrace in Pierre, it hurts me deeply and now I only want to forget about her and move ahead into my new life.

I need to preserve my own strength and peace of mind- for my family's sake and for the unborn child growing in my belly. I need to stop worrying about what might happen to Martin on this campaign, as well. There is no doubt in my mind that the Army's superior forces will prevail in the upcoming engagement and undue worrying will only cause me and my family harm. Still~ it's hard not to fret.

The river leads north into a seer country. Although there were a series of sickening bends and switchbacks a day or so out from Pierre we are unimpeded now and sail down the middle of the river at high speed. The captain believes we will arrive in Bismarck within the next two days- barring any more delays.

Annie and I sit back by the Gatling guns so we're well out of the way of the captain and his crew. Martin is making a new set of photographs- mainly of Marsh, the boat, the munitions and some of the crew. He plans on sending what he has south to Yankton so Solomon can either frame the photos or paint them- according to the recipient's wishes and monetary circumstances.

Now that Annie's little friends have left she is back to doing lessons by herself, an exercise that has lost its luster. Her ragdoll, which was supposed to be a little boy to go along with Mary's girl-doll has reverted back to being feminine and goes by the name of Maryanne- a reminder in Annie's heart of her first, real friend.

It is so sad, sometimes my heart breaks for her but she seems to be taking Mary's loss in stride. To most children, life's experiences are elastic and ever-changing, and Annie is okay with that. She now yearns to make land-fall in Bismarck and I don't blame her.

The boat was fun at first-exhilarating even- but now I want to feel dry, steady land under my feet. In fact, the only thing I want to do is settle down and prepare for the arrival of my baby. I have wondered, more than once, whether Martin might consider settling down in Bismarck after the Army's engagement, at least until the child is born.

Martin told me that he has heard of a proper boardinghouse Annie and I can stay at while he is away. Seeing the look on my face when hearing that news, he smiled and held me in his arms.

"Oh, don't look that way, Nel. This house is nothing like what you and Annie stayed in, before, in Yankton. It is owned and operated by a very nice widow named Mrs. Fairweather, and it is in the good part of town. The captain recommended it to me and says that he has stayed there himself, more than once."

I shrugged and replied, "Okay, Martin. I understand."

I was being a bit of a pill, I knew, but I still hadn't quite gotten over the fact that he would be leaving Annie and me behind when the cavalry departed for Montana.

Giving him a kiss on the cheek, I added, "Don't mind me, dear. I just wish Annie and I could go with you."

He nodded. "I know, Nel, but even *I* am glad you are staying behind where I know you'll be safe from harm."

I just sighed and let him go on his way, unmolested by my concerns.

Oh, the one thing I forgot to mention is I am writing in a brand new diary! After the McDonald family scurried off to their new lives in the town of Pierre, Martin, Annie and I had gone to the post/ telegraph office, a little café and, finally, a mercantile for some fresh fruit, soap, coffee, sugar and yarn.

We were under strict orders to be back on board within three hours' time or risk being left-behind, so it was a whirl-wind of activity, most of which concerned my keeping a sharp eye out for Annie who had sprung from the boat like a young bear from a trap.

Despite our short time-table, Martin somehow found the time to purchase some candies for Annie and a new diary for me! My old diary is starting to come apart at the seams and I have even begun to write cross-hatch, which is necessary but very hard to make sense of.

Later that same evening, after we had eaten a light supper, he presented the new book to me with a smile. "Here, Nel... so you can keep recording your life."

I gasped in joy. This diary is quite a bit larger than the last one my sister had given me and its blank pages beckon. "Oh, thank you so much, Martin! I love it!"

Grinning, he said, "I enjoy it too, my dear. I don't want you to go blind cross-writing the way you've been doing, and this way you can record what goes on in Bismarck while I'm gone, okay?"

For some strange reason a chill of foreboding ran through my veins for a moment, but I shook it off. I ran to where he stood with a pleased expression on his face, and gave him a fierce hug. "I will record everything I see, Martin. I promise!"

Lately, he has been helping me with my writing. My mamma did a pretty good job in educating me- the best she could do, at any rate, with what schoolbooks she had on hand.

Still, since I have begun writing, I have discovered just how hard it is to maintain good grammar... not to mention proper spelling. I won't let him actually read my diary... there are too many private thoughts within and feelings spoken of that are inappropriate to a husband's eye, but whenever I ask how to spell a word or compose a sentence he is generous with what he knows- which is a considerable amount.

I married Martin through sheer necessity but I am learning, to my delight, how truly marvelous, educated and talented he is. Every day, I thank my lucky stars.

Our passion for one another is unabated as well. Although my mornings are a sometimes a little rough, by evening my body is alive with sensuous sensation. More than once, Martin has convinced one of the sailors, a youngster by the name of Darryl Spencer, to spend time with Annie after dinner so we can enjoy some private time in our cabin.

Looking upstream now, as the wind whips the hair back from my face and the sun bathes my body in its warm embrace, I remember the night he brought me my new diary. Seeing the look in my eyes- and the yearning-

Martin strode from the cabin and reappeared a few minutes later with young Darryl in tow.

After he left with my little sister to play Tiddly-Winks on the twilit deck, Martin peeled my blouse from my shoulders and traced a line of fire from my forehead, to my shoulder-blades, breasts, nipples and belly button with his tongue.

By the time my petticoats and skirt fell to the floor and I stood naked before him while he knelt between my legs licking and sucking at my warmth, I was quaking... literally panting with desire.

I swear, I never knew love could feel like this or that passion is a living thing... so animalistic, so raw and powerful, the strength of it sometimes leaves me weak in the knees and powerless against its pull and thrust.

When I could take no more of his sly manipulations, he led me to the bed and stretched out on his back. Then, I climbed on top on him and groaned as his length entered me. I bit my lips, sighing at the pleasure of it and we rocked together as one.

Finally, I couldn't help it... I screamed my passion out loud. He laughed deep in his throat and covered my mouth with his so the rest of the crew would not hear my cries.

Martin found his release and we wound down, shuddering and twitching together in the afterglow of our love. I knew then, for once and for all time that Martin was meant for me- and that I would follow him to the ends of the Earth and beyond- just so he would continue to let me feel the keen pleasure of his love.

Dear Diary,

Although the Far West made good time-very good time, according to young Daryl Spencer- we didn't arrive at Fort Abraham Lincoln until the morning of May 27th. To Captain Marsh's disgust we had missed the Army's exodus into Montana by ten days.

Martin was upset as well. We had heard about the 3rd and 7th Cavalry's grand exit from Fort Lincoln and he had hoped to be on hand to take photographs. He also wanted to be in amongst the troops who were on the march but now he was forced to wait.

Marsh assured him, though, the Far West was likely to over-take the cavalry within a few days and that he would be in the enviable position of taking photos of three separate battalions. Apparently, Custer had decided to divide the 7th into three wings before the troops even left Fort Lincoln.

Major Marcus Reno, supported by Arikara scouts

were to head north to engage with the southern end of the Indian encampment and Captain Benteen would be heading southward to thwart any Indian escapes.

Meanwhile, Brigadier General Terry, leading his own battalion, would bring up the rear, and planned to meet the Far West at the mouth of the Little Bighorn River.

At least, that's what I've heard! Apparently, the Army's plans are as fluid and ever-changing as the very waters we have been navigating and Marsh is gnashing his teeth in frustration.

He is also frustrated by news that Elizabeth Custer and a number of officer's wives are planning on dining aboard the Far West later this afternoon. He is a busy man and is, even now, spending every waking moment transferring forage, goods and ammunition onto the lower deck.

Still, being hired by the Army means he must uphold military tradition, so he has instructed his cook to prepare as fancy a luncheon for the ladies as possible.

He also asked Annie and I to attend the dinner, which I suppose I must, but I don't really want to. I have heard things about Elizabeth Bacon Custer that give me pause. She was rather well-born- the daughter of a prominent judge- and I've been told she is not above taking on airs.

This is the last thing I need, frankly. Martin will be leaving with Marsh and the Far West later on today or, at the latest, tomorrow and the only thing I really want to do is go to Mrs. Fairweather's boardinghouse and keep my husband captive in my arms for as long as humanly possible.

Meanwhile, there is a lot to observe here at the Fort Lincoln landing. A party atmosphere is still evident even ten days after the Cavalry's departure. Martin is making last minute plans and he and Annie are moving our baggage close to the gangplank for removal into town.

I'm watching the opposite shore that seems to be teeming with white settlers, soldiers and thousands of animals. I have been told that Bismarck is not normally so packed but all manner of people have come to either join the large Army heading into Montana, or service it in one way or another. There are still hundreds of mule-teams and skinners, soldiers, prostitutes, camp-followers and merchants milling about, selling everything from sex to fresh butter.

Martin strode up and said we would be leaving on the ferry in an hours' time. Said ferry was pulling up to the landing even now and I sat down on one of our trunks, using an old newspaper to fan my face. Thinking about the many hours I had spent knitting warmer cloaks for me and my sister, I rolled my eyes. It was hot and sweat blossomed from under my armpits and drenched the blouse under my breasts.

Captain Marsh walked up to us and asked if we would be joining him for luncheon. Martin took one look at my flushed, miserable face and begged off. "Honestly, Sir, I was hoping we could be excused… Nel is feeling ill and I still need to see her and Annie set up at the board-inghouse."

The captain looked as if he wished he could beg off, too, but he smiled and shook my hand. Removing a brand new straw hat from his head, he gave the two of us a small, formal bow. "Ladies, I am sorry I have to put you off here but the Army insists. I did speak to Mrs. Fair-weather, and now that most of the Army has left she says there is a fine room you and your sister can stay in while we're gone."

I stood up with a grateful smile and held out my hand to shake. "Thank you, sir, for your kindness. I will miss the boat, I think."

He grinned. "Yes, she grows on a body, for sure." Shaking my hand, he tipped his hat to Martin and Annie and scurried back to his work. A few minutes later, we heard a tinny hoot and saw the ferry heave into view. It was filled to overflowing with troops, civilians, freight and horses but making good time.

While the ferry unloaded, I couldn't help but stare. We were suddenly surrounded by all manner of people who were bound for the fort. One man held an elaborate rack in the air that show-cased umbrellas and straw hats. I realized, suddenly, where the captain had obtained his new head-gear!

Martin studied the hats closely, as well. Now that heat had descended upon the land and, with it, mosquitos as large as hummingbirds, I understood that straw hats were quite desirable. Seeing that they were reasonably priced at only 25 cents, I nudged his elbow and asked, "Why don't you buy one, Martin? It will come in handy in this heat, don't you think?"

He grinned in agreement and moved away to hail the salesman.

Three blowsy, heavily made-up women wearing low-cut, satin gowns and lacey parasols strolled by. A heavy musk lingered about them, seminal and sweet. I sneezed as they stared at the men in saucy appraisal- especially Martin. Then I stood up and glared as one of them twirled her parasol under his nose in invitation, but she just laughed and sauntered away.

Another man stood arguing with the ferry operator. He was pushing a wheelbarrow mounded up with sacks of flour, metal baskets of eggs, butter, tins of lard, sides of bacon and wheels of cheese. "Alright, dern it!" he groused. "I'll pay for my load just like it's a passenger, although that don't seem right… don't seem fair a-tall! Say, you wouldn't happen to be interested in a pound of butter? Only a buck, you know… undercuttin' the competition by a dime!"

I realized something then… war is, at the heart of it, a profitable affair.

There was a bit of a commotion and I turned around to see two nicely-dressed women making their way down the incline to the boat's gang-plank. I couldn't be sure but I assumed, correctly, they were Custer's wife and the wife of another officer. Elizabeth sailed ahead of the other lady like a ship under full- steam and when she saw me sitting close to the Far West's gang-plank she swept her skirts aside and sniffed as though I were nothing but a bag of rubbish left in her way.

Sighing in relief that Annie and I were no longer expected to share lunch with this pretentious woman, I stood up to rinse my face in our cabin and say my final fare-wells to the riverboat known as the Far West.

Dear Diary,

Martin is gone, along with Captain Marsh, a number of officers, doctors, a barber and politicians onboard the Far West up the Missouri, in route to the Yellowstone River and its tributaries. I feel like my heart might break if it weren't for a new friend.

Everyone in this town seems to be resting easy, secure in the knowledge that the Army's superior manpower and arms will have the edge over the hostile natives but I can't seem to shake the feeling that something is horribly wrong- that doom lies in the very air around us like the looming thunder-clouds that sail over town every afternoon and drench us in warm, fat raindrops.

Martin spent most of his last day here situating me and Annie in Mrs. Fairweather's nice house, renting a mule to haul his heavy camera and picking up last minute supplies for his trip into Montana. It was a far cry from what I *had* been expecting- a long, leisurely love-making session followed by an even longer nap.

I had also entertained the thought that Captain Marsh might continue to run behind on his schedule, which would mean I could spend one more night with my lover but a hastily drawn note, delivered by Daryl, informed Martin that the boat was hauling anchor at 4:00 pm and that he'd better be on board or he would be left behind.

So much for that… at 3:30 on the 27 of May, I stood by the gangplank again, saying goodbye and farewell to my husband and trying to keep from bawling in fear.

Even Martin, now that the time had come to say good-bye, seemed a little worried. He was a brave and intrepid young photographer who had seen more than his fair share of battle-action during the Civil War. But as he stared past me, west, into Montana he muttered, "My only wish is that General Terry's commanding the 7th rather than Custer."

"Why? I heard that Custer is really good. Is he not?" Like a spoiled little girl I was ready to argue Martin out of going, but I should have known better.

He put his finger under my chin and lifted my face so he could stare into my eyes. "Nel, it hardly matters to me who is in command, see? I am here to record events as they unfold, no matter the outcome. It's my job!"

I blinked back frustrated tears and nodded. Mustering a smile, I hugged him one last time and kissed him as he turned toward the gangplank. He blew Annie and me kisses from the deck and waved his new straw hat in the air as the Far West was poled backward into the rivers current.

Captain Marsh, his co-pilot and young Daryl waved at

us and Marsh blew his whistle three times in farewell- to Annie's delight. I watched the boat sail away until they were only a speck on the water, and felt my heart pinch with a nameless dread. Looking up, I saw another lady standing alone on the other side of the dock.

She was a pretty thing with shiny brown hair and red-rimmed blue eyes. She dabbed at her tears with a hanky and caught my frank appraisal. "Hello!" she called out. "Did someone you know just leave on the boat?"

I answered, "Yes, my husband is a photographer from Yankton... Martin Leibowitz. He is supposed to follow Custer and take pictures of the engagement. My name is Eleanor and this is my sister Annie."

She walked up to me with her hand out-stretched in greeting. "Pleased to make your acquaintance. My name is Sally Williams and my husband, Thomas, is a reporter for the Chicago Times. He is traveling with a senior corre-spondent named Charles Diehl. Maybe my husband will meet yours and they can compare notes and photographs for the paper!"

I smiled at her friendly manner. "Perhaps... that would be nice. Maybe they can keep each other safe, too."

Tears filled her eyes again and I felt like a spoil-sport. Touching her arm, I added, "I'm sorry. I'm two months gone and the slightest thing makes me cry. I don't mean to be gloomy."

She smiled. "Congratulations!" Continuing, she added, "You're not the only one who feels sad, you know. We've been here for a month or so and many people are saying that the Army is outnumbered by the Indians, ten to one and that Washington DC is doing their best to hobble the troops."

I frowned, not having heard these rumors yet. I suddenly wished I could just take wing and fly to the Far West- pluck Martin up in my claws and wing him back home with me, safe from the Indian war.

Now it was Sally's turn to apologize. "Oh Eleanor, please excuse me. I am also a reporter, although an unsung one, and used to speaking my mind- no matter the cost. Trust me, my mouth has gotten me into hot water more than once!"

We smiled at one another and then she exclaimed, "There are those clouds again... it looks like it's going to pour. Why don't you and Annie follow me back home and I'll fix us a cup of tea?"

Oddly enough, she led me straight back to Mrs. Fairweather's house and we shared a laugh, realizing we were staying in the same establishment. First stopping by the kitchen, she bought three cornbread muffins with fresh butter for a nickel and then we followed her upstairs to her and her husband's room.

It was exactly like our room but well-lived in with clean laundry drying on a rope by the woodstove, a paper-cluttered desk and some toiletries piled up on the vanity. "Sorry for the mess," she laughed. "Thomas and I were trying very hard to finish an article for the paper before he left and I didn't expect to entertain visitors, either!"

I grinned, liking the young woman immensely, and helped her wash a couple of cups. After tea and muffins Annie curled up on a small couch and fell asleep while Sally and I talked. We sat and visited for a couple of hours and I told her about my diary. She seemed quite interested in my writing and claimed that there was a good market for eye-witness reports of the "New-West" in her home town of Chicago.

"Maybe you will let me look at the quality of your writing? I don't mean to pry into your personal affairs-not by any means, but I'm not kidding when I tell you our paper is just dying for some new editorial stories... and they pay well, too!"

I promised to show her a few of my less personal entries and thought about Martin who never failed to encourage me in my writing efforts. Then, like a goose, I asked Sally whether she had ever heard of my sister Patsy or my Auntie Chloe.

She giggled and said, "Well, Chicago is a huge city and unless your sissy and aunt are known outlaws they are only two people in a crowd of almost 250,000 souls!"

Gulping in disbelief, I stared down at the toes of my boots. I could hardly even imagine such a gathering of people in one place, it seemed impossible. Embarrassed, I said, "Oh, I didn't realize. I wonder how I'll ever find them."

Sally studied my face for a moment and said, "How old are you, dear? If you don't mind my asking..."

"Sixteen," I answered with red-blushed cheeks.

Grinning, she said, "Well, you have me now, and I'm so glad I found you. Once the time comes, I will help you track down your sister and aunt, okay? It shouldn't be too hard. Meanwhile, I'm an old married woman of twenty-five and we can keep each other company while our husbands are gone, all right?"

Feelings of joy peeked through the storm-clouds in my mind and we smiled at each other in easy companionship.

Dear Diary,

Every night, oppressive feelings of loss and bereavement fill my mind until I think I might scream but my days are busy now and filled with interesting things- thanks to my new friend Sally.

The day after we first met, Annie and I saw her at breakfast in the downstairs dining room. As promised, I had cut out a few passages from my diary for her to look at. I couldn't hand over the whole thing, of course... I didn't want her to know about my sexual awakening or that I am actually a murderess.

But I did let her read about my buffalo sighting and some of our adventures on the Far West, like the Indian attack, the Negro family's lynching and the "Grasshopper" maneuvers Captain Marsh is famous for.

Mrs. Fairweather had made a large pot of porridge with apples and biscuits and while Sally read my words,

Annie and I ate and listened to some of the table talk amongst the other boardinghouse patrons.

There was an ebullient salesman named Briggs who sang the praises of a new medicinal tonic he was selling and a doctor named Marcus Willoby who had recently set up a practice in Bismarck. There was a widower named Digsby at the table, as well. Apparently, he had sold his house after his wife passed and spent his days working as a traveling cobbler.

Every single one of them had the Army's incursion into Montana on their mind and weren't afraid of talking about it. My ears practically bent in two trying to take in their differing viewpoints.

Briggs said, "If anyone can bring those Injuns to heel, it's Custer. He may be puffed-up but he's unsurpassed at sniffing out a native encampment…"

To which, Dr. Willoby rolled his eyes and sneered. "Custer is a buffoon of the first order. I served as a medic before I took up my own practice and had the misfortune of serving under him in Kansas. You know, don't you, that he left his regiment behind in hostile territory-twice? The first time he took off chasing after a bull buffalo and ended up shooting his own horse out from under him." The doctor's face was growing quite pink as he recounted his memories.

"The second time he left the regiment behind was when he received a letter claiming his wife, Libbie, was having an affair. There were missing and wounded men after our tussle with Black Kettle's tribe but he didn't give a good Goddam! He left every Jack man of us to fend for himself!"

Mrs. Fairweather, a plump, sweet-natured lady in her

mid-sixties was serving fresh food from the sideboard. Clearing her throat she said, "Gentlemen, please refrain from swearing in my dining room... at least while there are ladies present."

The men turned toward us ladies and apologized for their wicked tongues. I smiled in forgiveness, although I had heard far worse spoken on the riverboat. "Your discussion is quite interesting, though," I said. "Please, go on with what you were saying."

Mr. Digsby spoke for the first time. "Custer's biggest mistake, recently, is getting in bad with President Grant. I heard he turned State's evidence against Grant's own brother, Orville, and Secretary of War, William Belknap. It's a wonder he even made it back to Fort Lincoln- Grant was all for putting him in prison for treason!"

Brigg defended his idol. "All that aside, General Custer's the man for the job and an American hero! At least he looks the part with his nice, long hair and nice outfits, unlike that stiff-back, General Terry! By God, I stand by my words!"

"Words that would carry more weight if you knew that Custer is no longer a general but a Lt. Colonel and his head is shorn as tight as a sheep's right now!" Sally exclaimed.

"Wha... you don't say! But why would he go and do a stupid thing like that?" Briggs squeaked.

"Too many fleas and ticks on the trail, is what I heard," Sally replied with a grin.

Two of the three men turned toward my friend, smiling in agreement but Briggs turned red with frustration. "If you know so much, young lady, then you know that career soldiers always go by their highest rank!"

Sally shrugged. "Of course, you're right. I'm only saying that Custer was busted back in rank for good reason and I think we wouldn't be amiss in praying for the welfare of our troops."

The doctor spoke into the silence. "Do you ladies have menfolk in the action?"

She nodded. "Yes, my husband, Thomas, is a journalist for the Chicago Times and Mrs. Leibowitz' husband, Martin, is an independent photographer assigned to Custer's regiment."

Doctor Willoby said, "Well ladies, I will certainly keep you and your husbands in my prayers."

Suddenly, my tender belly gave a lurch and I stood up with my napkin pressed to my mouth. "Excuse me, please!" I mumbled and ran to the downstairs privy room.

I don't know if it was my pregnancy or the contents of the men's discussion that made me heave into the indoor toilet but I retched until I was dizzy. When I finally came out both Annie and Sally were loitering in the hallway.

"Are you okay, Nelly?" Annie, who had taken most of my morning sickness in stride until now, actually looked scared for me.

"Oh, I'm fine, sis. Don't worry a bit." I wiped beads of sweat away from my forehead and took a deep, calming breath.

"Nelly... is that what your friends call you?" Sally asked.

"Nel is fine, Sally. Nelly's a little girl's name and I'd rather not be called that now, if you don't mind."

She shrugged. "Sure, I understand. Say, why don't we take a little walk? It's a pretty morning and I want to talk to you about your writing."

A few minutes later the three of us stepped out into a pretty June morning. The sky was clear (for now, anyway) and birds twittered gaily in the many willow trees lining the boulevard. I had brought a little money with me in order to buy some foodstuffs and therapeutic paper and we sauntered slowly toward Main Street, taking in the mild weather with pleasure.

Turning to Sally, I asked, "Do you really think Custer is a bad leader?"

She sighed, but her inherent honesty prevailed. "Yes, I do Nel. That doesn't mean he will do a bad job on this campaign, though. In a way, Briggs is right. There probably isn't a better Indian fighter than Custer, so for both our sakes, I must believe that Thomas and Martin are in good hands. Let's sit down there for a moment and catch our breath, okay?"

She pointed toward a wooden bench by a small park filled with geese, kids, mothers, nannies and, of all things, kites. Annie stood and stared at the flying toys and I determined to buy one for her at the mercantile if there were any to be had.

To our left, a number of fine ladies were also taking the sun. Looking closer, I realized it was Elizabeth Custer and a number of officer's wives having tea under the shade of an old elm tree. The grand lady, herself, was standing up in front of the others reading a passage from a book in her hands. I grinned, noticing the many of the women looked bored to tears, although some of them seemed to hang on her every word.

"That is Custer's wife, Elizabeth." Sally murmured. "They are two peas in a pod…"

"I met her, two days ago," I answered. "Well, I didn't

actually meet her. My family and I were disembarking from the riverboat just as she and another lady were climbing onboard. She swept her skirt aside when she saw me. I guess she thought I had bugs or something..."

Sally snorted. "That's Libbie, alright, but I doubt she thought you had bugs. You are very pretty, you know. She probably thought her husband might have set his hat on you- if you know what I mean?"

I shook my head in confusion. "No... set his hat?"

Sally shook her head. "Word has it he's quite the lady's man and she probably felt threatened by your very existence."

I was shocked. "But... I'm a married woman!"

Sally grinned. "I know, my dear. As am I but, apparently, that has never mattered to Lt. Col Custer -or to his wife!"

I studied the tips of my boots, realizing again just how naïve I still am in the ways of the world.

"Anyway," Sally continued." Elizabeth fancies herself above all others. She's also writing another book and plans on publishing quite soon, along with her husband. Which brings me to you..." I turned to look at her and she was grinning from ear to ear.

"What?" I asked.

"Well, I think you're a fine writer... a born-writer and I want you to write for the Chicago Times. I can do some editing for you, if you like... there are a few spelling and grammar issues in what I've seen, so far. But, I am sure that even without my help, the paper would jump on your stories. They are just what the editor is looking for."

My jaw had dropped open, and Annie yelped, "Sis, that's good isn't it?"

I nodded, and said, "Really, Sally? You think I should give them my stories?"

She shook her head. "Absolutely. But, you won't be giving them away... the Times pays $5 per story... what do you think about that?"

I wasn't sure what to think but my heart glowed with pride.

Dear Diary,

I know it's been quite a while since I sat down and wrote on your pages, but I've been pretty busy. The day after I accepted Sally's offer, we went together to the telegraph office and sent word to the Chicago Times to be on the look-out for three "True-Life" accounts of the western expansion and the Far West's exploits on the Missouri River.

The following day we received confirmation and a welcome note from the paper's editor, along with a bank draft authorizing me to receive $10 upon receipt of my two articles. I was so proud, I could have leapt for joy.

Sally has been helping me with some of my grammar and punctuation issues and I promised to pay her for her efforts but, she shrugged and said, "Don't worry about it, Nel. I am going to receive an extra dollar for every story you publish- it's kind of a finder's fee."

Relieved, I thanked her again and we went back to

work. Most of the time we work in her and her husband's room. It's already set up with a desk, pens and paper, a dictionary and assorted necessary's. I worry, sometimes, that Annie and I might be in Sally's way but she's assured me that our company is more than welcome.

I am relieved. More than once, I have noticed her red-rimmed eyes and the loneliness she feels at her husband's absence. I don't think she is a gloomy-sort but she is a realist and the more she hears on the street about the Cavalry's engagement to the west, the more worried she feels.

It's the same for me... and now, even Annie. I don't think my sister really understood the meaning of her new friend's (and uncle's) absence or how long he would be gone.

When Martin first left, he had given Annie a mighty hug and told her that she would be in his thoughts and prayers every day. I realize now, though, that she thought of his absence as quite temporary- a matter of days- rather than the reality- he was gone for however long the engagement lasted- and maybe gone for good.

I do my best to keep my feelings and my tears to myself but, like so many children do, she seems to have a sixth sense about things. Between Sally and me, Annie is beginning to really worry about the fate of our husbands.

Because of this new anxiety, and knowing that I have been spending too many hours, lately, polishing my writing, I decided to spend more time with my sister... at least, three hours a day playing, exploring and generally having fun.

Today, Annie and I went back to the little downtown park. We fed the wild geese and flew the bright red kite I had purchased for her. There has been no sign of Elizabeth or the other officer's wives since that first morning. On one hand I'm glad but on the other hand, now that I am a published author, I long to hear her writing.

I know that some of her work is wildly popular and I want to hear how she puts her words on paper. Thinking that I could inch toward her group as she reads aloud to them in the park and, perhaps, hide behind a tree so she can't see me eavesdropping, I'm frustrated now that she's keeping to the other side of the river, safely ensconced within the fort's walls.

Still, it's a relief to see Annie smile as her kite sails high into the air. As usual, my pregnancy makes me feel tired by mid-afternoon and I admit that I almost fell asleep, but then her high, musical voice caught my attention. Jerking awake, I stared through the slowly-shifting rays of sun at a tall figure who was leaning over and talking to Annie in a familiar manner.

Alarmed, I stood up and began running in her direction only to pull up short and stare. Lt. Adam Burrows stood next to Annie with a half-smile on his face. I could hardly believe it and blurted, "What are you doing here?"

Realizing how rude I sounded I blushed but Adam smiled and said, "I wonder that myself, Nel, but in answer to your question, I am convalescing due to an injury I suffered under General Crook's command."

Now that the fog of sleep had dissipated, I could see that he was leaning heavily on a cane. His left arm was slung tightly against his chest and his face was wan and pale. "What happened to you?" I gasped.

He shook his head. "The stupidest of mistakes, I fear. My horse sank a hoof into a gopher hole and went down with me under him. Broke my left arm in two places and dislocated my shoulder." Sighing, he added, "Worse yet, I had to put my gelding down."

I saw his bright green eyes darken at the memory of it, and I put my hand on his sleeve. "Well, I'm just glad you weren't killed."

He smiled. "Thank you, Nel. But this means I am now out of the action, which is disappointing. My mother is sending me to West Point while I gain back my strength. I have retained my ranking as Lieutenant, but will go to the school with accommodations which means I will likely be promoted to Captain upon graduating."

"Congratulations!" I said, truly pleased for him.

He gazed into my eyes for a moment and I could feel his stare probing my very soul. "What?" I asked.

"Where is your husband, Nel" he asked. "Has he gone into Montana with the troops?"

"Yes… why?" I said, feeling worried, suddenly, and prickly. I had been on the receiving end of Adam's dislike for Martin before and wasn't in the mood to hear any harsh words spoken now- especially since my husband was in no position to defend himself.

Adam shrugged. "No offence meant, Nel, truly. It's just that our Wyoming scouts have been telling us that Sitting Bull's encampment is, at least, three times bigger than anticipated. Latest intelligence also informs us that Custer, Reno and Benteen's forces are scattered far and wide and that the hostiles know about their approach. I fear that Terry's forces are in grave danger."

My heart was beating fast and the hot sun throbbed on my head.

"Nelly? Are you all right?" I heard Annie call to me

from a long distance away and when I opened my eyes, I was lying in Adam's arms, blinking up into the trees' ever-shifting shadows.

Sitting up and peering around I said, "What happened?"

Adam grimaced. "I happened, that's what. I was telling you about Custer's campaign and you suffered a shock. I am so sorry, my dear."

"Nel!" I looked to my left and saw Sally running in our direction. Her eyes were wide with fear and she gave Adam a light shove as she knelt at my side. "Nel, are you okay? Is this man bothering you?" she was staring past me at Adam with hostility.

"No! This is Adam, I mean Lt. Burrows, and he is an old friend." I said and struggled to my feet.

"Oh, pardon me, sir!" Sally said, "I thought you were molesting my young friend and over-reacted."

Adam nodded. "Well, it's good to know that Eleanor has a champion on her side, now that her *husband* has left..."

For some reason, although I don't think Adam realizes it, he cannot mention the word husband or the name Martin in my presence without a heavy shadowing of scorn... or anger. It made me bristle and I was about to say something nasty but I paused.

Remembering what Martin had said weeks ago- that the "green-eyed monster" was controlling Adam's emotions, I realized that my husband was right. At the time I didn't think that Adam could care about me enough to feel jealousy. But now I understood what Martin had meant... and I agreed.

Taking a deep breath, I said, "Adam was just telling me

what the troops from Fort Fetterman have learned about the Indian encampment. It's quite illuminating, Sally. Perhaps we can sit down, out of the hot sun, and Adam can tell you what he knows?"

Crisis averted, Adam, Sally, Annie and I went to our favorite little café on Main Street. We had a nice luncheon and talked for a couple of hours about Custer's campaign.

Finally, Adam stood up and said he needed to report back to the fort doctors before they declared him missing in action. Promising to meet up with Annie and I before he boarded a coach back to Yankton in a weeks' time, he took his leave.

The three of us watched him step outside and then we sat still for a moment, staring at each other in alarm. Then we got up and headed back to the boardinghouse with heavy hearts.

Dear Diary,

As promised, Adam has come to call a number of times over the last few days. Too often, in fact. It's not that I don't enjoy his company or appreciate the time he spends babysitting Annie while Sally and I work on our stories for the Times. It's the way he's acting... as though he is courting me.

Sally just smiles. "You could do worse, you know... Adam is quite a looker and from what you've told me- his family has money."

"That's not the point!" I exclaimed. "I am a married woman. He has no right to act this way."

Inexplicably, her blue eyes filled with the tears that always seemed to be on the verge of falling. "Of course you are, dear," she answered softly. "It's just that, in these uncertain times, it's not a bad thing to have a contingency plan in place."

I wanted to say something hot in return but seeing the forlorn expression on her face and knowing she only meant me the best, I relented and stood up to give her shoulders a light squeeze.

It has been thirteen days since Martin sailed up the Missouri on the Far West and I have yet to see a letter from him. Thomas had left town with the Army on the 17th of May. One large sack of mail arrived eight days after the cavalry's departure but there has been no word since then. It seems to me that every day that passes without a word from her husband, Sally loses more faith in a happy ending.

"Regular mail arrives today, Sally." I offered. "Perhaps we'll hear about how our articles are doing in Chicago. And, you never know... one of Terry's runners might arrive today with word from our husbands. We both know that horrible weather in the Montana Territories is putting a lid on the campaign."

Sally scrubbed the tears from her eyes and shook her head. "Of course, you're right, Nel. Please excuse my poor behavior."

Thinking about the spare money I had in my pocket and wishing to see my friend's smile again I said, "Why don't we go out to breakfast this morning... my treat. I think we could all use some fresh air. And maybe, by the time we're finished, the mail packet will be in."

Sally stared at me for a second and answered, "That is a fine idea, dear. Just let me splash some water on my face and we can go."

A few minutes later, we were walking down Main Street. Rain clouds were threatening again, but the day was unusually warm and quite humid. About a block away from the café, we saw Adam sitting on a bench reading a newspaper.

I smiled in delight. "If the papers are in then so is the mail. Do you want to go to the post office first?"

"That sounds good. We'll have something to read while we eat." Then she called out, "Good morning, Lt. Burrows!"

Adam jerked as if he'd been slapped and looked up at our approach. Instead of the charming, flirtatious smile he almost always wears in our presence, his face was cold... almost mean.

So mean, in fact, I stopped in my tracks and stared... so did Sally and Annie. "Why, Lieutenant, whatever is the matter?" Sally asked.

He stood up, folded his paper in two and handed it to her. Glaring sideways at me, he snarled, "Seems like we have been keeping rude company, Sally." His green eyes traveled insolently up and down my body as he added, "I guess we should both take better pains to really know our... "Friends".

His voice dripped venom and tears pricked at my eyes. I had no idea what he was talking about, but whatever he had heard about me had turned his ardor into hatred. He turned on his heel and strode away just as Annie cried out, "Adam, are we going to the park today?"

Ignoring her, he disappeared around a corner. Stricken, I put my arm around Annie's shoulder and stared up at Sally who had opened the newspaper to gaze down at the front cover. As I watched, her mouth dropped open and then, a wide grin stretched her lips.

That expression was one of the things I liked most about my friend, but right now, considering what had just happened with Adam Burrows, I was not in the mood for her hijinks. "Well, what is it, Sally?" I snapped. "What has happened?"

She winked and answered, "Well, why don't you tell me... Monique?"

"Mon... oh!" I stammered. Although it seemed like a lifetime ago, the name that was put on a certain painting had just come back to haunt me. "Give me that!" I demanded.

Laughing out loud, Sally handed the paper over and watched my face as I studied the large picture on its front page. I couldn't help it, but my cheeks blushed beet red.

For one thing, the woman in the picture was beautiful. But, more importantly, Solomon's talent was apparently too great to disguise for the likeness to me, despite the painted lips and powdered face, was abundantly clear.

Reading the caption, I felt like I might faint-

THE DAKOTAN

Yesterday, at The River Queen's grand opening, a masterpiece was revealed; Meet the famous French Courtesan, Monique la Fleur, who will preside over our gentlemen's club for all eternity!

"That's not me!" I blurted. "I mean, it is, but I'm not a courtesan, Sally. Please believe me!"

She nodded. "I know you aren't dear, but how on earth did this come about?"

I wished I could explain but that would mean

revealing far more than I want to about that perilous time in my life.

Improvising, I said, "This was painted by Martin's father, Solomon, before we were married. Martin really didn't want him to sell the painting to the hotel, but I think Solomon is quite proud of his work. Besides, they paid a lot of money for the commission."

I took a deep breath. "I honestly didn't think it would resemble me half as much as it does." Looking into my friend's face, I asked, "You do believe me when I say I'm not a courtesan?"

Sally snorted with mirth. "Of course I believe you! If you are a French whore you are the most innocent prostitute I've ever met!"

"So, you've met a lot of those, have you?" I quipped.

"I have, in fact!" she retorted. "A lot of newsworthy stories come from the Burroughs, you know... both Thomas and the Chicago Times editors will send me to talk to the street girls rather than a man..."

She sighed, folding the paper in two again. "Maybe we should just go back to our rooms, for now. I believe you are quite innocent in this ... affair, but word does get about. I'm afraid that if too many people see you loitering around town you'll draw undue attention to yourself- and some of it very bad attention, indeed."

Glancing about at the busy boulevard, I suddenly felt a hundred eyes drilling holes in my back. That was a ridiculous notion, of course, most of the people in town had barely stirred from their beds, yet. Still, Sally was right, we needed to get back to the boardinghouse as soon as possible.

Thinking about Adam's violently angry reaction to

seeing my image in print and how Mrs. Fairweather obsessively reads every paper she can get her hands on, I can't help but wonder just how long the famous Madame La Fleur will be welcome in her prim and proper establishment?

JUNE 15, 1876

Dear Diary,

It's been three days since Adam saw my portrait in the Dakotan newspaper and we have seen neither head nor tail of him. Well, fine!

Still, it stings a bit. Although I haven't appreciated his proprietary attitude toward me, I did enjoy the notion that Annie and I had a friend about town- someone who knew more than just rumor about the Cavalry's engagement to the west ... and someone who seemed to care about what might become of us.

His absence has made me miss Martin even more than I did before; his warm lips, ready smile and, more importantly, his mature temperament. I have begun to realize that, although Adam will *eventually* become a fine man, right now he is still just a boy-prone to rash decisions and racked by unruly emotions.

Since the Yankton newspaper hit Bismarck, Annie and I have stayed in either our room or Sally's. There is no

real reason to venture outside but we both feel confined…
jailed in our tight quarters.

The night we first saw the front-page portrait, Sally
asked Mrs. Fairweather to join us in her room. At first,
the older woman gaped and blushed at the picture but
after hearing an explanation for its existence, she sat and
stared thoughtfully out the window.

"You know, when I was a young girl," she murmured,
"I was never pretty enough to get myself into hot water
with a man, but I can see how it might happen. Over my
long life, I have seen countless girl's ruined by their
impetuous natures… and my heart breaks for them."

She turned to face me. "Considering the fact that your
painting was done by your own father-in-law, who is an
artist, and you ended up marrying his son, I think that
you should be forgiven. However, I have worked hard to
maintain the dignity of my house. If people in this town
start putting two and two together and try to sully this
establishment's reputation, I will ask you to leave. Are we
understood?"

I nodded, "Yes, ma'am, I understand."

"Good!" she said, getting to her feet. "I'm going to tell
our other guests the same thing. I know you won't tell
anyone about the paper, but I can't be sure about my
other boarders. I shall advise them to keep their lips
sealed or suffer the consequences."

She paused for a moment, adding, "I'm thinking,
specifically, of Mr. Briggs. That man's mouth is so big and
wide, I fear that one day he'll take a false step and disappear inside it, forever!" She giggled and, for a moment, I
saw the young girl she once was.

"Thank you, Mrs. Fairweather!" I called out as she

stepped into the hallway. Then, turning to Sally, I added, "And thank you, too, Sally. It never even occurred to me that Mrs. Fairweather might kick me and Annie out."

She shrugged. "Thomas and I have had a lot of experience with houses like this. The proprietors are sometimes as prickly as porcupines when it comes to their domain's reputations- their livelihoods depend on it."

"But, why?" I asked. "I mean, why would people think so ill of a simple painting? It wasn't too revealing, was it?"

She frowned and said, "Nel, it's not the painting itself. It's the scandal behind it... the implication that you are a French courtesan. Don't ask me why, but I have found that many people dearly love to besmirch other's characters... whether it's deserved, or not. I should know- I've been a victim of malicious gossip for years now!"

"What?" I gaped. "Why?"

She smiled. "Because I am a woman working in a man's world, that's why. Although things are improving, many of the men at the Chicago Times hate me- hate the very thought of me working at their precious paper. Never mind I'm college educated and have more talent than most of them put together!" Her face had turned red and I wished, for a second, I hadn't asked.

She stood up and stared down at me. "Just remember this, Nel. Many of the people you meet in your life will wish you ill... not for anything you have done wrong, but for the fact that you are beautiful- and they are not. Or, that you are young, and they're old. There are a hundred things that will turn an otherwise decent person to spite."

She sighed. "Sometimes I think its sheer boredom that sets tongues to wagging and often, the hateful things they say will have nothing to do with *you* at all. These folks can only feel big if they can make the people around them feel small. I'm sorry, but the sooner you can prepare yourself for this, the better off you'll be."

Her face was grim and I realized that, for some reason, Sally had often been shown the treatment she was warning me about, now. I smiled up at her and her expression lightened.

Grinning, she said, "Well, now that's over, I think we should just take dinner in our rooms and get back to work. What do you say?"

A wonderful thing happened this morning... two wonderful things, actually. It's a good thing, too. Annie and my imprisonment has led to some quarrelsome days and I know that my sister is fixing to get up to some sort of mischief if we don't escape our room soon.

The first thing that happened was Sally. Around noon, she knocked on our door with presents for each of us. One was a little toy soldier for Annie to play with and the other was a lovely lady's hat for me. It is a soft, dove-gray, low-crowned affair complete with a little veil that can be dropped down over a woman's face for privacy's sake.

"It's a mourning hat, actually, but it won't be remarked upon if you wear it outside, "Sally said. "Many ladies wear the veil when the skeeters come out or when the sun's rays are too bright. I thought that, if you wear this, we can go outside without you being spotted."

According to her, none of the people she ran into every day had put two and two together yet, and she thought that even if the rumor mill had begun to spin by now it would soon subside for lack of interest.

I felt so overjoyed I gave my friend a fierce hug and cried, "Let's go for a walk now!"

Laughing, she said, "Okay, Nel. Annie, are you ready to escape the dungeon?"

Annie jumped for joy and hollered, "Yes, yes! I am so ready!"

Just then, there was a knock on my door. Turning to look, my heart sank. I wondered if Mrs. Fairweather had arrived to kick Annie and me out or if the town's citizens were aiming to see me and my sister sent out on a rail.

I looked at Sally, who shrugged, and opened the door to see Lt. Burrows standing in the hallway with a bundle of papers in one hand and a bouquet of flowers in the other. He looked shy and rather miserable as he held the parcels out.

"Hello, ladies," he said. "First, I need to apologize for my wretched behavior to you, Nel. I am so sorry I over-reacted to that picture in the paper. I know, now, that you are not a courtesan or anything of that ilk."

"Figured that out for yourself, did you?" I snapped.

He hung his head. "Yes, with Sally's help, I did… please, forgive me Eleanor. I was just sick with jealousy and I can't seem to keep from acting like a horse's ass when I'm around you… excuse my French!"

I stared sideways at Sally who grinned in response. Then I turned back to face the young man. "Well, thank you, Adam, for the flowers and the apology. I guess we should just let the whole thing drop, for now."

He nodded with a happy smile. "Thank you, Nel… really." Turning to Sally he added, "Now, I don't know who is responsible for the mistake but these letters and this large envelope arrived at the fort by military courier four days ago, from Montana."

Sally gasped and grabbed the papers from Adam's hand. Sorting through them she grabbed two letters for herself and handed one to me and another letter to Annie. The large sealed envelope was addressed to Solomon.

Both letters carried Martin's bold, spidery signature~

TO MY BELOVED WIFE, ELEANOR and
TO MY DARLING NEICE, ANNIE.

"Please, come in and sit down, Adam." I said and sank into the nearest chair to read Martin's long anticipated letter as the lieutenant found an armchair to sit in.

This is what my husband wrote~

To my beautiful wife, Nel.

Due to the mind-bending speed with which Captain Marsh applied his boat and crew, I am now in Montana.

We are moored at the mouth of the Yellowstone River awaiting Custer's return and that of his two separate wings of command - Captain Benteen's regiment and Major Reno's troops. When they return, I will most likely accompany Custer to Sitting Bull's encampment.

General Terry is due to arrive any day and I hear he is quite put out with Custer's behavior. It is rumored that the brevet general is treating this campaign as some sort of holiday and he is stoutly refusing Terry any authority over him or his beloved 7th. I honestly don't know how any proper Army can operate under these circumstances.

Meanwhile, as snowy puffs of cottonwood seed fill the air and the smell of primrose prickles our nostrils with the first blush of summer, I can't help but think of my lovely young bride and the paper roses she held under her nose one day as she sat for a portrait with my father.

I know now I fell in love with you that day and that I will continue to love you until the end of my days...and beyond.

I hope that you and Annie are well in my absence and that our child is still safe and sound in your belly.

I am here to do a job and to secure our future together as a photographer of some good repute. But, rest assured, my heart yearns for you...your smile, your touch, your body.

Sincerely from your loving husband,

Martin

PS- Nel, please send these pictures to my father. He can develop the film in our shop at home better than I can right now.

You do remember where I stashed our extra cash? Just get some and forward this packet to Yankton ~with my love and affection.

While you're at it, take an additional twenty dollars and buy yourself and Annie a treat, okay?

Martin~

Dear Diary,

A wretched thing has happened but I'm recovering now and want to continue my diary where I left off so that my passages make sense.

Sally was pleased as punch with her letters. She had been smiling ever since she read her husband's correspondence and seemed in a frenzy to write more articles for the Chicago Times.

I should have said so a few days ago, but I was weary after writing my last entry and took a nap rather than mention the fact that there was one other letter in the bundle of soggy papers Adam handed over- from my sister Patsy! Because of everything that has happened lately, I almost forgot that I sent her a telegraph, but it was gratefully received and has now been answered.

Although I didn't mention how they had died, Patsy and Chloe were deeply saddened by the news of Mamma and Davey's passing and asked for more detail. She also asked about Daddy, and wondered what on earth we were doing in the Dakota Territory. Then she went on to apologize for her absence.

She wrote that she knew it would be either him or her in the long run-had she stayed to endure any more of his abuse. She is only sorry now that she hadn't thought to spirit the rest of us kids along with her to Chicago. She has no idea how that might have been accomplished, but her heart aches for us.

She and Auntie Chloe hope we can, eventually, make our way to live in Chicago, close to them. She also told me that she and her young attorney, Marcus Tremont, are engaged to be married in August. She wants Annie, at least, to come and stay with her and her husband so she can gain a proper education and believes that the wild country we are in is no place for a child.

She wishes me and mine well and is waiting, impatiently, for more news. So, I am going to send her a letter today. I have a lot to say, actually, about my father, my dear new baby and how my husband has gone somewhere beyond the western horizon with General Custer's 7th Cavalry.

I also want to tell her about my column in the Chicago Times and that I am actually an acquaintance of the famous riverboat captain, Grant Marsh of the Far West.

I'm sure she won't hardly be able to comprehend what has become of her two younger sisters but, that is the nature of change, I guess. Family members are swept apart and sometimes are never able to find each other again.

I hope that as soon as Martin comes back and, after my baby is safely delivered, the three, no four, of us can board a train and head to Chicago for a visit. I don't want to lose Patsy along with the rest of my kin. (Besides, perhaps my big sister is right... this is rough country and I would love Annie to attend a proper school so she can prosper in life.)

Anyway, the day after I received Patsy's letter, Annie and I made ready to send Adam off to Yankton on a stage-coach. Sally had begged off since she was in the middle of three different stories and wanted to send them to the Chicago Times the next morning.

Annie took a bath and I cleaned up after she finished so we were pretty and fresh. I had taken Martin's generous offer in good faith and purchased two new dresses earlier that morning.

Annie's was a pretty pink with a white satin sash and mine was as green as an apple with tiny yellow flowers embroidered on the bodice. The best thing about this new frock is how loose in the belly it is. Although I am not showing yet, I'm sure that I will soon and it is a comfort to know that I will have something decent to wear as my pregnancy advances.

I was relieved to know the Lieutenant was heading home to his Mamma and on to West Point. Although he is bright and handsome, his attitude is far too familiar for me. I believe he will pursue my hand in marriage if Martin is killed in action but this is not something I want or desire. His almost constant flirtation is getting on my nerves.

It also causes me to stay awake long into the night, wondering if there is something the lieutenant actually knows and is keeping from me. Rumors circulate all over town, all the time.

The road between here and the Montana Territory is still fairly fluid and people arrive on a daily basis with tales of the military's actions against the Indian nations.

One teamster said that General Crook's regiment was wiped out, to which Adam snorted and replied, "I can't wait to hear what "Old man Cook" has to say about that!" (Apparently, Cook's forces *had* been repelled from Sitting Bull's encampment but the general was claiming victory anyway.)

Another man, one of Custer's hired musicians, got drunk three nights ago and announced that sending his band home from the front-line was a sure-fire way to doom the campaign. He was tossed through the bat-wing doors of the saloon and told to shut (the hell) up before he jinxed the soldiers.

There are so many conflicting reports, my feelings see-saw from confidence to terror, twenty times' a day. I honestly don't know much more of this I can stand and I looked forward to taking a nice stroll in the afternoon warmth in a pretty new dress and saying farewell to the young man whose attentions I once yearned for but now leave me feeling cold and more alone than ever.

Annie and I stepped onto the street and, as always, I dropped the little, gauzy veil over my face before heading downtown. As the heat of summer descended upon the town of Bismarck, unfortunately, so did the grasshoppers. Great, buzzing clouds of them skittered and twitched in front of us as we strolled down the road.

Annie thought they were hilarious and loved trying to catch them in her hands but they gave me a skittish feeling. Watching my sister suddenly disappear into a dark fog of insects, I felt the weight of them on my clothing, hair and skin and experienced a moment of pure panic.

I stopped walking and tried to pluck a couple of the bugs off my veil and when I looked up, the bugs had vanished and so had she. I stared about wildly and screamed, "Annie, where are you? Annie!"

I looked right and left and started running down the street but I didn't see her- not at the park we usually visit or the café we frequent. As my heart started pounding in fear I realized that I was probably over-reacting, but I just couldn't imagine what had become of her in the one moment I had looked away.

Then, I looked up and saw something my eyes couldn't fathom and my heart denied.

My father, Frank Higgins stood at the mouth of an alleyway with my little sister's arm clutched in his left hand and his dirty right hand over her mouth. Her eyes rolled in fear and she struggled fiercely, but he shook her roughly and grinned at me.

"You'd better come here, Sis. You and I have some talking to do."

Dear Diary,

I am still recovering from my injuries and tire easily, so I rested after my last passage, took a light dinner with Annie and Sally and slept almost ten hours yesterday. I am refreshed now, though, and ready to explain what happened to Annie and I after Frank Higgins arose like a vengeful spirit and did his best to kill me.

I remember being so flabbergasted at the sight of him standing in front of me that my feet were rooted in place even as he dragged my sister into the gloomy alleyway between two buildings. He had aged and withered horribly since I saw him last.

His hat was off and his salt and pepper hair was grimy with dust and sweat. It hadn't been cut in months and those frizzy, wild locks clung to his misshapen skull like a greasy blanket. Despite that, I could clearly see a deep dent in his head... a dent I had put there, myself.

His brilliant blue eyes-always his best feature- were

faded now and stared in two, different directions. His right eyeball drilled holes into me as his left wandered, lazily, up at the sky and down at the street.

His mouth seemed permanently fixed into a lop-sided sneer and his right arm seemed to be next to useless. Twice, as I watched in horror, the palm covering Annie's scream flopped away and Frank had to lift his right hand back up with his left to place it back over her mouth.

His clothes were absolutely filthy. He looked like the worst sort of hobo but his one good eye glittered with intelligence and incomprehensible malice. He jerked Annie off her feet and ran into the alley, glancing behind to see that I was following.

I didn't want to- I was horrified, scared and ashamed but he had my sister in his clutches and I knew, without a doubt, that if I didn't follow, he would murder her in cold blood.

I picked up my skirt and ran after them into the side street between a sewing-machine repair shop and a "Land" office. The hustle and bustle of the busy street muted and the only thing I could hear was my own pounding heart and Frank's shallow grunts.

He moved ahead of me about a half a block and then stopped. Even as I watched, my father slammed Annie's body against the brick wall of the repair shop and held her at eye-level by the throat.

I kept running and screamed, "Let her go, Daddy! You're hurting her!"

Skidding to a stop, I saw him grin and squeeze Annie's neck in his left hand. Her legs kicked hard and I could see her face turning red. "Daddy! Drop her, please! Take me instead!"

He paused and his grip loosened. Annie gulped for air and her eyes searched my face, "No, Nelly, don't!" she whispered.

Frank studied my face for a second and snapped, "I'll let her go if you come here. Do it, now, or I'll throttle the life out of her!"

Gulping, I stepped toward him and he let Annie fall to the ground as if she were nothing more than a broken doll. I saw her hit the dirt and gravel-hard, and exclaimed, "Annie! Are you alright?"

She was weeping now as if her little heart would break and she crawled away on skinned and bleeding hands and knees. I saw no more, though, for the minute Frank let my sister go, he grabbed me by the throat and shoved me up against the brick wall.

Putting his face up to mine, he grated, "You think you can bash my head in and leave me for dead, you little whore? You think you can marry some Hebe and hang dirty pictures up on the walls in Yankton and I wouldn't notice?"

He shook me, hard, and my head slammed into the bricks. "Well, I took care of that old Jew... that so-called artist who hung my girl's picture up at the River Queen and called her a whore. Took his money and burned his shop to the ground... and him with it!"

His face was wild and his left eye spun in his head like a marble. He stared at the tears leaking from my eyes and grinned. "Well," he continued, "Now it's your turn! You tried killing me off and now you're gonna pay for what you done!"

I couldn't breathe but I tried to defend myself. "But

Daddy…" I croaked. "You were out of your head and trying to hurt Annie!"

He shook me again, like a bull terrier with an unfortunate rat. Then, he squeezed his left hand until I saw stars and heard a high-pitched whine in my ears.

"Daddy!" I heard my sister's voice coming from a million miles away. "Daddy, stop it! You're killing her!"

It didn't matter what Annie said, it was too late, and I knew it. Blood pulsed and pounded in my head and I could feel my soul leaving my body Then, I felt my weight dropping downward and something heavy slammed into my belly so hard that what little air remained in my lungs flew out of my mouth in a mighty wheeze.

Frank Higgins had slugged me as hard as he could and even as I gasped for air, he wound up his left arm again and punched me in the face. Stars burst before my eyes and I felt my knees give way. The ground rushed up at me and I met it as lightly as a feather.

I lost consciousness for a moment but gained it back quickly enough when I saw his boot coming at me. The only thing I could think of at that moment was the safety of the child in my belly and I curled up into a ball to protect my womb.

His large, hob-nailed boot met the back of my neck and I gagged at the excruciating agony of it. "Daddy, please- I'm sorry," I swallowed the blood in my mouth but felt it spill over my lips, staining my new dress and the ground beneath my head.

He reared back to kick me again, the whole time bellowing incoherently. I closed my eyes and prepared to meet my maker because I knew that one more blow, like the last one, would spell my end.

But, nothing happened, except for a deep gasp. Peering up at where Frank stood poised over me in his fury, all I could see was ten inches of sharpened steel protruding from his chest like an obscene metal tongue.

My father stared down at the regimental sword that pierced his body with his eyes opened wide in wonder. He put both of his hands on the bloody blade as if in prayer, swayed and fell backwards like a fallen tree.

I looked up through rapidly swelling eyes and saw Lieutenant Burrows standing over my father's body with shocked eyes. Then I felt, rather than saw, my sister kneel by my side.

She was weeping bitterly. "Nelly! Oh, Nel, are you okay?" she sobbed.

I tried to nod, tried to comfort her and thank Adam for saving my life, but I fainted and didn't wake up until later that night.

Dear Diary,

That first night, after the attack, my memory was spotty. I remember how Annie had kicked out as her body struggled for air. I recall my own terror when Frank punched me in the stomach and the fear I felt for the health of the tiny baby in my belly.

Mostly, I remember pain. My neck was lurid with bruising from the bottom of my chin to the top of my clavicle. The left side of my face was swollen and horribly bruised as well, causing my left eye and lips to puff up with pressure.

The worst thing, though, are the heavy, grinding cramps I felt in my womb. I could actually feel moisture leaking from my belly onto the sheets below my body and I wept with horror. I just knew that my new baby was struggling to survive Frank Higgin's assault and, at that moment, I knew that if my father were not dead already, I would murder him for what he had done.

When I awoke, I was in my bed with Doctor Marcus Williams bending over me. His pale blue eyes studied my injuries and his soft, white hands were exceedingly gentle. I almost wept at the kindness of his gaze. Annie and Sally stood on the other side of the bed.

Sally looked absolutely furious, but Annie just looked scared and hurt. Her throat was also bruised and her little hands were wrapped in bandages. I remembered how she had landed on all fours on the hard ground of the alleyway.

I reached my hand out and tried to say, "Sis, are you okay?" but stopped talking immediately, the pain was so intense. The shock of it must have showed on my face, for the doctor murmured, "Best not to talk right now, Nel. Your throat muscles are quite bruised and will remain swollen for a while."

Tears filled my eyes as the memories of Daddy's rage came flooding back. I thought of the things he had said and done and then I gasped as the pain in my womb registered. I struggled to sit up and croaked, "My baby! How is my baby?"

Sally put her hand on mine and said, "The doctor thinks you and the baby will be fine, Nel, but you need to rest."

The old doctor nodded his grizzled head and agreed. "Yes, complete bed rest- for a week, at least. I think your baby is alright but this is a crucial time to stay still and let nature do its work."

I sighed with relief and lay back on my pillow. Then I had an idea... gesturing to Sally, I asked for a pencil and a piece of paper. Nodding in understanding Sally walked

over to a pile of papers on the bureau, grabbed some
sheets and a pencil and handed them to me.

I wrote-

Daddy is dead?

Sally said, "Yes, thank God! Adam ran him through
when he saw what Frank was doing."

I considered that notion for a moment and wrote-

How did Adam know?

Annie smiled and whispered, "I ran and found him,
Nelly. He wasn't too far, either. When we didn't show up
at the Stage line office, he came looking for us."

I stared at my sister's face for a moment and wrote-

**You are very brave, Annie. Thank you for
saving me.**

She smiled and touched her sore throat.

Finally, I wrote-

Where is Adam now?

Annie was going to answer me, but Sally put her hand
on my sister's shoulder and said, "That's enough talking
from you, sweetie. Your throat is damaged too, and you
need to let it heal, okay?"

Annie shrugged and walked over to lay down on her
cot. Sally turned back to me. "Right now, Adam is downstairs talking to the sheriff and waiting for a military
lawyer to show up from the fort."

She must have seen the fear in my eyes because she
added, "He will be alright, Nel. It was a justifiable act and
there are witnesses to prove that fact. Besides, I heard that
your father was wanted for the murder of some woman
named Darla Hopkins, and the possible arson and homi-
cide of… " she paused and angry tears filled her eyes.

"I'm so sorry, Nel, but it sounds like Frank killed your father-in-law, Solomon Leibowitz."

I turned away from the look on Sally's face and closed my eyes in sorrow and exhaustion. I remembered Frank's wrathful words and my heart broke as I recalled Martin's father- that sweet and talented old man who felt such pride and fierce love for his only son. I thought about how he had welcomed my sister and I with open arms and his terrible fear for Martin, who wanted to make a name for himself as a famous photographer so he could support his new family in style.

And, I thought about my daddy, Frank Higgins.

Had he always been crazy and I just hadn't noticed until recently or were his life-long rages just a symptom of his insanity? If things had been different... if Mamma hadn't taken her own life, and Davey's, could Daddy have been cured with time spent in a sanitarium?

Maybe, if I were a kinder, more patient daughter, I could have cured him!

All of these thoughts swirled around in my head like a flock of panicked birds until I finally fell asleep.

I woke up at dawn the next morning and realized I felt better. The cramping in my belly had stopped and my mind had cleared. I was still sad, of course, and dreaded writing to Martin about what had happened to me and, more importantly, to Solomon because of me. But, to be perfectly honest, my principal feeling was relief.

Frank Higgins was dead, and I couldn't help but rejoice. I knew that God would not approve of my satisfaction but I would deal with that later. For now, at least, the yoke of "Murderer" that had been weighing me down with guilt and remorse was lifted.

Annie saw that I was awake, and smiled. Walking over to the woodstove, she poured me a cup of tea with honey and brought it to me to sip. "I'll let Sally and Adam know you're awake and go downstairs to get a bowl of broth, okay?" she rasped.

I nodded my head and when she turned away, I reached out and touched her shoulder. I still couldn't talk, but I looked into her eyes and whispered, "I love you, sis."

She grinned, resilient and happy. "I love you too, Nel. It'll be okay now."

I watched her skip out of our room, and thought, *Yes, things will be better now, just so long as Martin comes back to me safe and sound.*

PS~ I'm going to sleep a little more now, dear Diary... and, I hope you can forgive me my honesty. I would have loved my daddy with all my heart- but he never gave me the chance to do so and, although I doubt it, I hope that God will forgive him his crimes, for I simply cannot.

Dear Diary,

Although it has almost driven me mad, I've languished in bed for four days. Dr. Willoby has given me permission to get up tomorrow morning and walk about, just so long as I'm extremely careful and do nothing to cause my body or my baby a shock.

I can't help but roll my eyes at this- it's not like I go seeking adventure or violent confrontations but I must admit... those things seem to find me anyway, and I vowed to take it easy.

I have managed to get some writing done including a letter to Martin, a long letter to my sister Patsy and another letter to Solomon's bank, letting them know that Martin is alive and well and will be returning to Yankton soon to take care of his father's affairs.

Annie is raring to go outside and play. Her throat was hurt when Frank slammed her body against the brick wall but she can talk now (boy, can she ever talk!) and she's feeling bored with me and my constant scratching.

My throat apparently suffered more extensive injury- it is still quite swollen. But, this morning I was able to eat Mrs. Fairweather's porridge and even a piece of milk-soaked bread. I have never tasted anything as fine! Although it is plain fare, anything is better than the thin chicken broth I've been living on the last few days.

Hearing a bit of a commotion outside, Annie got up from her bed (where she had been playing Army with her ragdoll and the little toy-soldier) and ran to the window. Peering down, she exclaimed, "Hey, Nel. They're putting up decorations!"

I frowned. "Decorations? What is it?"

"Red, white and blue things... sheets, I guess you call them," she answered.

Remembering, I realized that Bismarck, along with every other town in our union was fixing to celebrate our country's Centennial birthday. The fourth of July wasn't for another week or so, but Bismarck's citizens were planning on doing it up proud.

I couldn't resist... throwing the covers back, I rose from my bed and joined my sister at the window. She stared up at me with a frown.

"You'd better not let Doc Willoby catch you, sis," she muttered. "He'll put you back in bed for another week!"

She looked put out at me but I grinned, knowing that my baby's precarious grip on life had strengthened and he (or she) was out of danger now. "You're just worried that I won't be able to take you to the park tomorrow!" I laughed.

Affronted, she replied, "That too, I guess."

"I just want to get a look, honey. Move over so I can see."

Annie stepped aside and I peered down at the street. Sure enough, red, white and blue bunting was being nailed to the front of a solicitor's office and a mortuary across the street and, further up, I saw that streamers were being strung overhead from the gaslights on either side of Main Street.

Sally, who was at the Bismarck Tribune office at the moment, had told me the town was planning a parade and a city-sponsored picnic at the park on the 4th. There were speeches planned, a political rally and readings of G. A. Custer's new book, MY LIFE ON THE PLAINS. There would also be an introduction of a new soft-drink called Root Beer, and a condiment called ketchup!

It sounded quite grand and, after what happened last week, I thanked my lucky stars I would be able to attend. I only wished that Martin would arrive back home in time to attend the festivities with us. Feeling weary, suddenly, and slightly chilled, I stepped away and made for my bed.

Annie looked concerned, "You *are* okay, Nel, right?"

I smiled, "Sure, Annie. I'm fine. Just got out of bed a little too quickly… it made my head swim!"

"Would you like a cup of coffee, Nel? The doctor says you can have some now if you want…"

Annie looked worried and I said, "Yes, that would taste great! See if you can rustle up a sweet bun or two while you're at it, too." I rifled through my purse and handed her a dime.

Annie left the room with a happy smile and I closed my eyes. My body was fine, I knew, but my heart was stricken with fear. When I had glanced outside I saw something that sent chills through me.

The town looked normal as could be and the people on the streets below my window seemed perfectly fine, as well. It was the western skyline that had frightened me.

Looking up, I had seen a large, black cloud etched on the horizon. Although the sky's overhead were blue and bright, that dark cloud was skull-shaped and seemed to pulse with an evil light of its own.

It was not lost on me that Martin was somewhere beneath that darkened canopy, along with Custer, Terry, Reno, Benteen and the whole of the 7th cavalry.

The next morning dawned bright and clear and my room was filled with people. Sally, Doctor Willoby, and Adam were all watching me as I took my first (authorized) steps.

Adam had been found innocent of murdering Frank Higgins due to eye-witness testimony and his own powerful Army attorneys. He was putting off going back to Yankton, though, until after the fourth of July, although a stagecoach will be leaving in two days' time.

When I questioned him about it, making sure he knew how very grateful I am for his timely intervention, he shrugged. "I know how you feel about me, Nel and I promise to back away and not pressure you with my devotion. Still, there is no reason I can't delay my departure for a few more days. School doesn't start until September and I can heal as well here as at home."

Not knowing how else to discourage his attentions, I just sighed and thanked him, again, for saving my life.

Now, as I walked slowly across the floorboards, Doc

Willoby asked, "How do you feel, Nel? Any cramping... dizziness?"

I smiled. "No, I'm fine, really." I whispered, carefully. I didn't dare tell him that I had already gotten out of bed, and I glared at Annie when I saw her frown and bite her lower lip.

"Well then," Sally said. "Maybe it's time for us to go outside and get some air! You ought to see the park and the courthouse. The town has put on its best finery!"

"Yes!" I agreed and Annie whooped with joy.

The doctor and Adam took their leave and Annie and I left the shelter of the boardinghouse for the first time in days. I couldn't believe how hot it was, and looking to the west, I saw no sign of the ominous black cloud that had haunted my imagination yesterday.

Thank God... I hate to think of myself as prone to "vapors" but that strange vision had tested my resolve and given me horrible, forbidding dreams all night.

The three of us walked slowly down the street and turned right on the corner of Main Street. Sure enough, there were red, white and blue streamers everywhere, including the little park where a small band-stand and podium were being built for the holiday. A group of musicians were seated nearby and I could hear the opening notes of Custer's favorite song, Garryowen.

Sally was telling me that Martha Jane Canary, AKA Calamity Jane had been seen about town the last couple of days and had been kicked out of no less than four different saloons for stating that "Custer and his troops are damn fools and will come to no good 'A-Toll', if they don't leave the Big Horn Valley and right quick!"

Although I had heard that Miss Canary didn't know a

whiskey bottle she didn't love, I also knew that she was a fine scout, and my blood ran cold. "Have you heard anything else, Sally?" I asked.

"Lots of rumors, but that's all, Nel. We can't believe everything we hear, can we?"

Her tone held conviction... a strong under-current of worry, as well. I was pondering my reply when a familiar figure broke away from a group of people in the park.

As we watched, Elizabeth Custer ran up to us with red, swollen eyes. "Sally! Sally Williams and... Eleanor, is it?" she cried. "Please, I need you to tell me what you know. Also, I would like one of you to interview me. I have some things to say to President Grant and the American people!"

Dear Diary,

I studied Custer's wife as Sally drew up short and said, "Libby, I'm sorry, but you know perfectly well that the Chicago Times will not print a direct statement to President Grant! I don't care who you are!"

Elizabeth stared at my friend for a moment and then turned her gaze on me. I was somewhat shocked by the grand lady's appearance, mainly because she did not seem so grand -up close. In fact, she seemed rather pallid with long dark hair, bushy eyebrows and a pale, pinched mouth.

Of course, no one looks their best when they arc crying and upset, and Mrs. Custer seemed to be both. Still, she managed to offend as she stared down her nose at me and demanded, "You are that Nel person, correct? The one who writes fluff pieces for the Times?"

"Yes, Ma'am, Eleanor Leibowitz," I said and stuck my hand out to shake.

She ignored it and sniffed. "Well, I swear, you could really use a thesaurus... and a dictionary!" She smiled at Sally adding, "No offense, meant."

Sally *was* offended and made her displeasure clear. "Libby, we've known each other a long time and I'm used to your ways but I would thank you to leave off insulting my young friend, here. She has more talent in her little finger than either one of us has in our whole body!"

Mrs. Custer studied my face and tears filled her eyes. "Of course, you're right, Sally. Eleanor, please accept my apology but I am undone, simply undone. Could I, at least, give you an opinion about my husband's engagement?"

I looked at Sally and she shrugged. "Your words are, technically, OP-EDs, dear. You can relate Mrs. Custer's words without presenting them as fact. Facts are my job-mine and Thomas'."

Elizabeth smiled and said, "Shall we sit down over there with my friends? They are the wives of many a fine officer in the 7th..." Seizing my elbow, she whisked me away. Turning around, I called out, "Sally, will you look out for Annie for a little while?"

She grinned and said, "Sure, we'll be in the café having a soda pop."

"Come on, girl, I don't have all day" Elizabeth snapped.

I was fed up with the woman's bad manners... actually, everyone's bad manners! I knew that I should respect my elders but I had, suddenly, had quite enough of being pushed around and disrespected.

Stopping dead in my tracks, I said, "Mrs. Custer! My husband, and Sally's husband are both with the 7th Cavalry as we speak and trust me when I say, we are all upset and scared to death!"

Elizabeth stood with her mouth open in shock as if her horse had suddenly opened its mouth and sung Dixie.

"Now," I continued, "If you want me to send an article to my editor, I will, but please treat me and mine with some courtesy!"

Her face blushed red and she stammered, "Well, I never..."

Looking torn between dismissing me with prejudice and getting down on her knees to beg, I glared at Custer's wife and said, "What do you say, Ma'am?"

She thought for a moment and replied, "I say you're right, young lady. I am sorry... I guess I've grown too accustomed to issuing orders. Please, let me introduce you to my friends..."

So, I sat and wrote notes for the article as Elizabeth Custer whinged about President Grant, General Terry and Captain Marsh (who had refused to take her and some other officer's wives up to the Yellowstone on the Far West so they could be closer to the action and their husband's sides).

She went on to say that she and many other people were having terrible, prophetic dreams and that she believed Terry was purposefully putting her husband, George, in harm's way. (I would no sooner write that accusation as fly to the moon!)

Finally, after about an hour, Mrs. Custer dismissed me. She had, apparently run out of things to say and needed to catch the ferry back to the fort. She was being scrupulously polite now and pleaded with me to send her words on for public consumption just as soon as possible.

I assured her I would, and watched as she and her friends flounced away. I *did* plan on sending her story out but in a highly-abridged manner. Certain she would not be satisfied with my edits, I couldn't help but grin.

"Hello, Nel. What are you doing standing here all alone?"

Adam had walked up behind me and stood staring at me now in a protective manner. Sighing, I answered, "Oh, I just got done doing an interview with Mrs. George Custer... there they go, now." I pointed toward the retreating crowd of women.

Adam grinned. "Bet *that* was fun! Everyone knows she's a handful!"

I nodded, "Yes, she's a pistol but she's also scared. I think that the American public might be interested in the Army wives' fears..."

Adam kept his mouth shut, but stuck his arm out to take. "Look, Nel. There are Sally and Annie... shall we join them?"

Adam, Annie and I went back into the café while Sally walked to the post-office. She had taken one look at me and decided we should hasten back home as quickly as possible. Although this morning I had felt fine- raring to go, in fact, I was shocked now at how fatigued I felt. I guess my body really had undergone a shock and was not letting me forget it.

I sipped a glass of iced-tea and listened as Adam and Annie bantered back and forth in their usual, easy manner. If nothing else, Adam is quite gentle with my sister and I am grateful to him for making her feel safe and happy.

Sally came back a little while later with a smile on her

face. She had that look in her eyes- the look that told me she was hot on a new story.

"What's happened?" I asked.

"Well, a couple of things, actually, but there's one story that involves you and me, Nel!" she crowed.

"What?" I didn't know whether to be happy or scared.

She winked. "Just one of the most important thing to happen for women- ever!" She held me in suspense for a second and then she blurted, "A lady I know, Sara Spencer, addressed the Presidential convention on the 15th of this month, Nel!"

I must have looked less than over-whelmed, for she smiled and patted my arm. "It's all about women's rights... don't worry, dear, you'll begin to understand the significance of this news as you get older."

"Also," she added, "Alexander Graham Bell has patented his new telephone machine and the new Transcontinental Express train just reached San Francisco from New York in only 83 hours and 39 minutes!"

I *was* impressed by that! 83 hours- why that's just a little more than three and a half days! And the telephone machine... being able to hear a person's real voice from miles away- that seemed more like fiction than fact.

"Anyway," Sally said, happily. "I have a couple of good stories to write and I think it's time we got back home to do so. By the way, how was your interview with Libby?"

Tired, I murmured, "Interesting..."

She laughed, "I'll bet!"

Then she took my arm in her hand and led Annie and I back home to the boardinghouse, while Adam stayed behind, staring after me with thwarted desire.

Dear Diary,

There have been some strange- and terrifying- rumors circulating about town the last couple of days. I found out about it from Sally who spends a lot of her time working with the owner/editor of the Bismarck Tribune.

The whispers are varied but the theme seems to be the same... Custer and his 7th have been wiped out!

Well, people love to impart bad news... the worse the better, for what is gossip but melodrama and attention seeking? We *did* hear from a reliable source, though, (Lt. Burrows) that General Crook retreated from the Battle of Rosebud Creek, with word that the Indian encampment, led by Crazy Horse, was just too big to handle.

Stories are also being told that the great Indian chief, Sitting Bull himself, and a number of braves had walked to within firing range of Crook's soldiers, sat down on a knob of land and shared a pipe while bullets fell, harmlessly, around them.

That sounds like a tall tale to me, but it *is* known that the Indian forces around Sitting Bull's encampment are so strong that Crook's troops have retreated from the Rosebud and are licking their wounds at a place called Goose Creek in Wyoming.

If this is true, it spells trouble for General Terry's 4-Prong attack plan, as Crook's 3rd Cavalry was supposed to make up the southwest leg of the engagement. I know now that Calamity Jane, who had traveled with the 3rd, was not lying when she said Custer's troops might be in trouble... although she may have gotten some of the particulars mixed up.

Hearing this type of news has pushed both Sally and me into a state of suppressed panic. I often think about what will become of my sister and me if Martin does not return and my mind reels with uncertainty. Sally assures me that if worse comes to worst, she would welcome us back home to Chicago with her, and I thank her for that.

I think if the worst does happen, Annie and I *will* head to Chicago but it would be in order to find Patsy and Chloe. Perhaps Sally and I can remain good friends and I can still write for the Times, but all of that palls if I have to do it alone- without Martin.

Meanwhile, it's truly a test of nerves for all of us to go on with our lives, as usual, while the sting of gossip swarms around us like a nest of angry bees.

I have stayed in my room for the last couple of days since my interview with Elizabeth Custer. Feeling frightened by the exhaustion and the cramping I felt that night, I decided to take it easy and write my stories from the warmth and safety of my bed.

Having finished my story about Elizabeth Custer and

sent it off to the Times along with Sally's correspondence, I have been going back to the opening pages of my first diary, trying to decipher the cross-hatched words and marveling at how childish I sounded at the beginning.

Honestly, although only a little while has passed since I received the diary as a gift from my sister Patsy, I feel as though I have lived two lifetimes and have matured into a woman from the young, innocent girl I once was- just a few months ago.

This afternoon, Annie and I had just eaten some of Mrs. Fairweather's wonderful venison stew for lunch when Sally dashed into our room wide-eyed with excitement. "You'll never guess what happened!" she gasped, winded.

Alarmed, I sat up in bed and said, "What is it?"

"There was a gunfight, just now, on Main Street! I barely escaped with my life!" she answered.

"Sally, how were you involved?" I asked, eyeing her excited face.

"Purely by chance, really," she replied. "I was just standing on the boardwalk, talking to a lady I know when a bunch of men spilled out of the saloon across the street. Two men drew their guns and I learned that one of those men was the famous gunfighter, Jim Levy!" Sally fumbled in her reticule and producing her ever-handy paper tablet, started dashing notes to herself for a new, "True-Life" article.

She wrote and wrote, basically keeping Annie and I waiting with bated-breath, until I said, "And?"

Looking up, she blushed and said, "Sorry- I didn't want to forget the details." She put the notepad away and continued, "Anyway, Levi shot his opponent dead, but not before the man, whose name was..." she consulted her notes again. "... Troy Hansom shot an innocent by-stander named Evan Friedrick. He was only a few feet from where I was standing and watching!"

"Was Mr. Friedrick killed too?" I asked.

"Nah, he was just winged, but he's mad as a wet hen, I'll tell you that. He is, apparently, one of the most prominent German settlers in this area and even as we speak, he's rounding up his own personal posse to bring Levi to justice!"

"Isn't Mr. Levi in jail?"

"Oh no," Sally shook her head. "By the time the sheriff and his deputies showed up, Levi was long gone... and good riddance. I hear he's done this before. He's one of those quick-draw "shootists" who don't advertise their skills, unlike a lot of gunfighters who try to intimidate by reputation, alone. Apparently, he shouldn't play cards, though. The last gunfight he was in was over a poker game, too."

Sally was still standing by the door and I invited her to sit down and have a cup of tea. Plopping into a chair, she asked, "How are you feeling today, Nel?"

"I shrugged. "I'm fine, really. I did get a little over-tired the other day but mainly, I'm trying to avoid Lt. Burrows."

She grinned. "Like I said, you could do worse, but I understand. Are you coming out with me tonight?"

There was a summer ball planned at the mayor's house later on this evening. The press had been invited due to the numerous dignitaries who had come to town for the Centennial celebration. I had planned on going but, as usual, I worried about being too young and too gauche to attend such affairs without making a fool of myself.

Sighing, I looked Sally in the eye and said, "I want to go but I only have one dress that's appropriate for the affair and I was almost laughed out of another mayor's house when I wore it. Martin gave it to me as a present and I love it, but... could you look at it for me, and see what can be done to make it more presentable?"

Sally frowned. "I bet your ball-gown is perfectly fine but, if it will give you comfort, sure, I'll take a look at it for you."

I got out of bed and walked over to the chifferobe where my ball-gown was hanging. Pulling it out, I saw the gold material with the tiny silver stars spangled over it and remembered the pride with which Martin had presented it to me. The memory of it almost took my breath away and my heart pinched, painfully, with fear and the possible loss of the man I had grown to love.

Sally looked at the gown and smiled. "Why, this is lovely, Nel. I can't imagine why you thought it wasn't..." then her eyes narrowed as something caught her attention.

"Ah, ha!" she exclaimed. Reaching into the spangled folds she tugged lightly on the bodice and I heard something rip.

I gasped and tears loomed as I worried that my precious dress was ruined but Sally just grinned. "Honey, this is probably what people were laughing at," she said. "This paper was used to display the dress in the shop but it was meant to come off once worn... see?"

She handed me the tissue paper and I realized that the neckline did, indeed, dip where it was supposed to and I blushed at my own naivety... I must have looked like a fool at the mayor's dinner party!

"This skirt needs to be pressed on the bottom, though. How about I have Annie do some ironing so you look your best tonight?"

I looked at my little sister, who nodded. "Sure, Nelly. I don't mind," she said.

So, whether I want to or not, I am heading to a ball. I'll let you know, dear diary, how it turns out.

Dear Diary,

The ball started out beautifully but ended on a sour note. Having been so worried about embarrassing myself, I was surprised at how well Sally and I were received and, even if that were not the case, I'm sure that my fierce friend would've protected me from any barbed tongues.

When we arrived at Mayor Tristan Teisort's house, a butler escorted us to the backyard where a large buffet was set-up and a number of guests mingled in their finery. I could hear the sound of an orchestra tuning up indoors and the smell of roasted meat wafted on the warm afternoon air.

I was pleased to note that my dress compared favorably and, now that the paper had been removed, looked much better than some of the other gowns on display. My belly was only just beginning to ripen, so I was able to fit into the dress' waistline but my breasts were swollen and spilled, lushly, over the neckline.

Seeing a number of men, both young and old, turn to stare at me with appreciation, I clutched my lightweight shawl close about my upper body. Sally laughed and whispered in my ear, "Oh Nel, don't be a goose. Your dress is modest enough... look at the mayor's daughter!"

I followed her gaze and blinked. Sure enough, a pretty but rather plump young lady sailed through the crowd in a silk, crimson-colored gown, cut so low that the tops of her nipples were plain to see. The girl was clearly proud of her dress and didn't blink an eye as every man in her wake stared at her in open-mouthed desire while the women glared at her with hostility.

One grand lady named Mrs. Butters sailed up to me with her two young daughters in tow. Plucking my skirt up she peered at the material and asked, "My dear, this is lovely! Is it a French design? My daughters are in dire need of new ball-gowns but the choices in this ghastly town are quite limited!" Glancing over at the lady in red, she added, "I would rather die than see my girls dressed by Madeline Teisort's seamstress!"

Realizing that my gown was quite modest, compared to Madeline's, I said, "Thank you, Ma'am. My husband bought this gown for me at a dress-shop in Chamberlain. Would you like the name of the establishment?"

She smiled and said, "That would be nice, dear. I'll have my husband contact them with my girl's measurements." Looking around, she asked, "Is your husband here with you tonight?"

Shaking my head, I answered, "No Ma'am, he is with Custer now, somewhere in the Montana Territory, along with Sally's husband, Thomas. May I introduce my friend, Sally Williams?"

Turning to Sally, the middle-aged lady introduced herself and her daughters. "My husband is a judge here in Bismarck. That's him, over there... he can't come to one of these functions without being shanghaied by every politico in the territory!" She stared at the rotund, little man with a mixture of exasperation and fondness.

We visited a few minutes and then a bell rang, announcing the dance was about to begin. The crowd ambled inside and hearing the orchestra strike a chord, I quickly found a seat by the back wall. I wanted to dance... really I did, but the only dances I knew were country reels. There was no way I wanted to trip over my own feet at a formal ball!

Within seconds, though, a line of men had formed to ask me for a dance. I looked to Sally for help but she had just accepted a man's arm and as she followed him onto the dance-floor, she turned around and winked at me with an impudent grin.

Not knowing what to do, I sat in dismay. Mrs. Butters, having just sent her two girls onto the dancefloor, leaned toward me and whispered, "Girl, it's quite appropriate for a married lady to dance in a public event like this... go ahead and take a spin. I'll gather your call cards."

"Call cards... but I don't know how to dance!" I gasped.

She giggled and said, "Just hold on tight! That's what I used to do when I was younger!"

I had turned two men away by now, but I knew that I couldn't continue to do so without giving offense. Screwing up my courage, I smiled and nodded as a stout, middle-aged gentleman stepped forward and asked me to dance.

I told the man, whose name was Angus Swift, I was unfamiliar with the waltz steps and he grinned and said much the same thing as Mrs. Butters... "Just hold on to me, my dear. The four-step is as easy as pie."

And it was, once I got the hang of it. Mr. Swift and I talked a little bit as the first tune played and I learned he was a school master whose two sons were with the 7th. He was worried, too, about some of the latest rumors going around town.

I wanted to dance with the nice fellow again, but the song ended quickly and I was whisked off into another fellow's arms. This man smelled rather ripe and spent more time staring at my breasts than either talking or dancing and I was relieved when that dance ended.

Then, as I had feared, I was taken up in Lt. Burrow's arms. He was not only as handsome as the rising sun and dashing in his dress uniform, but his eyes drank in the sight of me and those old, familiar feelings returned to my heart- sharp pangs of passion and desire I wanted no part of.

Not wanting to hurt Adam more than I already had and knowing I owed him my life, I shook off his embrace and gritted my teeth against the temptation he posed, never-the-less.

Seeing the look of shame and revulsion come over my face, the lieutenant stopped smiling and led me back to my seat. He bowed and backed away with regret but I saw the sorrow in his eyes and knew that, despite my best intentions, he was crushed.

The music stopped for a while and refreshments were passed around. During the lull, I couldn't help but notice a group of young men loitering along the far wall. It seemed to me as if every one of them had trained their eyes on me and were concocting some sort of mischief.

I almost asked Sally if we could leave, but when I turned to her she was deep in conversation with her editor friend from the local paper. Knowing I was probably letting my nerves get the best of me, I sighed and sipped my champagne flip.

Soon enough, the orchestra started playing again and one young man from the group of ne'er-do-wells approached with a ticket in his hand. *Darn it*, I thought, *he actually has a dance card!*

Knowing I couldn't refuse, even though I distrusted the look in his eyes, I stood up as he approached with as charming a smile as I could muster.

He bowed with a mocking grin and drawled, "May I have this dance?"

I nodded and took his arm as the music soared. Turning toward him, he took me by the waist (something none of the other men, including Adam, had done) and twirled me onto the dance floor so swiftly, my skirt sailed out behind me.

Biting my lip against an affronted squeal of alarm, I glared up at him as he leered down at me. "Bon soir, Madame La Fleur... Just how much do you cost? My friends and I are willing to pay premium for your services tonight."

I knew, suddenly, that every freckle on my body had just blazed beet red and I gasped in shock. I honestly didn't know what to say to the rude young man but I knew that the chickens had just come home to roost.

I realized that he and his friends must have seen the "infamous" painting at the River Queen Hotel in Yankton

and I could hardly claim innocence since here I was now-
in the flesh. Still, I couldn't believe that even a highly-paid
(if fictional) courtesan would be called out so publicly and
I stuttered in anger and humiliation.

We had come to a stop in the middle of the dance floor
and the young man seized ahold of my left arm and
barked, "Well? How much?"

"Let go of me!" I gritted, and tried twisting away but
he pulled me back so hard I almost tripped and fell.

Then, I heard a familiar voice say, "Let go of the young
lady or I'll run you through!"

Adam Burrows had not gone far and he must have had
his eye on me because he stood behind me now with his
ceremonial sword drawn and a snarl on his face. The
music died down at the ruckus and the crowd stopped
to stare.

The horrid young man, whose name I didn't know,
seemed willing enough to push his claim. "Don't you
know, this here is the world-famous Madame la Fleur?
My boys and me got the money for a poke and we intend
on making her put out!"

The sword rose, menacingly, and Lt. Burrows whispered into the sudden silence, "Pistols, tomorrow at dawn
in the cemetery!"

Sneering, the young man took one look at Adam's
arm-sling and laughed. "You want a shoot-out over a
whore, fine. Tomorrow... first light."

Then the man walked away and I stared up at the infu-
riatingly handsome but determined face of my foolish
young friend in dismay.

Dear Diary,

Well, Lt. Burrows is gone now. Not, gone as in- dead, thank God, but on his way to the Army fort in Yankton- with prejudice. Honestly, this morning I came to believe that Adam would perish because of his ardent, if misplaced, devotion to me.

Needless to say, after the challenge was issued Sally and I took our leave from the ball. I was horrified and mortified. That dratted painting was rearing its head again and whatever pains I had taken to be no part of it were ruined now- thanks to those impudent, young men.

I feel sure that, despite the fact I am not a courtesan, my reputation in Bismarck is now ruined. More importantly, as I laid in my bed after we got back to the boardinghouse, I couldn't sleep a wink, I was so fearful over Adam's safety at the duel.

Tossing and turning all night, I finally arose at 4:00 am and got dressed. Annie woke as well, and although I tried to talk her out of witnessing the duel she insisted, saying, "Nel, Adam is my friend, too! I want to be there for him!"

Tears stood in her eyes and I realized she was right. She was too old now and had been through too much to deny her the opportunity of wishing Adam good luck, or if worse came to worst, goodbye.

Sally knocked on our door at 5:00. Opening it, I saw my friend standing in the hallway. She was grim-faced but determined. Bearding the goat, she said, "I'm bringing my notepad along, Nel. Despite the fact Adam is your friend- my friend as well- what he and the other men are doing is illegal and needs to be reported."

Although I wasn't surprised, I *was* a little shocked. Could my friend, (and Adam's friend) Sally, really just stand there and cold-bloodedly report the news as men were shot to death… over nothing?

I felt a chill and then I realized, for the first time, that Sally was something I would probably never be, unless my skin grew very thick, indeed- a true news correspondent… and a really good one.

Strangely comforted, I nodded and said, "Well, we'd better get going. The duel is at 6:00 am." The three of us trooped downstairs and were met in the front parlor by Doc Willoby and Mrs. Fairweather.

The lady of the house was dabbing a hankie under her eyes in distress, (she had developed a bit of a crush, I think, on the ever-flirtatious, Lt. Burrows) but the doctor was all business. "There is a good reason that duels have been outlawed, you know…" he grumbled. "It's just a waste of life, is all. Hopefully, the sheriff has heard the news by now and will put a stop to this nonsense before your young friend is killed!"

Annie rose to the defense, "Adam will shoot that man dead, doctor!" she said. "You just watch and see!"

The old man shook his head and turned to me. "I don't suppose Lt. Burrows ever mentioned to you he is left-handed?"

My mouth opened in shock. I hadn't known that and I thought, *and now the fool has challenged a man to a pistol match? What on earth is he thinking?* I didn't have a chance to fret about this newest intelligence, though, as the 6:00 hour was fast approaching.

Sally, Annie, Doc Willoby and I stepped out the door into a cool, slightly drizzly morning. To my surprise, the streets seemed quite busy and were filled with pedestrians. Then I noticed that most of the folks were, like us, heading out to the graveyard to witness the duel.

Affronted, my heart blazed with fury but I also understood that there was nothing I could do or say to stop them. The challenge had been issued in a public manner... and in a very public place, after all, and the citizens of Bismarck felt they had the right to witness the spectacle for themselves.

The graveyard is fairly close to town and the walk only took a few minutes. I saw Adam standing with another soldier on one side of the cemetery and the young man who had accosted me standing with his friends on the opposite side.

The rain grew thicker and more insistent and I remember thinking, *Why, they can't shoot it out in this weather, can they?* But, the men were undaunted. Both Adam and his opponent repeatedly drew their pistols and practiced their aim as their companions (or Seconds) whispered last-minute advice and instructions in their ears.

My heart was ready to pound itself out of my chest. I noticed, now that I had been told, that Adam did, indeed, favor his left hand but I also knew that the lieutenant's left arm and shoulder were still quite sore and tender.

Unfortunately, the young tough who had risen to Adam's challenge seemed to be a very quick draw and unencumbered by any kind of pain. As though they sensed Adam's weakness, the man's cohorts sneered loudly and their hurled insults carried, eerily, in the moist and chilly air.

Finally, a man walked through the crowd and stood between the two contestants. I recognized Sally's friend, C.A. Lounsberry, the editor of the Bismarck Tribune. Of course, it would stand to reason that the principal newsman in town would have heard about the engagement this morning but I still felt shocked that he would involve himself in such a sordid affair.

"Gentlemen!" he shouted. "Please step forward and hear your instructions."

Adam and Jim Sturgis (Sally had learned the man's name from her editor friend a few minutes earlier) stepped up to either side of the newspaper editor and listened to the rules of engagement. I strained my ears but couldn't hear a word over the pouring rain.

"What did he say, Sally? I couldn't hear..." I blurted, but she had moved to the side to get a better view of the action. An older man turned around and said, "Its 20 paces, Ma'am and first blood."

I didn't know what "First blood" meant but it didn't sound good. I wanted to stomp my feet and cry a halt to the whole affair but I watched, powerless, as the two men turned their backs to one another and started pacing in opposite directions as the editor called out, "One, Two, Three…"

Suddenly, I heard a commotion and two wagons pulled up. They were military wagons and as soon as the horses came to a skidding stop, a number of soldiers spilled out and stepped into the middle of the fray.

Fanning out, the militia trained their rifles and muzzle-loaders on Sturgis' friends, while two officers took Adam's arms, spun him about and clapped him in hand-cuffs.

Again, the rain fell so hard I couldn't hear what the military men said but, quick as a wink, Adam was hustled into one of the wagons and driven away toward the river and Fort Lincoln.

The ornery young men who wanted to purchase my favors protested the loss of their quarry, loudly, but being faced with the business ends of so many muskets they dispersed quickly and were, to the best of my knowledge, never seen or heard from again.

Annie, Sally, the doctor and I made our way back home in the pouring rain, along with half the town's population, none the wiser about Adam's fate but, later on this afternoon, a young Private knocked on my door.

The Private gave me a half-bow and handed me a letter. "Compliments of Lt. Burrows, ma'am," he said.

"Is he alright?" I asked.

The Private had stepped backwards and was preparing to take his leave but he paused, "The Lieutenant is fine, Mrs. He is in some trouble though, insubordination and rabble-rousing, and he is heading back home on a military wagon as we speak. The Colonel wants him safe and sound in Yankton while he recovers his strength and makes ready for his time at West Point, rather than chasing around after a married lady..."

I blushed, as if I were personally responsible for Adam's behavior but the Private grinned. "The lieutenant's friends all know it ain't you, Ma'am. That boy has been moonin' over you for months now. Better this way, right?"

"Yes, yes it's much better this way," I answered with a sigh of relief. "Thank you, Private."

The man gave me another half-bow and walked down the hall and out of sight.

Dear Diary,

It's the fourth of July, and Bismarck is celebrating our country's Centennial birthday! This is really big news and worthy of celebration, although our frantic need to conquer this huge, majestic country has not been easy or always fair.

I speak of the Indians, of course, whose land is being gobbled up, right and left, but also of the many pilgrims who have perished in their attempt to tame this vast and perilous land.

The natives struggle and fight against the incoming hoard of whites and, to us, their methods seem barbaric, but I am not fooled. Maybe it's because of Sally's patient but persistent lessons, I don't know, but unlike so many of my white neighbors, I feel that "our" means of gaining what we want are just as brutal.

It's not lost on me that the Black Hills and most of the

Montana Territories were *given* to the Indians for all eternity... until, that is, gold and silver were discovered and then our government's solemn handshakes and heartfelt promises dissipated and flew away like dandelion fluff on a summer's breeze. No wonder the Indians hate us so, and wouldn't trust us as far as they could throw us!

Sally and I have discussed this numerous times over the last few weeks and have agreed to not speak our opinions out loud. Too many of the citizens in this town hate the "Red Man" with a passion. And, I can't really blame them. The Sioux, Crow, Blackfoot and Cheyenne have been hard on many folks around here.

It's hard to forgive a race of people who have killed your father or brother, mother or daughter in retaliation for the theft of their land, especially now that so many of our troops are actively engaged in a war against Sitting Bull and his united tribes.

And that seems to be the key... Indians are not known for banding together and uniting in one common goal. Their warriors are encouraged, in fact, to act alone and to garner personal glory- not to fight as a unit against a common foe.

Now, though, the northern tribes *are* standing together as one great army and many people are worried that the might of our troops will not be enough to defeat them. Of course, this kind of talk discourages me and I hope and pray for Martin's safe return.

I'm also wondering- just how long will this engagement take? Martin didn't have a clue when he left, except for the fact he thought that once the troops were in place the rout would happen quickly. I guess I thought that meant he would be back home in two or three weeks-at most! But, for many of the troops, it's been well over a month and still no word from them.

Rumors trickle in of course, news both good and bad. Custer's been defeated! Custer has won the day! The reports are so varied and sometimes so far-fetched no one believes a word, by now, one way or the other. But everyone is worried.

Since the aborted duel took place and Adam was packed off to Yankton, I have stayed at home in my room. Sally assures me that most people in town couldn't care less who I am, but I'm weary of being painted with the black brush of shame.

Also, morning-sickness has returned with a vengeance. I no sooner leave the comfort of my quilts in the morning than I'm either grabbing the chamber-pot or running to the privy down the hall. I wish this would come to a stop almost as fervently as I wish my husband would come back home to my loving arms.

But, this is a special day and despite another bout of nausea a couple of hours ago, I am ready for the festivities. My new green dress was ruined during Frank's assault but I have cleaned and pressed the yellow and black one Martin bought me in Chamberlain.

It fits, barely, but Annie helped me take it out a little in the waistline so it will close in back (the open buttons are covered by a black, satin sash.) She is also wearing her best and when we inspected our reflections in the cracked mirror in our room, she grinned and said, "You look pretty, Nel... it's the baby, I think."

I smiled, although I thought I looked the opposite of

pretty, plumper than normal and flushed with the heat of the day. Still, a compliment is a gift and I hugged her and said, "You are pretty too, sis! Ready to go downtown?"

She nodded and said, "Yes! I want to try that root beer stuff... can we?"

Checking my purse for adequate funds, I smiled and said, "Of course. We can't afford to buy everything on offer but we have enough money to try a few new things."

We had fun, at least for a while. The streets were teeming with people, and booths of merchandise were set up all up and down Main Street. A band whistled and tooted in the park and party members hollered about the new Presidential nominees.

The day had dawned bright and blue and now the heat pressed down on us with hot, sticky fingers. Annie and I tried a new thing called Ketchup on fried potatoes and it really is good. Also, Annie has a new favorite flavor called root beer. I wasn't sure, at first, thinking it was an alcoholic drink but the vendor assured me it was just soda pop.

It was refreshing to sit under one of the big willow trees in the park, sip the root beer and listen to the hustle and bustle of the celebration. I guess that my reputation in this town isn't too badly damaged because the redoubtable Mrs. Butters walked up to where Annie and I sat in the shade and told me her husband had, indeed, ordered six new dresses, sight unseen from the dress-shop in Chamberlain.

She asked after my friend Adam with a side-ways glance, but seemed to accept my claim that we are only friends- nothing more. Then she sailed away saying that twenty loaves of her famous sourdough bread were going up for auction in a few minutes. The benefit was being hosted by the Lady's Auxiliary, and all proceeds would go to the wives and families of the wounded soldiers finding their way back from Montana.

Then, I saw Elizabeth Custer climb up the stairs to a small podium to do a reading from her husband's novel, My Life on the Plains. Turning around so I could hear the words better, I sat and watched her perform.

Annie was playing with a number of children she's grown fond of and I could see Sally chatting it up with some of the city-council members by the buffet tables. As always, lately, my body craved sleep by mid-afternoon and today was no exception.

Bees hummed in the shrubbery and the grasshopper's steady sawing lulled me into a doze. Then I heard a commotion toward the grandstand. I had earlier seen a number of Indian women and children wandering about the park. They were the Army scout's family's and seemed just as excited as the white folks at the Centennial celebration.

But now, for some reason, they were huddled together and talking in their native language about something.... terrible. Many of the Indian women screamed out in fear and pulled their long shawls over their heads in grief.

Libby had stopped her reading and stared down at the native women and children in alarm. Then she stepped off the stage and walked over to talk to them. They told her (apparently) that there had been a "Great Battle" to the west and that the White Man had been defeated.

Elizabeth knew some of these Indian women well-they were, in actuality, her neighbors at the fort, and she instantly believed the worst. Before anyone on the street, or in the park knew what was happening, she gathered the other officer's wives to her side and fled the festivities.

Dear Diary,

As you can probably imagine, rumors abound. The mayor tried to calm his citizens down after Mrs. Custer left the park, claiming that this might just be another misunderstanding but, like me, most folks thought that this story may be all too true, considering the fact that it was Custer's own Crow scout, Curley, who had brought the dreadful news back to Captain Marsh.

The Far West is, even now, motoring back to Fort Abraham with some of the survivors. Apparently the riverboat has been transformed into a hospital boat, is making record speed and should make landfall in Bismarck sometime tonight.

Annie and I are back home awaiting Sally's arrival. Although I may make it seem like she is callous in her quest for news, my new friend is anything but... tears were standing in her eyes and her chest heaved with fear and grief even as she said, "Go home, dear. I have to do whatever I can to find out the truth about this latest news but I'm scared to death. Like Martin, Thomas was supposed to be with Custer's unit."

I was feeling light-headed and nauseated after hearing the news in the park and watching the military tuck tail and head back to the fort. I wanted nothing more than to hide my head under the covers of my bed, despite my sister's disappointment. But, even *she* could see that the festivities were over.

Merchants and vendors stood alone in frustrated bewilderment as Main Street, the park and the city square emptied of people, the military band dispersed and plates of food were left uneaten and fly-covered on the many trestle tables set up for the occasion.

When Annie and I got to the boardinghouse we saw most of the boarders sitting around the parlor and the dining room table discussing what they'd heard. "Nel!" Mr. Briggs shouted. "Come in and tell us what you've heard!"

The cad, I thought, resentfully and said, "I'm sorry, Mr. Briggs but I'm unwell!" Then I flew up the stairs with my sister in tow. Once behind closed doors, all the tears I'd been keeping behind my eyes fell down my cheeks in a perfect storm of grief.

"Nelly! What's wrong? I don't understand… is Martin dead too?"

Annie was still too young to grasp the notion that my husband's fate was deeply intertwined with Custer's and if Custer and the soldiers in his unit had perished chances were good that Martin was dead as well.

I sobbed and hiccupped, "Annie, I'm sorry I'm upset

but I am so worried over your uncle! I can only hope and pray that he's still alive and well!"

My sister's eyes got big and round. "Oh," she breathed. "I didn't stop to think…" Then we were both weeping and clutching one another on the side of the bed.

A knock sounded on the door. "Nel… Annie, can I come in?" Doc Willoby called out.

"Come in, Doctor," I answered and the old man peeked around the door, "Nel, I'm sorry about Briggs. He has a big, stupid mouth. But, please, try not to worry. This could just be another rumor- you know that!"

"Yes, but Sally says this one has the ring of truth about it!" I cried. "If it's true that the Far West is bringing back wounded troops then the main battle must be over. And, why would Custer's own scout tell such a lie?"

Willoby nodded and his shoulders heaved in a sigh. He placed a tray of coffee and pastries on top of the bureau in the far corner of the room. "All's I know is this… your baby's health depends on your reactions now. Your body has already endured a great shock and the child inside you survived that time, but too much more and I could lose you both!"

I sat on the bed and glared at him for a moment, thinking, *What am I? A rock with no right to feel love or fear or sorrow! Must I really swallow the fact that I might have just lost the one thing in my life that gave me joy and comfort without complaint- lest I lose the child?*

Feeling a faint flutter in my belly, I almost gasped out loud. It was as if my baby was experiencing all my sorrow and anxiety as its own, and had reached out to comfort me in my distress. Realizing, suddenly, that the doctor's concerns were valid and that the being inside me was a person- actual and whole- and not just a biological happenstance, I covered my stomach protectively and took a deep breath.

"You're right, Doctor. I will try to remain calm- for the baby's sake."

Willoby smiled and brought me a cup of coffee and a sweet bun. "That's my girl..." he murmured so gently that tears pricked my eyes, again. Then, the old man sat with Annie and played the part of the "bad guy" against her rag doll, while I let my eyes drift shut.

I woke up later feeling much better but the mood in town is tense, uneasy. Sally went to the Bismarck Tribune office and has spent most of the day with her friend, Lounsberry. She stopped by twice to say that people up and down the Missouri River have reported seeing the Far West making great speed toward Bismarck. She also says the boat will probably arrive this evening.

Many, many people in town feel like I do. Most of us, of course, are not affiliated with the Army and Fort Lincoln but our husbands, fathers, brothers and sons are and we look forward to seeing them, and touching and kissing the survivors.

But not knowing *who* has survived is killing each and every one of us. The latest intelligence says that many of Benteen's and Reno's troops made it through the battle but there are over 50 badly wounded men on board the Far West.

Who are they? Has Martin survived to tell the tale...? Thomas?

All I can do is pace back and forth... worry and wait.

Dear Diary,

About 10:45 last night, my eyes flew open at a familiar sound... the Far West's peculiar but distinctive whistle. Annie must have been sleeping with one eye open as well, because she sat up and whispered, "Nel, are you awake? The boat is coming!"

I was ready to go... I had been lying on the bed fully-clothed except for my boots and as I sat up, I said, "You'd better hurry if you want to go to the landing with me..."

She ran to the bureau and started dressing in record time. Meanwhile, I tied my hair back in a knot, sipped cold coffee and thought about whether or not Martin might be onboard the boat.

Pictures of wounded soldiers would appeal to the anti-war, artist inside Martin's soul but had he survived the conflict? Worried tears filled my eyes but I bit my lip and said, "Ready? The Far West should be pulling into the harbor soon."

Annie nodded and grabbed her day cloak off a hook by the door. I really wish she hadn't insisted in coming along but she knew the boat, her captain and many of the crew members. She also had a stake in whether her new uncle was on board or not. My warning that there may be dead and hideously wounded soldiers on the riverboat didn't seem to faze her sensibilities and I realized, again, that she had grown up far too soon for her own good.

There was a soft knock on the door. "Nel, are you up?" It was Sally, who had agreed to accompany Annie and me to the boat on its arrival. Neither one of us could wait to see our husbands again and hold them in our loving arms.

The three of us moved as quietly as possible down the stairs in order not to disturb the rest of the house but we were surprised to find most everyone awake. Doctor Willoby was just putting on his jacket and his medical satchel was on the floor by his feet. I could hear Mrs. Fairweather moving around in the kitchen, smell food cooking and saw that her sons were bringing in armloads of extra wood for the woodstoves and fireplaces in every room.

As we stepped outside into the black of night, I was astounded to see lights lit in almost every window in town and realized that many of the citizens were waiting for the boat's arrival- for one reason or another. Some people, like us, were searching for loved ones, some were looking to relieve their friends of duty- like Doc Willoby for his old friend, Doctor Porter, who had been in on the campaign and some folks were just preparing for extra business, like Mrs. Fairweather.

We walked down to the docks and joined the ever-growing crowd. I saw the boat, fully-lit and crawling as close to the shore-line as possible. The bottom deck of the boat milled with darkened shapes and I could see by the light of many lanterns that men were lying on the deck-boards in every state of injury possible. Army men and civilians were loading the soldiers onto stretchers, and waiting impatiently for the ramps to be lowered onto the ground.

I saw Captain Marsh in the soft glow and it looked to me as if the man had aged a century, overnight. His normally tidy hair stuck out in angles and his face was hollow-eyed and haggard. I also saw a horse in a make-shift stall, whinnying eagerly at the sight of land. (I would learn, later on that night, the equine passenger known as Comanche was being considered the lone survivor of Custer's Last Stand as his owner, Captain Miles Keogh, had apparently fallen in battle.

Sally rushed off to find her friend, Mr. Lounsberry, who was standing and talking to one of General Terry's officers, Captain Smith, who held a huge suitcase full of dispatches from Terry, himself.

A few minutes later, as I watched soldier after soldier being carried on stretchers from the boat to either a doctor's office or the mortuary, Sally walked up to me. "Nel, I was just informed that my Thomas didn't make it. He fell, along with reporter Mark Kellogg in Custer's engagement."

My mouth fell open in shock. "Oh Sally," I choked. "I... I'm so sorry!"

Annie heard the news and ran to my friend, flinging her skinny arms around Sally's waist in silent grief.

Sally smiled with sadness. "I knew it, though..." she whispered. "I don't know how- but I think I felt his passing the moment it happened. Somehow, in my mind, I've been ready for this night and don't feel shocked at all." She stared into my eyes. "Do you think I'm crazy?"

I shook my head. "No! No, I don't think that at all! It's just that… why can't I feel Martin?" My voice had risen into a soft wail and I turned around and stared at the boat.

Sally put her arms around me and murmured. "He's not on board, Nel, I asked already. Nobody has seen or heard from Martin since Custer sent him after Benteen's wing. I'm so sorry, dear." We held each other close even as the soft cries of other weeping wives and families reached our ears.

"Listen," she said. "I promised the editor of the Tribune I would help him send the news out to the nation. There are, apparently, dozens and dozens of dispatches in that suitcase that need to be sorted through and sent out and I see John Carnahan, the telegrapher, arriving in his buggy now. Will you be okay?"

I nodded. "Yes, and you? Do you want my help with anything?"

She shook her head. "No. The best thing for me right now is to stay busy. Maybe, in that mess of papers there is word from Martin… if so, I'll bring it to you as soon as possible. For now, though, I think that you and Annie should head home. You need your rest… promise me you won't do anything rash?"

I nodded, and said goodbye as she rushed off to report the news. Turning around, I studied the boat again and watched as Grant Marsh walked down one of the ramps and headed toward Annie and me.

Up close, Marsh looked even worse than I thought. He

was practically reeling with exhaustion but his eyes sought mine and he held his arms out to us in comfort. "He's not with us, darling girls," he said softly as Annie and I wept in his embrace. "I asked every surviving member of that God-awful rout on the boat but no one has seen your husband. I'm so sorry."

"When will the rest of the troops come back?" I asked, thinking I guess, that maybe one of those soldiers would have heard about Martin's fate.

Marsh shook his head. "That's just it... most of the cavalry survivors will stay on. They are still active military and there is a lot of work to do- what with searching for bodies and burying the dead. Even as we speak, Terry is dividing up the troops again and sending them after the retreating Indians."

He sighed and staggered slightly in fatigue. "I'm guessing there will be a few stragglers coming in, mainly civilians now that the Army is moving west but my part in this debacle is over- for the time being."

Looking down at my face he added, "I have to get back onboard but I want you to head home and get some sleep, Nel. Custer, from what I gather, made some terrible mistakes and has left a lot of widows grieving in his wake."

He gave me one, final squeeze. "I'm going to hit the hay as soon as I can but, later on today, I'll take my boat to the fort and inform Mrs. Custer about her beloved, 'Autie'. Trust me when I say, that's not a conversation I relish."

Then, the good captain turned on his heels and walked back onboard the Far West as my heart broke in two.

Dear Diary,

This is the first time in days I've had the energy or courage to write in these pages. I know, though, that eventually I will regret any more abrupt endings, like the one that has marked the end of my marriage. Okay, I'm sorry. This is not a good way to start. Let me begin again...

The night the Far West pulled into Bismarck and I found out that Martin was missing in action, Annie and I went back to our room at the boardinghouse. I was inconsolable but spent the better part of two hours trying to stay calm for my sister's sake.

I made tea and we sat, weeping, until the early light of dawn. Once Annie fell into an exhausted slumber I stared out the window, paralyzed with sorrow and fear and, honestly, didn't know what to do now or where to go from here.

I knew that we couldn't linger for too much longer in

Mrs. Fairweather's boardinghouse. It was expensive, for one thing, and I didn't need the constant reminder of why Annie and I were there in the first place. I knew we had another week left before I had to pay again to stay, so at least I had a little time before I had to make any decisions.

But, what now? Should I go back to Yankton? What was there for us but the burnt-out husk of Solomon's shop? The bank was there, of course, and I knew I could use some of my inherited cash but how could I explain Martin's absence?

Would the bankers believe my husband was lost or would they hold onto the Leibowitz estate indefinitely until solid proof was offered of Martin's death? The thought of it all made my head spin, dreadfully.

Plus, I wasn't ready to leave yet. What if my husband was still alive and somehow making his way back to me now? No one had seen or heard from him since before the battle... maybe he was holed up somewhere, wounded. My heart quailed at the thought of Martin making his slow and painful way back home to us just to find that we had left him behind when he needed us the most!

My head whirled with fatigue and I knew I needed some rest so I lay down on my bed. Just as I closed my eyes there was a soft knock at the door. I got up and opened it to see Sally standing in the hallway. She looked as forlorn and exhausted as I felt.

Holding out a letter, she said, "I found this, Nel. It looks like it was written the night of the 25th."

I took the letter and felt my heart pounding hard. It was as if a ghost had come swimming up out of nowhere and tapped me on the shoulder. I started to open it and paused. "Do you want to come in while I read it?"

Sally shook her head. "No, dear. I'm washed up. I really need to get some sleep so I can think clearly. A telegraph arrived, just a little while ago, from the Chicago Times. They want me to come back and step into Thomas' shoes as senior war correspondent." She sighed and gave me a weary smile. "Quite the coup, eh? Rather a hollow victory, though, considering."

"Well, Annie and I will be right here, if you need us, okay?" I said.

Sally nodded, "Yes. Let's all get some sleep and later on we'll try to figure out, together, where we go from here."

I gave her a hug and watched as she walked, slowly, to the room she and her husband had once shared together but now was hers-alone. Then I stepped back inside and read Martin's last letter to me.

June 25
Dearest Nel,

This has got to be quick, as I have been sent packing by Custer and I must make haste to catch up with Captain Benteen and his mule-teams.

I am heart-broken to hear about my father's passing... and grateful that you survived your father's latest, horrific attack. I am so busy, right now, I don't know that my heart has quite accepted the truth in either matter, but know that I hold you blameless.

I will be home just as soon as possible and I believe that the 7th is ready to muster forward. The Indian encampment is very close and the troops will move on the morrow.

I admit, I'm so angry I could slap the smug smile right off of Custer's face, but what am I supposed to do? Once he heard that a correspondent from the new United Press and his photographer are on scene, he sent me packing like yesterday's fish!

Oh well, despite Custer's own raging vanity, I have compiled a number of candid shots of him and his troops. I also have no doubt that more good shots are in the making.

I love you, my dearest wife and can't wait to see you again soon!

With ardent affection, I remain~
Your faithful servant,
Martin

P.S. If the worst happens, Nel, please take this letter to my father's bankers in Yankton. There is better than $25,000 in Solomon's account, which, of course, will go to you and dear, little Annie upon my demise.

All my love, dearest...

Annie and I slept late into the afternoon. Although we were both heartsick, at least we were better rested and ready to find out more about what had actually happened to General Custer and his troops.

We cleaned up a bit and headed down to Sally's room. She opened the door just as we arrived. She looked fatigued but ready to face the world in her indomitable way.

"Ah," she said. "You're awake, good. Let's go downstairs and see what Mrs. Fairweather has on for supper, shall we?"

Suddenly, my stomach gave out a loud growl of protest and I realized I hadn't eaten since yesterday morning. Annie laughed at the sound, God bless her, and I felt relieved that she had regained her sense of humor.

There were quite a few people, some of them total strangers, sitting around the big dinner table and Mrs. F scurried about serving up piles of biscuits, platters of roasted chicken and bowls of fresh garden greens. All of them seemed to be talking at once and everyone had heard a slightly different version of the 7th Cavalry's battle at the Little Bighorn.

Mr. Briggs, ever the blabber-mouth, was saying, "Custer is a fallen hero! If Benteen hadn't of up and left with the mule teams we would have won the day against those savages!"

Another man, whom I didn't know from Adam, challenged, "You don' know what ye'er talkin' about, goddammit! If Benteen hadn't a left when he did the whole army woulda been slaughtered!"

Another man chimed in… "It was Reno who failed, you know. He had the upper hand when his troops came in on that encampment from the south, but he chickened out at the last minute and proceeded to get shit-faced instead of fight!"

All three men were shouting at once and suddenly, Mrs. Fairweather's son, Benjamin, stepped into the room from the kitchen. He was about thirty-years-old and fairly bulging with muscles from his regular work as a blacksmith.

He spoke softly but his deep, bass rumble silenced every tongue in the room. "Next time I hear any of you using obscene language in my mother's house, I'll use you as a tie-down pin at the smithy!"

For all my worry and sorrow, I couldn't help but grin at the shocked expressions on the men's faces. Mr. Briggs, who had run afoul of Benjamin before, blushed and muttered, "Sorry, sonny. We won't curse no more, I promise!"

"See that you don't," Ben answered and stepped back into the kitchen to feed more wood to the cook stove.

Sally spoke into the silence. "Does anyone know how many men were lost?"

One man, whose name was Stephen Myers and had served as an interpreter for Major Reno said, "Last I heard was; out of the 7th Cav's- 750 officers and enlisted men 268 were killed and another 62 wounded. That number's bound to change, though."

"Did you ever meet a photographer named Martin Leibowitz?" I asked.

Immediately, the man's eyes sharpened. "Leibowitz, you say? Young man, not too tall, but handsome in his own way with black hair, and brown eyes?" he asked.

Heart pounding, I nodded silently. "Yes, he's my husband."

Stephen's face fell and he studied his plate. "Yes ma'am. Now that I recall, he spoke of you, often. He and I grew to like one another quite a bit and spent a lot of time together while Custer, Benteen and Reno scouted Sitting Bull's trail."

Pausing to take a sip of coffee, Stephen continued, "I knew that we would go our separate ways once the attack commenced, but I was shocked that Custer sent Martin off to find Benteen's unit, since I was under the impression Martin was Custer's own, personal photographer. Still, the last I saw your husband, he was making haste to catch up with the mule train while Custer rode down the Medicine Trail Coulee."

He gave me a tentative smile, adding, "Who knows,

Ma'am… maybe going after Benteen was just the ticket. I heard that of all the troops, Benteen's command suffered the fewest casualties…"

"Yeah," Briggs snarled, "cuz he tucked tail and hid!"

At which point the debate started up again. My heart was twisting with grief and I was finding it hard to catch my breath so I stood up, excused myself and fled the room.

Dear Diary,

The next day, Sally told me she would be taking the east-bound train back to Chicago in three days' time. She is pleading with me and my sister to come with her but I don't know if I'm actually ready to leave yet.

I told her I will have an answer for her by tomorrow and I know Annie and I should go, but the thought of leaving Martin behind gives me nightmares. Still, Chicago is where my Auntie and sister are, and my job is there, too, although I have yet to meet my editor and fellow journalists.

Every day since we heard the news about Custer's loss, Annie and I take a walk. I have discovered a place at the far western end of town where one can stand up on a high rock and see miles down the road leading into Montana. I'm rewarded most of the time for my vigilance, although not in the way I want, because many a wanderer has come down that road on their way back from Custer's campaign.

I have seen cook-wagons and teamsters, merchants, blacksmiths and prostitutes walking toward town, bedraggled and worn down with weariness. I even saw two, giant wolfhounds ambling up the road one day and a number of men surrounded them saying that they were Custer's own beloved pets.

Unfortunately, however, I've seen neither hide nor hair of Martin. This is bad enough but the area in town I've been haunting seems to be host to the worst type of people. I would have been more worried about that if my eyes weren't glued to the road leading west but today, Annie and I had a scare.

The large standing rock I referred to earlier is on the far-side of a livery corral. Across the street are two run-down houses that are home to a number of prostitutes and next to those, there is a café/saloon. The whole area reeks of stale booze, livestock and human waste and my sis and I have had to pick our way through snoring, passed-out drunks who have fallen asleep right in the road where they fell. But I have been compelled to search for Martin, despite the risk.

Annie and I had spent a couple of hours perched on that giant stone and, so far, no one had come in from the west. I turned to her and started to say, "Are you ready to head home, sis?" when I saw two people staring up at us from the ground.

One was a big, mean-looking woman, with stained, velvet skirts and one of the biggest bosoms I have ever seen. The other was a small, rat-faced man in a bright red vest with a piece of grass sticking out of the corner of his mouth. I figured that she was probably a prostitute and the man her pimp. They grinned as I caught their eyes.

"Why don't you two gals come down off that perch so we can get a look at ya…" the man said.

I grabbed Annie's arm, but thank God, she seemed in no hurry to meet the two miscreants! Looking up at me, she glanced down at the ground by the far-side of the boulder and I whispered, "Jump! I'm right behind you!"

My sister scrambled down to the ground and I followed suit even as I heard the woman swear, "Hey, get back here, dammit!"

The man ran to catch us but Annie and I swung wide and left the pimp and his whore far behind. For the first time in days, I felt like laughing even though my exhilarated giggles were more an expression of fear than relief.

Annie was laughing, as well, as we tore down Main Street and finally slowed our pace as we turned the corner leading to the boardinghouse. Somehow, I felt as if I had just been liberated- not only from the enterprising grasp of those two low-lives but also from my frantic need to search any longer for Martin.

It was a strange feeling but profound… as if Martin's ghost had just given me permission to leave. It made me want to cry out loud but laugh as well. Stopping, I took Annie's hand in mine and said, "Are you ready to go to Chicago to see your sister and Auntie?"

Annie looked torn but eager. "Yes, Can we go now, really? I don't think…" her pretty cornflower blue eyes filled with tears. "I'm sorry sissy, but I don't think that Uncle Martin is coming."

I hugged her close and we wept. Then I said, "I don't

think so either, Annie. And now I think we should follow Sally back to Chicago on the train, okay?"

She nodded. "Okay," she agreed and we stepped inside the boardinghouse to pack our belongings.

Sally, Annie and I left the next day, along with many others, heading eastward to the city of Chicago. It was not easy, though. My elation was short-lived, although I had no doubt that we were doing the right thing.

As the train pulled away from Bismarck I stood on the back deck and stared as far West as I could, hoping against any hope that I would see my husband riding up hard behind us and waving his straw hat in the air to catch my attention. Of course, nothing of the sort happened.

All I could see was the quickly diminishing town, shimmering in hazy waves of heat, and clouds of grasshoppers which were, even now, demolishing every green thing in the area. I waited, though, and stared until the locomotive made its way around a bend and Bismarck was lost to sight. Finally, I stepped inside and made my way to where Sally and Annie were seated.

As I joined them, I could hear most of our fellow passengers talking about the 7th Cavalry's stunning loss. I knew this was bound to happen... the whole country has been galvanized by the news of Custer's defeat. I had steeled myself but it was still hard to sit and listen to what, in my eyes, amounted to the loss of my husband.

One older man seemed to be the most vocal and whenever he spoke, all the other men shut-up and listened. So did Sally and I and I wasn't surprised to see her notepad in her lap as she penned the discussion in her odd short-hand.

"Okay," the old man said. "You all think you know what happened but here is the real skinny, according to my good friend, General Terry. He has, of course, sent official papers on to Washington but I will be the one who presents testimony to President Grant."

He paused in a dramatic manner and a man on the bench in front of me said, "Well… we're waiting, Col. Hemsworth."

Hmmm, I thought. *That man is far too old to be an active soldier in the Army, so maybe he is retired?*

As if reading my mind, Sally leaned over and whispered in my ear, "Colonel Hemsworth *was* the Secretary of War, Nel. He is retired now but still acts in an advisory capacity for President Grant. Let's listen closely… this man might be our best source yet…"

So, I pulled out my own little notebook and wrote Hemsworths words down as if my life depended on them.

Dear Diary,

Annie and I have arrived in Chicago and, with Sally's help, are safely ensconced in my Aunt Chloe's large home. It is a bitter-sweet feeling for me... my home *was* in Martin's arms but now that particular shelter is a thing of the past, which hurts more than I can describe.

Still, Chloe's home is warm, comfortable and, above all, safe from the trials and tribulations of the frontier. Annie is starting to blossom and is looking forward to going to the big, brick schoolhouse down the block in six weeks' time. And I feel sure that my baby has its best chance of survival here in the city with a hospital only a few miles away and the love and adoration I'm sure will shower down on him, or her from my sister Patsy and my auntie Chloe.

I will describe my current life in more detail but before I do, I want to go back to that first day on the Northern Pacific Railway locomotive and the story Col.

Hemsworth told us about what is now being described as "Custer's Last Stand".

Realizing that every, single man, woman and child in the railcar were hanging on his every word, the old man sat back and, after lighting a giant stogie, proceeded to tell his captive audience what General Terry had told him about the engagement.

"Terry thinks it was a matter of poor communication, more than anything that brought Custer's unit to such a pass... Terry and his troops were bringing up the rear, you see, as was proper but it was next to impossible to issue immediate orders with all three wings of command scattered every which way but loose!"

The man's voice had risen in defense. He closed his eyes for a second and took a deep breath before continuing. "Anyway, Custer had already split his command into three parts... Major Reno's battalion was supposed to approach Sitting Bull's encampment from the south side, Captain Benteen's wing would come in from the north and Custer's troops would close the net from the east."

Suddenly, his eyes fixed on Sally. He cleared his throat and my friend glanced up at him with a small smile. "You!" he muttered. "You are that reporter from the Times, right?"

Sally nodded. "Yes Sir," she replied. "Sally Williams. My husband Thomas was killed in the battle while trying to report the news."

The gruff old man suddenly seemed frail and far more sensitive than I had given him credit for. Pulling out a snowy, white hanky he blew his nose and wiped a tear from his eye. "Yes, Mrs. I knew your husband, bless his soul, and always thought of him as a fair reporter. Please accept my condolences."

Sally's smile faded and for a moment and I thought her hard-won composure would abandon her completely, but she seemed to physically shake off such nonsense as raw emotion and said, "Please sir... go on with your story. We all want to know the truth of what really happened."

Hemsworth smiled and murmured, "Well, this is one side of the truth, anyway..." which made Sally's eyes widen in surprise and appreciation.

Continuing, he said, "In essence, the officers in charge had made a good plan- surround Sitting Bull's camp and force the Indians into a peaceful surrender. Unfortunately, our intelligence was inaccurate." He sighed.

"It was originally estimated that the natives in that village numbered in the low thousands- maybe 1,200 to 2,000 Indians in all, but we found out later that they numbered over 8,000 strong and many of them were fighting braves...

By this time, however, it was too late to turn back. Custer was far-removed from Benteen, just as Benteen was out of reach of Major Reno's unit. And, as it turned out, the fourth wing commanded by General Crook had failed to arrive on time at all, leaving a funnel open for the Indians to escape capture."

He stopped speaking for a moment and took a deep pull off of a flask in his vest pocket, which left room for one man to ask, "Is it true that Reno was as drunk as a skunk?"

Hemsworth glared and snapped, "I am not at liberty to attest to any one of those brave soldier's behavior! I do know that Reno lost only 18 men out of 350 and that was under intense pressure and over-whelming odds!"

The man who had spoken up blushed but countered, "I'm sorry, Sir, but you *must* know what's being said! Reno was drunk on his ass and Benteen pulled his troops so far away that there was no way his soldiers could have helped either battalion!"

Hemsworth started to reply but the man barreled on. "And, what about Custer's refusal to bring the Gatling guns along, not to mention the cannons?"

There was a general stir of emotion and Sally and I practically set our notepads on fire trying to keep up with the exchange. The old Colonel sat and stared with displeasure at the rabble-rouser until the hub-bub died down. Then he spoke into the silence.

"There is no way that non-combatants like you and I can judge what an active military unit does or does not do in battle, Mr....?"

The man blushed. "The name's Nelson- John Nelson."

Hemsworth nodded. "Mr. Nelson. You must know that. I can tell you this much though... the terrain in the Little Bighorn region of Montana is nearly impassable. It's filled with high bluffs, ravines, cliffs and coulees. It's a mud bog too, which is why the Indians call it the Greasy Grass Valley."

He paused for a moment with his finger in the air as if to ward off any more outbursts. Then he continued. "I know that if I were in Custer's shoes, I would have rejected the Gatling guns, too... they are simply too ungainly to travel over that kind of terrain. As for the cannons, remember- we all thought the Indians were far fewer than they turned out to be! And we agreed that lugging the cannon overland was over-kill!"

He sighed, looking terribly weary and sorry, perhaps, that he had volunteered to talk about it with us. "As for the rest, I believe there will be a military tribunal concerning each commanding officer's behavior during the engagement. This is customary after any loss in the battlefield."

He finished speaking but added, "Many people like to point the finger of blame, Mr. Nelson. That is the only way they can make sense of the world we live in and the terrible things that happen to good people."

He glared, pointedly, and finished, "But, despite what people whisper, we must all remember that out of the 7th Cavalry's 750 officers and enlisted men, 268 were killed outright and another 62 were wounded! That's the take-away here… not who did what wrong or right!"

Hemsworth stood up and said, "Now, if you'll excuse me, I'm going to the dining-car."

In the last five days, I've heard every possible variation on what happened at the Little Bighorn but, I keep going back to the old Colonel's final words.

People really *do* like to spread the blame. Some people mourn the loss of G.A. Custer as if he was their own glorious son and blame Reno and Benteen for his eventual downfall. Others are trying everything in their power to vilify the man's every action and blame Custer for the cavalry's failure to subdue Sitting Bull's combined forces.

I, myself, fall somewhere in the middle and only wish now, in hindsight that my poor Martin had been nowhere near that doomed campaign.

Dear Diary,

As you can plainly see, it's been quite some time since I wrote in your pages but things have been hectic for me- a time of deepest sadness and the most tremendous joy. But, let me go back and fill in what's happened since Annie and I came to Chicago.

The first week or so after our arrival I plunged into the darkest despair. As the baby in my belly grew, so did my feelings of sorrow. I found myself, by the last week of July so despondent I could hardly get out of bed in the morning.

I missed Martin, and my friend Sally who had gone back home to her own apartment and was busily filling her days with work at the paper. She sent me a number of invitations and constantly dogged me to come in to work with her and meet the editor who had hired me.

I didn't want to, though. I know, now, that depression had set in but at the time it felt more like fear. I have never lived in such a big city and its almost constant buzz and bustle unnerved me. Horses clopped down the thoroughfares whinnying and merchants screeched about their wares morning, noon and night.

I had never seen so many people in one place before, either, and their voices- strident and belligerent- threatened to deafen me. The only thing I really wanted to do, at that moment, was board the train back to Bismarck or Yankton where things were rough as cob but, for the most part, quiet.

Patsy introduced me to her young man who seemed quite bashful and a little chubby but followed my vibrant sister around like an adoring puppy. I was happy for her, truly, but found it hard to muster anything in the way of enthusiasm.

My aunt, Chloe, had grown quite elderly since I had seen her last. Although, at sixty-three, she is still full of health and vigor, she has become crotchety and less than charitable. She was particularly impatient with *me*, it seemed.

"I honestly don't know why you continue to moon over that young Jew the way you do!" she declared one day. "You have to know that the marriage itself was less than legal- as you are a Protestant woman- but how long did the union last, after all? Days... weeks?"

She stood by the side of my bed and snapped her fingers in frustration. "Poof! That's how long your love affair lasted, my girl, and it's high time you pull yourself out of the doldrums and get on with your life!"

Chloe, who had lived through three different unions and seemed to feel no regret, whatsoever, at the passing of those previous husbands was affronted by my misplaced grief. I knew she meant no harm... she was, in her own gruff way, worried about my state of mind.

Still, I sat up in my bed and snapped, "He was my husband, Auntie, legally and in every other possible way. I loved him and please, *excuse me* if I take a few days to mourn!"

My voice dripped with sarcasm and she reared back, affronted. Then she sighed and sat on the edge of the mattress. "I'm sorry, my dear. I was never tactful, you know that. It's just that men come and go. For all that they are supposed to be the strong ones in a marriage, it's we women who are left behind to carry on."

I glared up at her in resentment and started to defend my marriage again, but she said, "Tsk, tsk. I didn't mean that about your man being Jewish, either. Honestly, I'm not even sure what it means to be Jewish! Just as long as he wasn't a devil-worshipper, I suppose."

She grasped my hand in hers. "What I meant to say is this. You are now a widow with a child on the way. You must get out of this bed at once and start to live again!"

So, begrudgingly, I hauled myself out of bed and started to live again. First, I started taking long walks with my little sister who showed me a nearby park, shops, playgrounds and the school she would soon attend. The weather was fine... brilliant blue skies overhead and a cool breeze that lifted the hair off the back of my neck with cunning fingers.

Then, I made arrangements to join Sally at the Chicago Times where I met my editor, Mr. Nathan Holmes. He seemed a very nice fellow and raved over how well my little column is doing in the Times every other week.

A few days after that, a parcel arrived at the house from the bank in Yankton. I stared at the note for $25,798 and felt my head spin. By all accounts, I am now a very wealthy widow although the knowledge tastes like ashes in my mouth.

Still, I was happy to give my dear old auntie some money for room and board. She confided in me that she wishes I would buy the house from her since she has an old "friend" in Georgia who, since his wife has passed on, could use a companion in his dotage.

I remember keeping a straight face at that rather scandalous piece of information, but escaping post-haste so I could giggle into my pillow at the image of Chloe and her elderly mystery lover in delicious sexual abandon!

Two days later, I received a visitor. Patsy came to my door and knocked and I saw that she was in a high state of excitement. "What is it?" I asked nervously.

"You have a gentleman caller, Nellie. Put on something nice, why don't you?" she wrinkled up her nose at the mud- stained apron I had donned to pick tomatoes and cucumbers out of the small garden in Chloe's back yard.

"Well" I asked, "does this gentleman have a name?"

"Yes, and don't say no, darn you!" she cried.

"Ah ha!" I replied. I had heard that Adam Burrows was in town visiting relatives before he made his way to West Point. His presence here did not make me swoon, however, and Patsy frowned.

"Why, I can't believe your attitude, Eleanor, honestly! I have never seen a more handsome man and you, yourself, told me he comes from a very wealthy family. Don't you want to move ahead in the world?"

Patsy knew perfectly well that money was not an issue

for me since I had received my inheritance from Martin. She had, after all, received a rather hefty dowry from my own personal fortune. I was about to say so, but looking at her thin, freckly and somewhat plain face, I realized that she had developed an instant crush on the lieutenant.

I grinned. "Calm down, Patsy. Just let me freshen up a bit and seat the lieutenant in the parlor, okay?"

Satisfied, she smiled and said, "Don't keep the man waiting, sis!"

I took off my apron and stared in the mirror. I was looking well, even I could see that. My face was thinner than it had been but the sun had browned my skin and made my eyes seem even bluer than they already were.

I remembered, for a moment, how Martin used to trace my cheekbones and whisper, "How fine you are, Nel," but then I shook the memory off and went down to greet another young man.

AUG 3RD, 1876

Dear Diary,

Our interview went well, although Adam was as determined as ever, now that he knew Martin was no longer in the picture. I was pleased to see him but he hadn't been in the room five minutes before he got down on one knee and proposed to me- the cad!

Patsy was just bringing a tray of iced tea into the room when she saw the lieutenant kneeling at my feet, holding an elaborate diamond and ruby ring in the air.

My mouth was hanging open in shock even as Patsy let the tray drop to the floor. "Oh my God!" she shrieked. "Auntie... Annie... Nel's getting married again!"

Of course, pandemonium ensued as the maid rushed in to clean up the spilt tea and broken crystal and my aunt and sisters joined the fray. The whole time, though, Adam stared up into my face knowing that my answer was still, no.

Putting my hands to my burning cheeks, I yelled, "All of you, please, get out!"

Everyone, except Adam, froze and then made their silent way out the door. Adam arose from his place on the floor and placed the wedding ring back in his pocket.

His face was filled with disappointment and I rushed to him taking his hands in mine. "Dear, dear Adam. I do care for you, you know that, right?" I asked.

He nodded silently but his cheeks were burning in humiliation. "Yes, I know, Nel. I'm just not good enough for you, is that it?"

I shook my head. "No! That's not it at all. If anything, I don't think I'm good enough for you! It's just too soon... I still love Martin and the child in my belly is his!"

He studied my face for a moment and then his shoulders drooped. "I know, Nel. What I meant to say, before we were so rudely interrupted..." We shared a small smile. "... Was, will you become engaged to marry me? I have two years of school to attend before I can become my own man. But, if you will agree to wait for me, I promise to raise your son or daughter as my own."

His eyes searched my face and I saw how young and earnest he truly was. "I have loved you from the first moment I saw you," he added, "and the only thing I want is to be a good husband to you."

I was tempted... more than I can say, but I clutched his hands tighter and replied, "I am so honored, Adam. And, in my own way, I love you, too. But I must decline-for now."

His face fell and he dropped my hands.

"Adam, please listen to me!" I pleaded. "I won't be with anyone else... that much I will swear. And, if you still

desire me by the end of your schooling at West Point, I
will seriously consider your offer. Is that fair?"

He hesitated for a moment and then he grinned.
"That's fair, Nel… really! I didn't mean to ambush you,
you know. I just tend to lose my head whenever I'm
around you."

I nodded with relief. Looking past Adam's shoulder, I
could see Annie gesturing madly and the day-maid
waiting in the foyer with a new platter of tea. I smiled and
said, "One thing I *do* know is that Annie's head is going to
explode if she doesn't get to hug her favorite lieutenant's
neck."

He turned around and said, "You get in here,
gorgeous!" and Annie flew into the room with a joyous
shout. Then Patsy and Aunt Chloe filed in and we spent
the better part of two hours catching up.

It was late afternoon by the time he took his leave and
both Patsy and Chloe were annoyingly possessive over
the man they perceived would be my next husband. I,
however, was more depressed than ever.

Adam is most handsome and a gentleman to boot, but
I knew, in my heart of hearts that I didn't love him. Maybe
my feelings will change, over time, but for now the only
man whose touch I longed for was only a memory.

Adam came to call every day for the brief time he had left
in Chicago. But, finally, we saw him off at the railway
station. He seemed as happy as a lark and treated me as if
we were already betrothed. He never came close to being
too forward, but I had begun to regret my promises.

Never one for half-measures, Adam Burrows headed
off to West Point convinced that he had a bride waiting

for him upon graduation and I sighed as he blew me kisses from the back platform of the departing train.

The temperatures were in the high 90's and after the train took off I started to feel a little faint, so I was happy to head back home in the carriage to spend time in the cool shade of Chloe's garden.

Annie and Patsy were chatting happily about going shopping tomorrow for new school clothes and Chloe was snoring softly on the opposite side of the buggy. I leaned close to the window and let the rushing air cool my brow as we approached Chloe's well-kept but modest house with its gray shingles and white trim.

The carriage slowed to a crawl in the front drive as the sun streamed down through the branches of the giant elms and oak trees lining the street and I blinked as a dark, narrow figure detached itself from one of the tree's trunks. Blinking, I tried to focus as my heart started pounding in excitement.

Then, I was out the door and running... somehow, against all odds, Martin had found his way home to me!

EPILOGUE: JULY 7, 1878

DEAR DIARY,

THIS WILL BE my last passage, dearest diary. I am so busy now caring for my beautiful daughter Martina (Tina for short) and my baby boy, named Solomon; writing my column for the Chicago Times, and taking care of the famous photographer, Martin Leibowitz, I hardly have time to sneeze, much less doodle in a diary.

Still, as I make my final edits, I can't help but look back on the summer of 1876 in awestruck amazement. I honestly don't know how Annie and I survived those turbulent times... but for the grace of God.

The loss of Custer and his 7th Cavalry still weighs heavy on the hearts and minds of our nation's citizens, and the debate rages on. Libby has made it her life's mission to clear her husband's name, while others in his regiment, particularly Captain Benteen, lay the cavalry's loss to Sitting Bull squarely on Custer's shoulders.

Well, the consolidated Indian tribes at the Little Bighorn might have won the battle that day but they surely lost the war. Most of the natives have been run to ground and are firmly trapped on reservations where there is not enough food or supplies and the great buffalo herds have disappeared.

The War Chief, Crazy Horse, was murdered by U.S. troops last year and Sitting Bull has fled to Canada, leaving most of his people behind. It seems that not only was the battle of the Little Bighorn Custer's last stand... it was Sitting Bull's last stand too.

I still shudder when I think about my Martin, lost in the early morning dusk while he searched for the cavalry's mule-train and Captain Benteen. I asked him what had happened and, even now, he's not sure.

"Nel," he murmured in the soft after-glow of our marriage bed, the night he came home. "It's all still a blur, but this is what I do recall. Custer had dismissed me and told me to report to Benteen if I still wanted to take pictures. I remember how the general pointed into the darkness and said, 'His troops went that a-way.'"

Martin sighed. "I wanted to throttle the man, seriously, but I knew his mind was made up, so I skedaddled as quickly as I could to catch up with Benteen's unit. I recall that the sun was just starting to rise and I found myself on a high bluff. Something caught my eye then and I looked to my right and down..." His arms tightened around me and his beautiful brown eyes grew wide.

"For the first time I actually laid eyes on Sitting Bull's village. It was enormous... huge. I estimate that the actual encampment measured a half mile wide and over two miles long! I knew then, in my heart, that Custer was in deep, deep trouble...

I almost turned around to warn him... I was only about a half mile away at that point, but something else caught my eye- a slight movement, maybe, or the sun's reflection off of an arrow or rifle barrel- I don't know." He sighed.

"As my eyes sharpened, I realized that what I had thought were rocks and low shrubbery on the ground were actually the prone bodies of Indians who were sneaking up and surrounding me and the rest of our troops. Nel, there must have been hundreds of them! I honestly could hardly believe my eyes... it's kind of like when you study a puzzle and, at first, you can't make hide nor tail of it and then, gradually, the shapes begin to make sense."

He searched my eyes for a moment and continued, "Believe it or not, my first instinct was to get down off my mule and take some pictures. Stupid, I know, but I thought a photo like that would fetch a lot of money! Anyway, needless to say, I never had a chance because the next thing I knew I was struck by an arrow... me and my mule both!"

He reached down and unconsciously started rubbing at the wound that had almost killed him and *did* kill his rented mule. "I had just enough time to realize that I was a dead man before I fell off my mule and the mule fell on top of me. I really can't decide which was worse... that gigantic war arrow piercing my thigh or the weight of that dead mule pinning me to the ground!"

"At any rate," he said. "I passed out and woke up later on the back of a travois. I was dressed like an Indian and the pain in my leg was so intense it was all I could do to keep from screaming out loud. But, any time I moaned Little Owl would put his hand over my mouth and glare until I knew I had to stay silent."

Martin grinned at the shock on my face. "Yes, believe it or not Three Bull Man and Little Owl were my saviors that day. And, I believe that was because of Annie..." He reached into one of his travel bags and pulled out a frayed piece of faded orange yarn.

Handing it to me, he said, "Apparently, Annie and her little friend gave Three Bull Man a poppet before they left the boat. They didn't have time to make him an actual doll but it served its purpose...

That Cheyenne brave believes his dolly is filled with BIG magic and when he and Little Owl saw me lying there, squished under my own mule, they remembered who I was, dressed me up to look like an Indian and spirited me back to their village.

It took almost a week to get there and the whole time, they were on the lookout for hostiles, tending to my wound and trying to keep me alive- for Annie's sake!"

Martin hugged me tight as tears rolled from my eyes. I recalled the young Indians from the boat, their brutal justice against the men who had raped my friend, Natalie, and Three Bull Man's superstitious awe of Annie's ragdoll.

"Long story, short," Martin said. "Those two Indians saved my life. It took about a month before I was well enough to travel, though. Little Owl had taken the money out of my money-belt to decorate his teepee but he was willing to give me back enough to catch a coach to Yankton.

When I got there I sent a telegraph to Mrs. Fair-weather and learned that you and Annie had moved on to Chicago. The rest is history, I guess... maybe, in time, I will remember more of what happened but for now, I'm just glad to be alive and with you."

SINCE MY HUSBAND found his way back home to me our relationship has matured. Our passion for one another still burns brightly but I also know now just how sweet and clever Martin is. We have laughed together and cried, too; over Solomon's untimely murder, the damage Frank Higgins inflicted upon me and Annie and at the loss of so many good friends he made while following Custer into Montana.

Although his right leg still pains him sometimes, he works very hard and is now a photographer of very good repute. He actually has to work almost night and day, sometimes, to keep up with his orders. I help him out occasionally but its Annie's distinct pleasure and pride to be known as the famous Mr. Leibowitz' personal assistant.

I delivered my beautiful daughter in December of 1876 as snow fell in soft, cottony splendor and my heart filled with joy as I saw her father pick her up in his arms while tears of happiness coursed down his cheeks. We named her Martina and she is the spitting image of her daddy.

Ever the pistol, she is even now demanding I take her "OUT!" to play with her puppy! My son, Solly, who looks very much like me, is sleeping in his bassinet.

My aunt Chloe left for Georgia not long after Martin

came home and we hear from her occasionally. It sounds as if she is quite happy- perhaps even in love- and says that she and her new fella will be taking a ship to Athens, Greece next summer.

Annie, (Martin's savior) is doing well in school and plans on becoming a famous photographer. She loves my husband with all her might as does, surprisingly, Patsy.

At first, when Martin limped up to me on the day he arrived at Chloe's house, she seemed quite disappointed in him. Of course, Martin was alarmingly thin, his hair was too long and his face wan and pale. Also, it's hard to compete with Lt. Burrows golden good looks.

Since then, though, my older sister has come to see the beauty that radiates from his ready smile and his liquid brown eyes. But, honestly, Patsy does not have the time to moon over my husband or any other man as she is expecting her first child in less than a month's time.

I see Sally every week and she is doing well. When we meet for lunch, her eyes snap with pleasure as she reports that the Chicago Times considers her- a woman- to be one of their best correspondents! "Take that, you stupid men!" I have heard her say- more than once.

I am also pleased to report that Adam Burrows is getting married to a beautiful young woman named Sarah Fuller, the daughter of a West Point instructor, named Colonel Miles Fuller. He was heart-broken, at first, and acted as if I had been holding my husband's survival a secret just to thwart his attentions.

In no time, though, he wrote that he had met the girl of his dreams and would be married in a years' time! (Mind you, this was only a few weeks after he had declared his undying passion for me! Ha!)

Now, as I stare up at the famous painting of Madam LaFluer which Martin purchased, at great cost, from the River Queen Hotel in Yankton, all I can think of is how blessed I am... so blessed to be with the man I love~

But, I must close. Solly has woken up and is punching the air above his head with his tiny fists in search of his mamma and food. Tina is clamoring to go outside, the puppy is barking his head off and I can see Martin making his slow but steady way up the street toward home.

So, for once and for all- good bye, dear diary, good bye.

AUTHOR'S NOTE

I WANT TO THANK YOU FOR READING MY NOVEL, *FAR WEST: The Diary of Eleanor Higgins*. The only thing I hope for is that you enjoyed it and, if so, you will leave a positive review!

I WOULD BE REMISS if I forgot to mention the people who helped bring this novel to life... specifically:

Nathaniel Philbrick- The Last Stand

Evan S. Connell- Son of the Morning Star

Charles River Editors- The Battle of the Little Bighorn

Charles Haven and Ladd Johnston- Custer's Last Stand, A Brief Biography of George Armstrong Custer and finally,

Charles A, Mills- Custer's Last Stand- Portraits in Time

. . .

IF ANY MISTAKES were made while trying to sort out the facts of what happened to Custer and his beloved 7th... they are all on me.

A LOOK AT DEADMAN'S LAMENT BY LINELL JEPPSEN

The year is 1872. Twelve-year-old Matthew Wilcox leads a charmed life on his family's sprawling ranch in Washington Territory until a series of tragic events leave him orphaned and in the clutches of a vicious band of outlaws. Threatened by the gang leader's perverted cousin, Top Hat, Matthew also faces Indian attacks, dangerous wildlife, and a deadly snowstorm. He survives but burns with an overwhelming hunger for revenge.

Thirteen years later, Matthew - now a Spokane County sheriff - realizes that Top Hat is riding again with a new gang called the Mad Hatters. It means risking his friends, his family and the love of a good woman, but Matthew must find the man who destroyed what he once loved most in the world. To that end, he and his posse venture into Idaho gold country to capture the Mad Hatters.

Top Hat, however, has a different idea. He turns the tables, heading to the sheriff's hometown of Granville and going after everyone Matthew holds dear.

What follows will haunt Sheriff Wilcox for the rest of his life as he confronts the hatred, vengeance and retribution buried deep in his own soul. Matthew will do anything, though, to put an end to A DEADMAN'S LAMENT.

NOW AVAILABLE ON AMAZON.

ABOUT THE AUTHOR

Linell Jeppsen is a writer of science fiction and fantasy. Her vampire novel, *Detour to Dusk*, has received over 44-four and five star reviews. Her novel *Story Time*, with over 130 4-and 5-star reviews, is a science fiction post-apocalyptic novel, and has been touted by the Paranormal Romance Guild, Sandy's Blog Spot, Coffee time Romance, Bitten by Books and 64 top reviewers as a five-star read, filled with terror, love, loss, and the indomitable beauty and strength of the human spirit. *Story Time* was also nominated as the best new read of 2011 by the PRG. Her dark fantasy novel, *Onio* (a story about a half-human Sasquatch who falls in love with a human girl), was released in December 2012 and won 3rd place as the best fantasy romance of 2012 by the PRG reviewers guild. Her novel, *The War of Odds*, won the IBD award for fantasy fiction and boasts 18 5-star reviews since its release in February of 2013. It also placed 2nd, as the best YA paranormal book of 2013 by the PRG.